Frog Realm

Frog Realm

Artifact of Protection

A Historical Fantasy Novel

George L. Babec

MSTMicro Publishing
Knoxville, TN
http://www.mstmicro.com

Copyright © George L. Babec 2018

10 9 8 7 6 5 4 3 2 1 0

Library of Congress Control Number: 2018913707

ISBN 978-0-9970222-5-4 (paperback)

ISBN 978-0-9970222-6-1 (e-book)

~

First Edition
November 2018

Perception is blind without knowledge.

Honor, Loyalty, and Bravery.

Danger, they're coming!

CHAPTER 1

The air was thin and cool with patches of mist still lingering in the low lying dells of the jungle floor. Monkeys were playing high up in the canopy such that leaves were raining down and twirling in the air around them. Necalli could hardly catch his breath. He arched his back and rose up from the saddle to try to fill his lungs. His heart thumped wildly and the leather reins of his battle horse were moistened by his clammy palms. Every muscle tensed with anticipation and a desire to prove himself in battle to his father, the mighty King Ah-Cacaw, the jaguar, the great Ahau.

He turned his head back to glance at the immense forces that seemed to go on forever behind them, marching to the beat of a percussion of drummers. He could feel the beat of the drums deep in his chest.

The long march from the capital city of Tikal, throughout the night, gave him much time to think but too much time to become anxious. He took in a deep breath of the cool morning air and slowly exhaled.

The king looked over at his brave son sitting upon his horse riding between himself and his most trusted general, Moctezuma. His head held high and his strength shown by the muscles flexing in his arms and his stout chest proudly adorned with the leather sigil and armor of his father's heritage. The king could not have been more proud for his son had earned the respect of the mighty Moctezuma and had trained harder than anyone he had ever known, yet was humble and empathic.

The king's mind drifted to the day his wife Nelli finally gave birth to a son to carry on his dynasty. He could still see her beautiful, shining face as she held their newborn son in her arms. For so many years they tried to have a son but child after child only daughters. *Maybe that's why Necalli had compassion toward others being girdled by so many sisters or could it actually be tormented by so many sisters?*

Necalli held the hearts of every young lady of the kingdom and the Tenochcan people adored their prince; after all, he was good looking, sweet, and the son of the most loved king that had ever lived. Necalli was proud to ride at the head of the army with his deific father and the fearless General Moctezuma.

As he looked ahead, their pathway opened to a large clearing. Moctezuma gave the order and the conch shells blasted out the command; flags waved, and the powerful Tenochcan Army was deployed across a high sloping knoll, overlooking the vast skeletal armies of the mystical sorceress, Malinche. She plotted against the kingdom, joining with rival nations, and summoned the spirits of the dead to raise her supernatural army using dark ancient artifice. They were summoned by the powers of the nine levels of the underworld. The king could hardly believe the great throng before them. *How could this be happening? It's inconceivable. What power she must have gained since...* He feared for Necalli knowing that he was eager to prove himself in actual combat.

Once Malinche learned of the great secret that was hidden from her by the king, she drew on her great powers to deceive the nations and break the peace that the king had fought so hard to gain, for the king was not only a great leader of the Tenochca Kingdom, but he was the protector of the forbidden spring, also known as the spring of life, that was rumored to grant long life and even turn back aging. The king himself was well over a hundred years old, yet he looked and felt as if he was still in his prime.

Malinche desired access to the spring more than anything, for her powers could not sustain her forever. She had to act before she grew any weaker. She used her abilities to entice rival nations to join her in her attempt to come against the great king, even though he had always been fair and was well respected amongst all nations.

Necalli looked down the hillside at the ghastly enemy and the hair on the back of his neck stood up. His body quaked as he tried to come to grips in his mind with what his eyes were seeing. His skin crawled and prickled while he felt sharp tingles all over like he was being bitten by a thousand mosquitoes. He rubbed his arms and felt like he had bugs crawling all over him. He was not alone; the soldiers stood around him with raised eyebrows and wide eyes. They were also reaching down to rub their legs and rear ends like bugs were crawling all over them. Their mouths hung open and their bodies trembled. Many of them threw down their war masks meant to intimidate the enemy for they were of no use here.

Necalli closed his eyes for a moment and relaxed—he opened them again but they were still there. Their putrefying flesh hung from their bones with the stench of death in the air. What little garments they had were rotted and frayed. Most were like a pile of bones walking around aimlessly. One had no jaw and was missing the entire top of its exposed skull with half of its rotted brains hanging to the side and blackened upper front teeth.

The mass was fluently in motion as it seemed they could not stand still. They weaved about across the field, like a flag flowing in the wind, waiting for the order to strike forward. There were so many of them. Necalli looked at his father then Moctezuma. He could see the concern on their faces as well. A cold shiver quaked across his body. He turned his eyes to Moctezuma. "Surely we will prevail?" Moctezuma was in deep thought and said nothing. "Father, we must endow the troops with courage. No army has ever stood against us and lived."

King Ah-Cacaw looked at his son. "You will remain here with me and the reserve troops."

"But my Ahau, I mean to do battle."

"Your time will come, my son, but not today," the king said with a wavering voice.

"My Ahau, if we are to prevail I need Prince Necalli to lead a regiment of horsemen to flank their position," Moctezuma said.

"Use anyone you wish to command the flank, but leave my son at my side." The king peered directly into Moctezuma's eyes.

"As you wish, my Ahau." Moctezuma bowed his head, he dared not defy the great jaguar, but the look on his brow was distressing.

Malinche twirled her hand in the air creating green swirls of light that swooshed around her. She thrust her arm forward, the light dissipated out in all directions and the skeletal creatures advanced up the hillside. They scurried so fast, held back by nothing, it was like releasing hungry hounds thirsting for flesh. Moctezuma commanded archers and spearmen to shower the approaching enemy but to no effect. Most just went right through them and others stuck into what little flesh they had, but it was like they had no feeling at all, which meant no remorse, no hesitation.

Moctezuma looked at the king and he nodded at him. He unsheathed his sword and led the advance down the hillside. Each skeletal being that was struck down simply rose again moments later. Again and again they were stuck down just to rise once more. The terrified screams of the Tenochcan Army echoed off the hillside. They were being slaughtered. Necalli could see the devastation, even Moctezuma was growing weak with exhaustion and making no impact against the enemy forces.

"Father, we must do something."

"Send in the reserve troops!"

Necalli ordered the remaining soldiers to follow him into battle.

"Necalli!" the king shouted. He ordered his son to remain, but Necalli could not contain himself any longer. He unsheathed his sword and began to batter the enemy. He struck at the skeletal creatures and watched as they fell to a pile of bones and then reconstructed themselves. He fought as best as he could, but the enemy continued to advance until they reached his father's personal guard.

Necalli struck another, and before it could rise again he severed its head and kicked it down the hill. He watched—the creature lay still. He repeated his actions several more times with the same results. He gave order to spread the word that the creatures' heads must be separated and removed far from their bodies. Hours of fierce battle ensued, but finally the remaining Tenochcan Army began to reap with a strong arm. They annihilated the mindless skeletal creatures that had no true ability and the remaining enemy troops fled into the jungle. All that was left was Malinche's cavalcade.

Necalli and Moctezuma approached her command wagon and gave order to axe through the wooden doors. Once opened, Malinche tried to conjure a curse against them, but the king's moormit, Allusshia, armed with the powerful staff of Beesha, blocked her powers. They took Malinche captive, but when they marched up the hill they found the king mortally wounded with a cracked skull. They hurriedly returned to the capital where the king was treated by their best physicians, but there was no hope and the king passed into a deep coma.

Necalli looked at his father and fell to his knees. His eyes welled up and glistened over. He was all choked up but held back his emotion as best he could and wiped his eyes. He was so completely helpless to do anything. He would gladly take his father's place and blamed himself for not staying next to him as he was commanded. His head was held low. He couldn't even look at his mother or sisters weeping at the bedside.

His face drew cold. He stood up with a clinched fist. When the guards saw his face, they just moved well out of the way and said nothing. He walked briskly to the dungeon where Allusshia, armed with the staff of Beesha, guarded Malinche.

"Allusshia, can you do anything for my father?"

"Necalli, I cannot turn away from Malinche for she will destroy your kingdom, she seeks the forbidden spring."

Necalli's face turned red. He clinched his fists tightly and his lips drew together. "Then I will separate her head from her body." He took his sword from his sheath and prepared to behead Malinche.

"Bwahaha, go ahead, Necalli, take my head from me!" Malinche burst out in evil laughter.

"Necalli, wait! You mustn't."

"Why not? She deserves it for what she has done!"

"Yes, my prince, but you cannot. Come talk with me."

The beautiful humanoid moormit led the prince into the adjacent chamber to speak quietly with him. "Necalli, if you kill her now, she will become even more powerful. She is a spirit cast into a woman's body. If you kill her now, her spirit will be free and there will be no stopping her. She will spate her wrath upon the world."

"Then what can we do?"

"There is a way."

"Tell me."

"You can seek out Beesha, the greatest of the moormits. Ask her to create an Ispus to drain Malinche's power. Only then can we be sure she surely dies when you take her head."

"But where can I find Beesha? Nobody's heard from her for years."

"I know where she is, Necalli. I will tell you how to find my sister for I cannot leave while Malinche lives, but you must hurry. I cannot sleep or let down my guard. In only days I will grow weary, you must make haste."

Allusshia gave Necalli specific instructions so he could find her sister, then they returned to the chamber before Malinche.

"I can save your father, Necalli," Malinche said.

Her unbroken gaze drew him as she lifted her chained hand and sensually ran her fingers from her clavicle down between her breasts.

Her wet smile glistened. She was beautiful and desirable. Once in her gaze it was hard to look away. Seducer of kings they called her.

"Necalli, don't look at her or open your mind to her, she will entice you. She is able to entice any man who simply looks upon her or even take a weak mind from miles away."

"Silence, Malinche, or I will have you flogged."

"I am your father's only hope, boy. There is no other who can save him."

Allusshia became enraged and her anger sparked from the stela-stone in her staff as if a ball of lightning, striking Malinche.

"Hahahaha... Ha, you think your little magic tricks can harm me, you insufferable moormit! You will die soon. You will all die when I am free."

"Quickly Necalli, take the map and find my sister. Everything depends on this."

Necalli took the map and started to walk away. Allusshia grabbed his arm and stopped him. When he turned, she kissed him. He stood with a puzzled look on his face. Allusshia smiled widely. "It's good fortune to kiss a moormit."

Necalli laughed, notwithstanding the moment. "That's the first I heard of it."

Allusshia began to blush and giggled a little. "So how did it make you feel?"

"You're right. I do feel of good fortune. Maybe you should do it again."

They embraced and shared a long, passionate kiss. Necalli could feel the warmth and softness of her back through her thin, flowing garment as they embraced. A small electrical current flowed across Allusshia's skin. Necalli could feel a tingling sensation about his whole body and his tongue felt electrified as his touched hers. For just a moment his stress faded away and he didn't want to let go.

"How splendid, the prince of this magnificent kingdom is in love with a moormit. Bwahaha," Malinche said.

"Shut up! Whelp!" Allusshia said as she conjured another lightning ball that struck Malinche, knocking her host body unconscious.

"Finally, some peace and quiet! She is so stuck on herself, you know?"

"I'm glad you're protecting us from her. Someone I can trust."

"With my very life, my prince. You better be going now, there is little time to save your father."

Necalli gathered his armor and approached Moctezuma. "You must guard the kingdom while I am away."

"Necalli, this quest is foolish. You don't even know if this moormit is still alive, and even if she is, you may never find her."

"Moctezuma, I know how this sounds, but it's the only way to save my father," Necalli said in a sad, irresolute voice.

"Then let me send a legion of men to protect you."

"They would just slow me down. I must make haste and move very quickly through the forest for there is little time."

"Prince Necalli, you are the only son of the king. If he should die you should be here to take the throne. The future of the entire kingdom rests on you."

"Don't worry, I won't fail this quest, and when I return, the sorceress will be put to rest forever. Send men to watch over Allusshia, she mustn't sleep until I return."

"You should wait, at least until morning. The day grows dark."

"There's no time, I must leave now."

Moctezuma bowed before Necalli. "I will watch over your kingdom until you return."

CHAPTER 2

Necalli stood before his horse in the evening breeze. He stroked his forehead and fed him an apple. "We have an important quest, my friend. Be swift and surefooted." His horse let out a lovely little nicker and shook his head with approval. Necalli mounted up and they galloped through Tikal's great plaza and out of the front gate, which was just being closed for the night.

Necalli glanced back as he rode. The city was wonderful to behold with the slanting orange streaks of evening light illuminating the great Ceremonial Temple of the Four Lintels. There was no greater temple in the entire world except for that of the Temple of Naranjo, which King Ah-Cacaw won in battle from the god king Curl-Snout. They trotted past the Tree-Stones commemorating many such victories of his father and the many kings that came before him. There was the Tree-Stone of victory over the great Smoking Squirrel that took place long before Necalli was born and the Tree-Stone of the battle against the rebellious Jaguar-Paw-Skull who rallied the forces of Belize in an unprecedented uprising that lasted only days. One of the most impressive monuments was inlaid with unearthly stela-stones from the heavens. It recorded a great battle against the great Smoking Monkey when Necalli's father was a general leading King Caracol's armies.

Necalli continued on following a well-traveled path through the thick jungle. After about half an hour his horse just stopped. Necalli leaned down and whispered it his ear, "What is it, boy?" The horse stomped the ground with his hoof. Necalli felt a cold shiver run down his back when he caught movement out of his right eye. A poisonous snake had coiled by the side of the pathway with his head drawn back, ready to strike. Necalli slowly backed the horse away and dismounted. He unsheathed his sword and beheaded the snake with the tip of his blade. He patted his horse. "Thanks for finding dinner."

He picked up the snake and put it in his bag. His horse perked up his head and became alert. His ears turned towards the woods.

"What do you hear?"

Just then Necalli heard the screams of a young woman, dampened by the vegetation of the jungle. He squeezed through the overgrowth and into a clearing with his sword drawn. He saw a young woman running from an enemy soldier who had escaped the battle. He expertly twirled his sword in his hand as he ran toward them.

The woman was thrown to the ground. The soldier leaned over her with her long, blonde hair wrapped around his hand, pulling tight. She screamed with tears running down her cheeks and grabbed his hand to try to loosen his grip. He smelled ripe with body odor. She could hardly bear the thought of him being so close to her. The soldier heard Necalli's steps crackling dried leaves. He released the young woman's hair and quickly drew his sword, standing straight up.

Necalli, running at full speed, never slowed. Their swords clashed mightily and bright sparks illuminated the blades in the twilight. The young woman crawled backwards up against a tree, watching intently as the men fought. Necalli pressed forward driving the soldier backward with each swing of his sword. The soldier realized he was no match for the prince and lunged forward desperately with his sword. He caught Necalli on his side, but his leather armor deflected the blade, giving Necalli a perfect opening. He thrust his sword forward through the enemy soldier's thick cloth armor and into his chest with all his might. The soldier let out a sigh, exhaled, and fell to the ground dead. As he fell, Necalli pulled his sword free and sat on a fallen tree to catch his breath.

The young woman ran to him and kneeled on the ground before him.

"Thank you, my prince."

"What is your name?"

"Tepin, my prince." She looked up at him with teary eyes.

"You are most beautiful, Tepin. I have never seen a girl with albino hair. How did you end up out here in the jungle?"

"The soldiers came at dusk and attacked our village just over the rise. I alone survived. They killed my father, sister, and mother. I was so afraid. I hid myself, and when they weren't looking, I ran as fast as I could, but he saw me and chased me." She bowed her head to the ground and cried. Her whole body trembled.

Necalli sat his sword against the tree and kneeled down rubbing her back. He felt her pulsing heartbeat as if it were his own as he held her. His eyes teared up and he sniffled. He could feel her pain in his chest and knew her helplessness.

He whispered, "Tepin, I'm so sorry you lost your family. I wish I could bring them back to you. I'm now on a quest to save my own father. The pain is deep, I know."

Tepin sat up and Necalli held her. She leaned her head against his chest.

"Can I come with you?" she whimpered. "I can help you with your quest."

"My quest is swift, there is little time."

"My prince, I promise I will be of little burden."

"Sweet Tepin, you are no burden."

Necalli cleaned his sword on some leaves of a bush and slid it back into its sheath. He sat Tepin on his horse and led them down the path for several miles until he found a defensive area to set up camp for the night. Tepin helped to gather dried twigs and wood to make a fire. Necalli cooked the snake he'd killed earlier and they both ate.

"Tepin, you seem cold."

"Yes, my prince."

"That won't do."

"My prince?"

"That. When we are alone, just call me Necalli. Sometimes I get really tired of hearing, 'my prince,' all the time."

"But you are the prince and a great general."

"I am just a man."

Tepin kneeled at his feet with her hands on his toes and sandals. "Necalli, you are a great man and will one day be a great king like your father. There is no one in this land as great as you. Nor could there ever be. You saved me at risk of your own life. That soldier would have ruined me forever. That would be worse than death. I am your servant forever."

"Tepin, that's sweet and honorable but not necessary. You'll serve no man whilst I'm alive. That I promise you."

She looked at Necalli and smiled as he patted her on the back.

The night air was chilly and a cool breeze fluffed Tepin's thick hair. She crossed her arms in front of her to try to warm herself.

"Here, Tepin, come sit close to the fire."

She sat on the ground next to Necalli and held her hands out to warm them. They both sat still for a while thinking. Then Tepin's lips turned downward and her face turned flush. She was overwhelmed and couldn't even process everything that had happened to her and her family only hours before. She didn't know whether to cry or just try to block it all out and pretend it never happened. Still being chilly, she scooted a little closer to Necalli for warmth, but he hardly noticed as he just stared out into the stillness of the night with the smoke of the fire filling his nostrils and the crackling of the fire tingling his ears. He started breathing heavily and felt a knot in his throat making it hard to swallow. The fire popped and an ember landed on his leg. He quickly brushed it off then took in a deep breath but he couldn't help but to let out a little whimper.

Surprised, Tepin looked up at him. "Necalli, you okay?"

His eyes watered and he couldn't speak for a second. He sniffled and wiped his nose with his hand. He began to speak, but his voice was raspy and he had to clear his throat.

"It's my fault," he said in a broken tone.

"What's your fault?" she asked softly.

"My father, it's all my fault. He told me to stay by his side, but I didn't listen and now he might die. All I ever wanted to do is have the chance to prove myself. Everyone always has such reverence for him and affords me the same respect, but what have I ever done to deserve any of that? My first chance to make a difference and I abandoned him on the battlefield and now he might die."

Necalli hid his quivering chin with his hand so she wouldn't see then looked away wiping his eyes. Tepin thought for a second.

"Necalli, I honestly don't think your father was worried about his own life. I think he was worried about you. I mean I remember how excited my parents got when they talked about the day you were born. The whole kingdom rejoiced because our great king finally had a successor. I think it was your life he was worried about and not his. You are the only hope for our future and for his legacy. My father would tell me about the great battles that he fought in and how your father sacrificed so much to unite the tribes and bring a peace that has lasted a generation. Without you everything would be lost. He loves you, Necalli, more than his own life, I'm sure. He would want you to be strong so his sacrifices would continue on through you."

Necalli hugged Tepin and breathed easier. His whole body felt warm and at ease.

"You're really something, Tepin. So smart and perceptive, you know that?"

She smiled. "I just want to be helpful."

"Maybe our meeting wasn't just by chance."

"Do you think anything happens by chance?"

"I don't know, but I'm glad you're here."

"Me too."

Tepin leaned her head against his shoulder.

"You remind me of my oldest sister a little bit. She's really smart, too, but also really annoying.

"So you think I'm annoying?"

Necalli laughed. "No, no, I just mean you're really smart."

Tepin felt at ease and giggled.

"I should have spoken to my mother and sisters before I left though."

"Why didn't you?"

"I mean what could I say? Sorry, it's all my fault?"

"I'm sure she doesn't blame you and I'm sure she's glad you're still alive."

"I miss them. I should have said something."

"I miss my family too."

"Oh, my. I'm sorry, Tepin."

"No, it's okay. I'm trying not to think about it. What was it like, growing up? Were you and your father close?" she asked, wanting to change the subject.

"We were very close, but it was like he was always very stout, always having to have the persona of excellence. I did enjoy traveling with him a lot, but I never really had a normal childhood. Sometimes I just wanted to go and run and have fun with the other normal kids, but, at the same time, for as long as I can remember, I wanted to be exactly like him. Well respected and considered for my wisdom, just as he."

"You never just took off and had a day for yourself to have fun?"

"There were a few times. Dacey would follow me around everywhere. She wouldn't let me be. Everywhere I went, there she would be, right behind me."

"Was she your girlfriend?"

Necalli laughed. "No silly, my little sister. She was the only one younger than me. I miss her so much."

"What happened to her?"

"My father married her off to a tribal leader when he was pulling in the outlying territories to secure our kingdom. It's the only decision my father ever made that I disagreed with. I would never make my children marry someone they didn't love against their will, but Dacey was so beautiful and everyone knew it."

"So I take it that you and Dacey were close."

"She was the only one to treat me normal. Never expecting anything from me. Never ordering me about. She just wanted to be like me. When I would practice shooting, she had to have her own bow to shoot with me. She begged my mother for a horse so she could ride with me. Plus she climbed trees like a little monkey," he said with a smile on his face. "She would always pester me until I tickled her and then scream saying how much she didn't like to be tickled. She was so young when she had to leave us. I rode with them for several miles and she never broke a tear. She was dutiful and proud, sitting up tall in the saddle. She refused to ride in the wagon with the other women. Other than my father she was the strongest person I knew. She wanted to be a fighter like me but father… No way that was going to happen."

"I wish I could have met her."

"She was so feisty. We would sneak out some nights and sleep under the stars next to a fire. When my older sister caught us sneaking in early, she threatened to tell father and would say, 'What if someone captured you and took you away?' Then Dacey would threaten her to keep quiet, or else. Life was always a bit exciting with Dacey around. I have a lot of respect for all my sisters though. I know they look up to me to be a leader, but it's also nice to have someone to talk to that will treat me like a normal person. Dacey was the only one I could truly trust. I could talk to her about anything and knew it would never leave her."

Necalli bowed his head down and closed his eyes for a second.

"Necalli, you can trust me. I would never betray you in speech or body."

Necalli smiled and got up to put more wood on the fire. They both found a smooth place by the fire to lie down for the night. Necalli looked up towards the sky and could see a lone star through the thick canopy and wondered if Dacey was looking up at that same star. Tepin took a deep breath and let it out slowly. Her mind opened up and a few tears dripped down her face as she listened to the sounds of the jungle animals while drifting off to sleep.

CHAPTER 3

Necalli was startled by a spider crawling across his face. He brushed it away quickly with his hand. He felt very warm in the chilly morning mist. Tepin had cuddled up with him during the night. When he realized she was next to him, he just lay there not moving a muscle. He looked at her beautiful hair and thought about reaching out and touching it, but then his mind wandered and he thought about the kiss that he and Allusshia had shared the day before. *What are you thinking about, Necalli? You can't love a moormit, the kingdom would never stand for it.*

A troop of monkeys had taken notice of them and started screeching in the trees. Tepin let out a little snort and rolled closer against Necalli. She woke up and looked up at him staring down at her with his head propped up on his hand. "Oh! I'm so sorry, Necalli. I was freezing."

"It's okay, Tepin, relax. It was quite cold during the night. We should be on our way, though, we have little time to waste."

"Necalli, can I ask where we journey? You never mentioned."

"We seek Beesha."

"Beesha?"

"You've never heard of Beesha?"

"I have not."

"She's a moormit."

"Is that an animal?"

"No." Necalli laughed. "She's a reclusive humanesk being of great power. She and her sister, Allusshia, are believed to be the last of their kind still in this world."

"So Beesha will save your father?"

"Not exactly."

Tepin tilted her head in confusion. Necalli smiled and sat her on his horse then climbed up in front of her. She put her arms around his muscular waist and held on steadily. They continued down the well-traveled path. Along the way Necalli told her about Malinche and his quest to save his father.

"So once Beesha creates this Ispus you can get rid of Malinche and then Allusshia can save your father?"

"Basically."

"Are the moormits like us or different?"

"From a distance they look human, but their ears, hair, and skin are different than ours."

"Where do they come from?"

"From the Otherworld."

"I thought that was just a myth."

"No, it's real all right. Trust me on that one. If you only had seen what I saw."

They continued on for several hours before stopping at a stream to refill Necalli's water flask. The forest had grown humid and they were thirsty. Everything was in beautiful shades of green, even the stones in the stream were covered in moss, almost as if they were in a slow motion dream. The sounds of the water were soothing to the ears and it was so clear that they could see small fish swimming around. Tepin kneeled on the bank with a slight breeze blowing through her hair. She cupped her hands and drew the cool water to her lips. Her long hair dipped in the stream and floated with the current. A little fish swam up and grabbed a bug floating on the water right next to her. She smiled and looked over at Necalli splashing water on his face and wetting his dark hair. For just a moment her grief had drifted away.

Necalli's horse let out a snarl and stomped his hoof. Necalli looked up intently and listened. Tepin took notice and felt a shiver run down her body. She ducked into some bushes and thought, *I wonder if there're snakes in here.* She got scared and squatted down low to the ground as she scurried over behind Necalli. He stood with his hand on his sword, looking around and listening. There was movement beyond the treeline. He and Tepin snuck up behind some poinsettia bushes where they could get a good view of the clearing just ahead on the path.

They could see a small caravan accompanied by several of the king's soldiers moving slowly in their direction. "It's just a supply cavalcade," Necalli said. Tepin let out a short sigh of relief. They stood to walk back to the stream when they heard the thundering sound of horses galloping in the distance. They turned to see a large band of soldiers dashing toward the caravan with swords drawn, shouting and yelling. A woman screamed as they clashed with the king's soldiers. Necalli was poised to run with his hand on his sword. Tepin quickly grabbed his arm, holding tight. "My prince, there are too many of them. You'll be killed!"

"I can't just let them run through our lands killing everyone."

"Please don't, Necalli. I don't want you to die and you have to save your father."

He paused and thought for a second. The few soldiers of the caravan were no match for the large enemy force and they were quickly struck down. Necalli couldn't stand hearing the screams. His lips tightened and he clinched his sword with all his might. His heart was scorned with displeasure. He knew he had to do something and could not wait any longer as his heart was throbbing deep in his chest. He broke free of Tepin's grip and charged out into the field with his sword drawn. Tepin let out a frightened sigh and stood motionless, not knowing what to do.

As Necalli ran across the field, he was noticed by several soldiers. They galloped swiftly toward him with swords in the air. Suddenly, the sky drew dark as if it were night and the sound of clashing thunder rung out so loudly that they could feel the concussion in their chests. Necalli and the whole band of soldiers froze in their steps, staring up at the sky. The ground began to quake underneath their feet and the horses let out fearful patters, jumping into the air, throwing their riders. Necalli kneeled down, his eyes opened wide with his eyebrows lifted high on his forehead. He quickly covered his eyes when a bright light shone out of the darkness. Lightning bolts flashed across the field like hundreds of thin, fluent strands wavering in the wind. A cloud of glowing particles seemed to float up from the ground in slow motion. The enemy soldiers cried out all together as they were pierced through by the lightning bolts like a thousand white flaming swords. The smell of electrical discharge filled the air in a horrid, pungent odor.

Necalli dropped his sword and fell to the ground as the lightning dissipated. Tepin let out a cry and hurried to grab his horse by the reins and ran toward him. She felt a funny tingling all over her body. The air felt thick as if it was restricting her, slowing her movements. Everything was completely silent, even her footsteps pressing down into the tall grass made no sound. *Please be alive, Necalli, please, please, please!* She approached him and rolled him on his back. "Ugh." She put her head against his chest to listen.

Necalli awoke and sat right up. Tepin let out a short squeal and fell backward on her behind. She leaned forward and hugged him. "I'm so happy you're alive. I have never been so afraid." She breathed heavily. "What was that?"

"I wish I knew. That was intense. I've never seen anything like it."

"Do you think it was Beesha?"

"I don't know, Tepin. She's still a long way off, but I guess it's possible."

The sky began to clear and scattered rays of sun started to beam through. "Necalli, what's that?"

A dark figure arose amongst the dead soldiers on the far side of the clearing. They ducked down closer to the ground and watched as it seemed to drift across the field. Necalli put his hand on his sword. They couldn't make out a face, but they could see two glowing green specs as if eyes beneath the dark hood of a long, black cloak. The figure seemed to float up and into the jungle. "Necalli, what was that?"

"I don't know, but maybe it was what caused the lightning and killed all those soldiers."

"Well, I'm so glad it didn't kill you."

They could hear a faint groaning nearby. Necalli tried to get up but felt a little dizzy and fell backwards. Tepin took his hand and helped him to his feet. He held his sword and cautiously walked with her right behind him with her hands on his sides. They stood behind an overturned wagon and peeked around the corner. They could see some of the dead soldiers were still smoking from the lightning burns. Tepin stepped on a small twig—snap!

"Who's there? Please help me!" a faint, deep voice cried out. They could see an injured soldier moving around, lying on the ground.

"Tepin, it's one of my father's men."

Necalli ran over and kneeled down next to him. He had a deep gushing wound in his thigh.

"Tepin, quick, grab that leather strap over there on that wagon."

"Prince Necalli! How are you here?" the soldier asked.

"Don't worry about that right now. We need to stop the bleeding."

Necalli used the strap as a tourniquet.

"We need to joint his wound," Tepin said. "I need some intestines from that dead horse over there."

"You've done this before?"

"Yes, many times."

Necalli cut a length of intestine into small strands.

"What's your name, soldier?" Tepin asked.

"Tupac."

"Hold still, Tupac, this will hurt a little. I have to clean the wound."

Tepin poured water onto his laceration and he tensed up, grinding his teeth. She stitched up the wound with a small, sharp barb from a Jungle Perch she normally kept in her little pouch.

"Here, Tupac, bite down on this leather strap," Necalli said.

Tupac let out a deep squeal with each puncture of the barb until she was finished.

"There, how's that feel?"

Tupac took a deep breath and let it out. "Much better now, thank you." Necalli helped him sit up and gave him some water. "My lord, I'm sorry about the caravan. We tried to fight, but there were so many. Then there was a bright light and I don't know what happened."

"Something killed all those soldiers. We don't know how, but it's a good thing Tepin was here to mend you."

"Thank you so much, Tepin."

She smiled and cleaned the blood from her hands.

"We really need to get back to the quest, Tepin, too much time has passed. Tupac, do you think you can ride?"

"Absolutely, I certainly don't want to stay here."

They helped him to stand. "Ahhh!"

He almost fell in pain, but Necalli held him tight. They boosted him onto one of the king's horses from the caravan. Tepin pulled Necalli to one side. "I need to ride with him, to help him to stay balanced. He's in a lot of pain."

"Okay, but we need to grab another horse, just in case. We have to make up a lot of time, Tepin."

"I know, I know. Wait... You should put on that cloak hanging on that wagon seat over there."

"Why?"

"In case there're more enemy soldiers in the area."

"She's right, my lord, there've been a lot of enemy forces scattered about the jungle."

Necalli picked up cloaks for each of them and grabbed some extra bedding from the back of a wagon. Several quartz-like crystals fell onto the ground from one of the blankets. "Tupac, what was the caravan hauling?"

"I don't know, my lord. Your father told us to follow the Tlamocazqui and defend him with our lives. He led us to an ancient underground temple. He went in alone for several days, and when he returned, he had something concealed in his linens. We were on our way back to the palace when we were attacked."

"You don't know what he was concealing?"

"No, my lord."

"My father didn't say anything else about your mission?"

"No, but he did say something strange to the Tlamocazqui as I was walking in."

"Something strange?"

"Yes, he said, 'We must thwart the Tezcatlipoca to take her power.' That's all I know."

Necalli stood and stared into the jungle. Both Tepin and Tupac looked in that direction, but there was nothing there. "Necalli, are you okay?" Tepin asked.

Necalli looked at her. "How did he know?"

Tepin put her arm on his shoulder. "What's wrong, Necalli?"

"He knew. Somehow, he knew."

Tepin tilted her head and pulled her hair back from her face. She stared at Necalli, lifting one eyebrow.

"My father must have known about Malinche's power. Why else would he send the Tlamocazqui to get something to stop her?"

"Necalli, I don't understand."

"Tepin, Malinche must get her power from the ancient Tezcatlipoca. I have only heard of them by word of mouth. My father ordered all books about them to be destroyed. The Tlamocazqui priest was after something that would neutralize her powers or at least block them somehow."

"You mean like the Ispus?"

"Yes, exactly like the Ispus, but all the priest retrieved was rocks. I don't understand."

"My lord, what has happened?" Tupac asked.

"Oh, you don't know."

"Please tell me."

"Malinche attacked with a huge force and my father was badly wounded. His only hope is for us to find Beesha."

"Beesha the moormit?"

"Yes and we must make haste. We should have found her by now. If Allusshia sleeps the kingdom will be lost to Malinche."

Necalli packed the stones and climbed on his horse. The three of them rode briskly for many miles. The path began to climb in elevation and their pace slowed. The sun tucked in beyond the horizon and the jungle started to darken. Before they knew it they were in complete darkness. They could hear the sounds of animals scurrying about them. The ground became moist and it was harder to hear the clopping of the horses as they marched. "Tepin, are you still back there?" Necalli whispered.

She answered with a soft, gentle whisper. "Yes, we're here."

"I can't see the path anymore; I guess we need to make camp for the night."

"It got dark so quickly; I didn't think it was that late."

"There could be clouds making it darker. The canopy is so thick we can't see the sky."

They stumbled around in the dark trying to gather wood for a fire. Once lit, they made camp for the night and ate some dried pork. The jungle was so thick that it would easily conceal the fire from view.

Tepin redressed Tupac's wound and laid out his bedding by the fire. "Thank you, Tepin."

"Rest now, you need to heal."

Tepin sat next to Necalli. She looked up at him and smiled. He didn't seem to mind her sitting so close so she laid her head against his shoulder. He rubbed her back a little and felt her long, soft, blonde hair. She took in a deep breath and slowly exhaled. "Necalli, do you think we're getting close?"

"I think so. Allusshia said we will climb above the jungle to a place where the path grows narrow with a steep cliff to the right and a deep void overlooking the jungle canopy on the left. A mile or two later, we will lose the path. From there it's about eight miles."

"Without the path, how do we find our way?"

"She said to continue for another mile or two and we will start to hear the sound of rushing water. We just follow the sound until we find Beesha."

"That seems vague. I hope we find her."

"Don't worry, I trust Allusshia."

Tepin could smell smoke from the fire and gazed at the glowing embers dancing with light. It was cozy and relaxing listening to the crackling pops.

"How are you feeling?"

"I'm really sleepy." She yawned and put her hand over her mouth. "Necalli?"

"Yes?"

She paused a few seconds. "Never mind."

"What is it?"

"Nothing, I'm just so glad you're okay. I was…"

"You were what?"

She began to sniffle and wiped her eyes.

"Tepin, tell me."

"I was so afraid you were dead in that field. I almost couldn't breathe."

"I'm not that easy to kill, although that green-eyed thing and the lightning had me a bit worried. How can a man have such power?"

"Maybe that thing was Beesha."

"I doubt it; she wouldn't have fled into the woods like that."

Tepin wiped her face and nose. Her eyes grew heavy and she slowly fell asleep. Necalli laid her down and covered her up. He lay down, too, and watched her sleep for a while.

CHAPTER 4

A colorful parrot landed on a nearby limb, flapping its wings loudly. Necalli jumped and grabbed his sword. "Stupid bird. Why did you have to wake me? I was having the most wonderful dream."

"What were you dreaming about?"

"Oh, Tepin, I didn't know you were awake."

"So what was your dream?"

"Wow, we need to get moving."

Tepin smiled and laughed. "Okay, you don't have to tell me." She bumped into Necalli on purpose. He started to laugh. Tupac awoke and sat up, gently pulling his leg across the ground. He massaged and scratched the area around his wound. His bandage was stuck to the dried blood. As he tried to pull it loose, he let out a sigh.

"Tupac, wait, let me take a look." Tepin washed the wound and worked the dressing loose. She redressed it tightly. "How are you feeling?"

"A lot better than yesterday. I sure could eat though."

"We ate the last of the supplies I brought," said Necalli, "but I'm sure we can eat when we reach Beesha. It shouldn't be long now."

"Listen to all those birds, they're so loud," Tepin said.

"I know. I wonder why."

A little ball of light descended from the sky and flew by Necalli's face. He drew his brows and wrinkled his forehead as he stepped back. "What in the world?" It just hovered there in the same spot with a little hum like a bumble bee.

Tepin gasped. Her eyes widened as she walked closer. She held out her hand and it floated over her palm. She slowly moved her hand about and it followed her movements.

"Tepin, be careful."

"It's okay, see. It's harmless."

Necalli laughed. "Looks like you made a new friend."

"I wonder what it is."

"I don't know. Yet another thing I've never seen before."

"Well, at least this one's not deadly."

They mounted up on their horses and rode up the path. The little ball of light followed along with Tepin. She smiled and watched it fly beside her. The air became less humid as their elevation increased. After a while the path started to narrow and they rose above the jungle on the left. They could see a great distance. The sky was so blue and the jungle below was fresh and green. The leaves were flapping in a slight breeze. The air smelled sweet, almost like sugar. A cliff to the right started to increase in height the further they rode.

"You hear that?" Necalli asked.

"What?"

"The birds, they all stopped."

"Necalli! STOP!" They pulled back on the reins and held their position.

"What is it, Tepin?"

"Am I going crazy or is the ground breathing up there?"

They all looked intently forward for a moment. "What is that?" Necalli moved to dismount but then... The beast lifted its head above the path, snarling and breathing heavily. "Whoa, it's a dazhidegou."

"What in the world is a dazhidegou?" Tepin asked.

Before they could even try to run the enormous four-legged beast with huge horns and a scaly body of armor let out an ear-ringing, reverberating roar. They could feel its breath in their hair and smell the horrid stench at thirty yards. It began to charge and before they could even try to turn and run it was upon them. The ground was shaking with each stomp of its huge hoofed feet. Only feet away, the little ball of light flew across the dazhidegou's face. It stopped suddenly and watched as the ball of light led it near the drop-off.

"Quick! YAH! YAH!"

They snapped the reins of the horses hard. They rode as fast as they could for the pass. The beast turned and gave chase right behind them. It only took half a moment before its huge horn was mere inches from digging into Tupac's back. An intense wave of blue light and a burst of wind passed right by them. The beast slid to a halt with clumps and dirt and vegetation flying up into the air. They could see a dark figure on the path in front of them, but they never stopped. They dashed though the gorge left behind by the dazhidegou and through a small stream before galloping up and out of the trench. As they raced up the pass they could see a man with glowing green eyes under a dark hood. As quickly as he appeared he was gone. Necalli looked up and could see a bright blue glow on the top of a staff moving across the ridge of the high cliff above them. They did not slow for quite some time. The horses were breathing very heavily and slobbered at the mouth.

"I think we're clear of that thing and we need to rest the horses," Necalli said.

"I was just thinking the same thing," Tupac said. "That thing, whatever you called it, isn't following us anymore."

Tepin caught her breath and started laughing. "I have never been so scared." She put her hand on her chest. "My heart is still beating like wildfire." She took Necalli's hand and placed it on her chest. "See?" He looked her in the eyes and laughed with a wide grin.

"So what do we do now?" Tupac asked.

"Well, you can ride and we'll walk until the horses rest up a bit. We're very close."

"Necalli, you hear that? Rushing water."

"You're right, we're definitely very close."

The trail narrowed as they walked until the path was gone. After about a mile the sound of rushing water increased. They stopped at a small stream to water the horses and fill their flasks. A twig snapped and the horses jumped. They all stood perfectly still until a young man yelled out and fell backwards down into the stream about ten feet away from them off of a high rise. He landed hard on his back.

Tepin jumped. "Oh my. Are you okay?" She walked over and reached her hand down to offer to help the young man to his feet. Just then, five men with swords drawn jumped out of the thicket. Necalli went to draw his sword...

"Hold it, lad. You don't want to die today," their leader said.

"What do you want?"

"Quiet! You over there, get off your horse."

"He can't, he's wounded!" Necalli said.

"I said shut up!"

One of the men went to grab Necalli, pulling his hood from his head. He stood and stared for a moment. "Wait, it's the prince!"

"No, it can't be, not out here."

The leader of the group looked at Necalli and bowed down before him. The others followed. "Pardon, my lord, we didn't know."

"Rise. Who are you?"

"I'm Gardack. The clumsy one over there is Nolin, my son." Gardack stood up straight and tall with his chest out. "We are the king's men, my lord."

"What are you doing way out here?" Necalli asked.

"We are trapped by a great beast down the pass. It killed fifteen of my men when we tried to return home. Wait, how did you get up the path?"

"It's a long story," Necalli said.

"Did you lose your men, sire? You must have many men with you."

"They are camped down below waiting for us," Necalli said as he glanced over at Tepin.

"Are you hungry, my lord?"

"We could eat."

"Will you come and share a meal with us?"

"That would be great."

Necalli reluctantly accepted their request, but they were starving. Tepin walked close to Necalli and whispered in a whiny voice as they followed the men, "My little glowie's gone." He put his arm around her as they walked. Nolin took his wet shirt off and wrung it out. Tepin noticed that he was quite muscular. She glanced over at him a few times and noticed that he kept staring at her. She pretended not to notice and stayed close to Necalli. She watched as Nolin whispered something to his father.

After some distance they arrived at a small cabin erected out of bamboo. Necalli helped Tupac off his horse and sat him on one of several old timbers that were placed around a makeshift fire pit. They made themselves comfortable and shared some meat that was cooking on a spit. "My lord, you still haven't mentioned how you got past the dazhidegou. Does it still guard the path?"

"Yes it does."

"How long have you been stuck up here?"

"For a few months."

Tepin walked a short distance to get some water and Nolin followed her. Necalli lifted his eyebrows, tightened his forehead, and squinted, giving him an evil eye.

"Why did you and your men storm us at the creek with your swords drawn?" Necalli asked Gardack, sitting across from him on a dead tree trunk.

"We were going to take your horses to try to make it past the beast."

Necalli glanced at Tupac. He was giving him a strange look with his shoulders raised and his head hunched. He was slightly shaking his head no. Necalli ceased inquiring about the men and finished eating. Tepin handed him some water and sat down.

"Tepin, can you help me into the woods for a moment?" Tupac asked.

"Sure."

Tepin helped him to limp into the woods to relieve himself. As soon as they were out of view he grabbed her by the arm and whispered, "Tepin, something's wrong."

"What is it?"

"I don't think these are the king's men. Trust me on this. You have to warn Necalli."

"Okay."

They made their way back to the camp and Tepin helped Tupac to sit while keeping his leg straight. She walked back over to Necalli. She wanted to whisper to him, but the men were watching her closely. She tried to act casual and sat back down on the log next to him.

Some time had passed and they had finished eating. "Thank you men, for sharing your meat with us."

"You're welcome, my lord."

Tepin looked up to see Nolin intently staring at her. He never blinked or broke eye contact. The other four men also seemed to be watching them.

Necalli desired to get back on his quest and was losing patience just sitting there. He took a deep breath and let it out in a little huff. He glanced at Tepin and noticed the concern on her face. He looked around at the men watching them and was hesitant to get up. He slowly stood and stretched. He noticed three of the man casually put their hands on their swords. He pretended not to see them. *Something's going on.*

CHAPTER 5

Allusshia's eyes were growing heavy. Her head kept bobbing, shocking herself awake. She took in a frustrated deep gasp of air and slowly exhaled, barely noticing one of the guards gazing directly at Malinche. She smacked him hard on the back of his head. "What are you doing? Snap out of it!"

"Oh, wow. Sorry. I don't know what happened." He shook his head to try to free his mind from Malinche's manipulation.

"It's only a matter of time, Allusshia. You can't stay awake forever," Malinche said.

"Oh, just shut up already! I can't kill you, but I can certainly hurt you and you're pissing me off!"

Malinche grinned confidently at Allusshia. The guards were relieved by a fresh set of men better able to resist Malinche's enticing. They talked with Allusshia to try to keep her awake. Her eyes were drawing so heavy and they were having a hard time keeping her alert. One of the guards returned with a tray of refreshments.

"Here Allusshia, drink this. It will help you stay awake."

"What is it?"

"It's black tea. It's made from tea bricks the king recently traded with merchants from China. It's quite good, but it's a bit strong. It'll keep you wide awake." Malinche smiled widely as Allusshia tried a few sips.

"Wow, this is so good."

Allusshia gulped down the tea in seconds. The men could hear her gulping and looked at her strangely. After a few minutes, Allusshia started to have a glow about her and a cool breeze blew through the lower dungeons blowing her hair around. The air smelled musty but with a hint of roses from the gardens above. Allusshia felt very odd and her heart started to race wildly. She began to laugh out loud and blew Malinche a kiss. "Mwah."

"What's so funny, Allusshia?"

"I wonder how Malinche would feel if I tied her hair to her toes."

"What?" the guard who had brought the tea asked with confusion.

"I know, let's stuff worms up her nose."

"Allusshia, what's wrong with you?"

She started to stumble around. One of the guards reached out to grab her, but as soon as he touched her body he was shocked intently, the force of it knocking him down and sliding him across the stone floor. He sat up in pain holding his hand, it was smoking.

Malinche started laughing loudly. One of the guards walked over and rapped her upside the head and face with the butt of his pike. With her hands bound, she turned her hand in the guard's direction and, using her powers, lifted him high up in the chamber until he was pinned to the high dungeon ceiling. His pike and gear fell to the floor far below.

Allusshia laughed and lifted her staff. The stela-stone started to glow bright blue. She swung the top of her staff in circles creating a whirlwind of blue eleamus that began to rip electrons out of the air with sparks and small lightning bolts. She thrust the staff of Beesha forward, striking Malinche and engulfing her body in eleamus. Malinche screamed over and over again in great pain. The eleamus swirled around her, burning her clothes away and heating her binding chains until they were red-hot. The guard pinned to the ceiling fell hard to the ground and was killed instantly.

CHAPTER 6

Gardack spoke out. "So do you still think you can save your father?"

Necalli was taken aback; he gave Gardack a funny look.

"Hold on. I never said anything about saving my father."

"Yeah, when we first met. You said you needed to save your father."

"NO! I didn't. How would you even know he needed saving if you've been up here for months?"

There were several moments of intense silence then Necalli drew his sword swiftly from his sheath. Gardack and his men jumped to their feet. Their swords hummed when they drew them. Two of the men came at Necalli. He jumped backwards over the log he was sitting on while Tepin ran over behind Tupac.

Necalli swung his sword mightily, cutting through one of the men's blades severing his crappy sword in two. The man looked at him with a surprised look on his face just before Necalli ran him though.

Another one of the men attacked Tupac. He leaned back and slipped to the ground from the log he was sitting on, blocking each blow with his sword. The man swung at him forcefully like he was chopping wood. Tupac tried to block each blow as best he could, but he was helpless to stop him. Tepin grabbed a knife that Tupac had stuck in the log after eating. She thrust it into the man's side. He yelled out and dropped his sword. Tupac leaned forward and thrust his blade up though the soldier's belly. Tepin helped him to his feet. Just as he turned to look, one of the men jabbed his sword through his chest.

"Oh no!"

Tepin stepped back. She covered her lips with her hands. The soldier looked right at her and began to take a step towards her. She stumbled backwards but was caught by Nolin. Her knees felt weak and she stumbled as he pulled her backwards. She cried out in fear when he put a knife to her throat.

"Don't move, beautiful. I don't want to have to kill you."

Necalli was fighting fearlessly. He lunged forward and the soldier he was fighting stepped backwards, tripping over one of the logs around the fire pit. Necalli swung his sword with his arm extended, severing the man's head from his body. He turned his attention to Gardack who had stood back watching the fight. He took a step in Gardack's direction but Nolin yelled out, "Stop or she dies!"

Necalli froze. He put his hands out to the side as he slowly leaned down to drop his sword. He felt the blood rush to his head and broke out into a cold sweat.

"Wait! Don't hurt her."

He was stunned and tried to think of a way out of this.

"I'm sorry, Necalli," Tepin said.

Necalli stood up with his hands in the air in front of him. "Please, don't hurt her."

"Tie them up," Gardack said. "You will never save your father, boy!"

That's Malinche talking, Necalli thought. He looked at Tepin. She was flushed and her eyes were open wide.

Gardack tied Necalli's hands behind his back and then tied him to a banana tree. Nolin threw Tepin to the ground. She let out a shriek when he pulled her arms back to tie around a tree.

"Stop, you're hurting her!"

Nolin put his knife to Necalli's throat. "Go ahead. Say another word."

"Don't you touch him!" Tepin said.

"Nolin! We need him alive. The girl you can kill," Gardack yelled.

"Father, you said I could have the albino woman."

"Later. We have work to do."

They walked off leaving Necalli and Tepin tied to the banana trees. Necalli could hear them talking in the distance.

"Don't worry, Tepin, we'll be okay."

She frowned, protruding her lower lip, and cried softly.

"They killed Tupac."

She bowed her head down and her body felt drained. Her eyes watered and a sole tear ran down her face.

"Tepin, it will be okay. We'll get out of this."

"Why are they doing this?"

"I think Malinche may have a hold on Gardack."

"How?" Tepin asked with a wavering voice.

"I don't know. Something's wrong. Something must have happened. I hope Allusshia and my father are okay. We need to get free right now. Way too much time has passed."

Tepin's arms were so tightly pulled behind her back that she couldn't move. Necalli pulled and pulled at his ropes, but they just seemed to get tighter the more he struggled. The ropes were cutting off his circulation. He noticed several swords had been left just lying on the ground from the soldiers that he and Tepin had killed, but they were too far out of his reach.

"I wish there was a way to pull one of those swords closer."

"I can't budge, Necalli. There's no way."

By nightfall Necalli had lost most of the feeling in his hands and fingers, but he never stopped trying to get free.

"Necalli, it's no use."

"Tepin, don't you give up on me."

She beamed at Necalli and relaxed her body. She leaned her head back against the tree whilst looking at him.

"I'm going to miss you, Necalli."

"Don't you talk like that. We're going to be fine."

She took a deep breath, held it in for a second, and then slowly let it out. A light misty fog drifted across the ground dampening their skin. Necalli rested his chin on his chest and it felt sticky and clammy.

Gardack soon returned with his son and the other soldier. They were carrying a furry black boar with stringy hair. It was strung up by its feet on a thick stick. They skinned it and put it over the fire. The distant sky was barely illuminated with shades of charcoal-gray fading into blackness. The campfire cast dances of light against the trees of the jungle. Bugs were chirping and whistling various tones that carried loudly and rung the ears. Necalli and Tepin sat still and silent. For a few moments it felt like they had been forgotten, but then Nolin walked up and kneeled down in front of Tepin. He ran his hand slowly through her hair and across her face. She bit his finger, drawing blood.

"Ouch!"

She scrunched up her face and closed her eyes tight as he slapped her hard.

"Get off her!"

Nolin looked at Necalli and laughed; then he turned his attention back to Tepin. He pulled her head back by her hair and kissed her neck. She struggled but couldn't move. Necalli struggled harder than ever to get free. Smoke from the fire got into his eyes and they burned. Nolin sat in Tepin's lap. She flung her body upwards to try to knock him off.

"Get—off—me!"

"Nolin, I'm going to kill you!"

Gardack walked over to Necalli and put his sword against his face. "Are you now?"

Necalli tilted his head back and looked up at him. He pulled his sword away leaving a small incision in Necalli's cheek. Blood began to run down his face and drip from his chin.

"You two take that girl into the woods. I don't care to hear her screaming."

They cut Tepin's bonds and she wanted to run, but her arms were so weak that she couldn't get up. They pulled her to her feet. She screamed and fought to try to get away. Necalli squirmed and pressed against the tree frantically, but he was helpless to do anything.

"Necalli!"

"Let her go!"

Tepin wouldn't walk so they dragged her kicking into the darkness of the jungle.

"Necalli help me!" she frantically yelled.

"Gardack, you're dead! This is your last night in this world."

Necalli could hear Tepin's screams in the distance. His heart raced and he could feel the blood pumping in his veins and throbbing in his wrists.

Gardack laughed. "Boy, you've failed. Just admit it. You might as well give up. You couldn't save your father and now you can't save that feeble little albino girl." He cupped his hands to his mouth and yelled loudly, "Shut that girl up."

Necalli looked up at Gardack's torn shirt. He must have snagged it on something and his side was bleeding, but he didn't seem to notice. Necalli peered at him.

"You're just a coward, Gardack."

He put the tip of his sword against Necalli's throat.

"You're going to be more trouble than you're worth, aren't you, boy? I should just finish you right now."

He raised his face and lifted his sword high with a tight grip. His lips tightened together. Necalli turned his head and cringed, waiting for it; he let out a short yell. Just then he noticed two bright green specs in the darkness slowly moving with a little bob like someone walking. His ropes turned to ash and he ducked down just as Gardack's sword swished above his head trimming the top of his hair as it struck the tree. Necalli rolled across the ground picking up a nearby sword, but his wrist hurt and he could barely hold on to it.

Gardack came right at him. His sword bore down the edge of Necalli's blade striking the hilt. Necalli could feel the sharp shock in his wrists, it hurt badly and he shook his hand to ease the pain. He ran while shaking his hand to try to get the blood flowing again. He grabbed a vine and kicked off hard from a tree, swinging around him. Gardack turned and tripped over a log in the dark, stumbling to the ground face first. He exhaled hard as his chest smashed into the black soil.

Necalli tried to gain a stance using both hands as Gardack got up. He followed Gardack's flickering shadows set by firelight. Gardack came at him, swinging with mesmerizing accuracy. He was surprised at Gardack's war craft. Each thrust was smart, direct, and strong. Even at his best Necalli realized it would be a tough match as he backed up with each parry while his thoughts were tied to Tepin. His whole body quaked like he was wrapped in a hot blanket as he realized he may lose this fight. For the first time he was scared, not for himself, but how could he rescue Tepin if he were dead or his father for that matter?

Their blades clashed with bright sparks illuminating their faces. Gardack kicked Necalli, knocking him to the ground. He plunged his sword down as Necalli rolled several times before climbing back to his feet. He was driven back further and further until he almost tripped over a bush. He ran around a tree and tried to take up a better position when a monkey howled loudly just above him. It was so loud it startled Gardack as he turned to lunge forward. Necalli almost dropped his sword and stepped back again shaking the blood into his hand. His heart beat so hard he could feel it in his neck and wrists.

Just as Necalli felt his strength returning, Gardack swung hard knocking the sword from his hands. He staggered backwards avoiding his blade. His head spun and he felt dizzy and couldn't catch his breath. Gardack stepped on the side of a log, groping for a stable place to stand, and his knee cracked. He limped backwards to gain his footing. Necalli went to pick up his sword but fell. He rolled to his front and reached for his sword, but Gardack pressed his sandal on his head. Necalli tried to whip his legs around to kick him, but he only pressed harder. He could barely see Gardack's smile as he drove his sword down—down into the dirt.

A thick puff of green smoke rose up from the ground. Gardack poked around with his sword but Necalli was gone. He looked around in the dark, confused and rubbing his chin. Then he could hear heavy breathing behind him. Before he could turn he felt the sharp blade ripping through his body and could see the bloody blade emerge from his chest. He let out a faint grunt and pummeled the dirt.

Necalli stood. He shook his head, perplexed. One moment he was on the ground, the next he was standing behind Gardack. *What happened?*

There was no time to catch his breath. He hadn't heard Tepin scream in some time and feared the worst. He found his own sword and ran into the dark of the jungle and slammed hard into Tepin running the other way. She screamed and they both fell to the ground. "Shhh, Tepin, it's okay, it's me."

"Oh, Necalli, they're right behind—" Nolin and the other soldier ran upon them in the dark with their swords drawn. At first they couldn't see them, but then Necalli rose up with his sword in his hand.

Enough's enough already!

He defeated his doubts and stood tall grasping his sword firmly, motioning Tepin to stay down. He watched the two men closely as they circled around him, poised to strike.

"I'm going to enjoy cutting you into little pieces, prince."

"Well, that's not going to happen, Nolin," Necalli said as he twirled his sword in his hand, feeling much better. Nolin charged in and their swords hummed when they clashed together. Necalli could feel the vibrations but held strong. Swish! He ducked down as he heard the soldier swing at him. He veered his sword back to the side, spinning around, and slashed at the man's arm with the tip of his blade. He turned and punched Nolin in the face. Necalli lashed out mightily with his sword striking the crossguard of Nolin's sword and he lost his grip, holding his hand in pain. Necalli pulled his sword upward and caught Nolin's forearm as he turned and swung at the soldier. Nolin cried out and fell to the ground. Necalli took the advantage and pressed forward. The soldier tired quickly. Soon his arm strength gave out and Necalli drove his sword into his belly. The man cried out, holding his stomach in agony.

"Necalli! Behind you!"

Necalli spun around with his sword extended and Nolin ran right into it, piercing though his neck. Tepin screamed and held her hands over her eyes. Nolin fell to his knees gurgling and then fell backwards onto the ground, trying desperately to hold on to life. He couldn't talk but made faint noises and was clearly stressed while Necalli stood above him placing the tip of his blade on Nolin's chest. He leaned down on his sword, pressing it slowly though Nolin's leather armor and into his heart. He lay in the dark with his eyes open and with blood-soaked skin.

"What a waste," Necalli said.

The soldier, holding his stomach with one arm and using the other to try to crawl away, made grunting sounds as he skirted across the dead leaves. Necalli walked over and the soldier wailed just before Necalli beheaded him with a single whop of his sword.

He reached out his hand. "Tepin, are you okay?"

"That was horrible."

"What they tried to do to you was horrible."

Tepin went to hug him, but before she could she stumbled. Necalli caught her as her body went limp. Her side felt slippery and he almost dropped her. The whole side of her body was covered in blood. Necalli felt a pain deep in his chest and a lump in his throat. He couldn't swallow and trembled all over. "Hold on, hatsuts," which is to say, "sweetie." He desperately rushed to the light of the fire. "Don't you die on me!"

He laid her on the ground. Her breathing was short and heavy.

"Please stay with me, Tepin."

After cleaning the wounds in her side he used an ember from the fire to sear the serrations. He found some cloth to use as dressings. She was alive but unconscious and breathing faintly.

Necalli pulled together some bedding and lay with his arm around her with his head resting upon his palm, listening to her breathing and desiring her to live.

CHAPTER 7

Necalli's horse stood above him in the morning mist and whinnied. When Necalli didn't wake, he nudged his shoulder and snorted. Necalli slowly opened his weary eyes and reached up petting his muzzle. "Good boy. I'm so glad to see you, buddy." Tepin turned her head and looked at them.

"Tepin! How do you feel?" he asked with bright eyes and a heavy heart.

She tried to move and sit up. "Ugh, my side hurts."

"You had several cuts and lost a lot of blood."

Tepin lifted her shirt and looked at the wounds.

"What happened in the woods? What did they do to you?"

"I refused to let Nolin touch me. He tried, but I fought him off. He got really mad and stabbed me in the side several times with his finger knife. It hurt so bad. I could feel it hit the bone. I played dead and when they laid me down for a few seconds, I got up and ran as fast as I could. Next thing I knew, I ran into you."

"I'm so glad you're still alive. Nolin and his father were cowards and no soldiers of my father's."

"Tupac said so; he said to warn you but…" Tepin frowned thinking about Tupac and just looked up at Necalli with sad eyes. "Necalli, what's going to happen to the kingdom?"

"I don't know. We need to finish this quest and find Beesha. It's been far too long. It should have only taken me a day and a half to reach her."

"I wish we could just live up here and forget about the world. You could hunt and I could cook. We could be happy."

Necalli hugged her gently and kissed her forehead. "That would be splendid, Tepin, but we have a responsibility to stop her. People like Gardack and Malinche only serve themselves. They rule to control the masses for personal power and gain. A true king is foremost a servant of the people who gives up his own desires for those he serves to provide them with safety and freedom to prosper and to pursue happiness. Our kingdom has lived free for a long time and thus has prospered greatly. Although it may not seem like it, the people of our kingdom would rather fight and die than lose their freedom. Regardless of the fate of my father we must prevail."

Tepin smiled boldly at him. "You are a true king and I will follow you to the end."

Necalli shook his head. "You are sweet, Tepin, but I don't want you anywhere near the fighting."

Tepin just smiled and blushed a little bit.

"Do you think you can ride?"

"I must, we have to find Beesha, right?"

Necalli helped her onto his horse and climbed up behind her. He held her tight as they headed toward the sound of the water. She leaned her head back against his chest.

After traveling for a short distance they came upon a high cliff. There was an immense sound of crashing water. They moved up to a clearing just ahead.

"Necalli, that's just incredible."

"I'll say. That's the most impressive thing I think I've ever seen."

"Yeah, it's like several miles wide. Ooh, look at the rainbow from the mist."

"Just imagine the power of all that water crashing down."

"I hope we don't have to cross that." Tepin laughed.

"The land bordering the other side is beyond our kingdom."

"Necalli, how do we find Beesha now? We found the rushing water."

"I trust Allusshia. We'll find her."

They traveled upstream along the river for about a mile until Tepin cried out, "Necalli, look. My little glowie's back." She held out her hand and it hovered above her palm, just as before. "I wonder where he went." The little glowing ball flew into the woods and then hovered back and forth. After a few seconds it flew back to Tepin, stopped for a second, then flew back toward the woods.

"Necalli, I think it wants us to follow it."

"Hmmm."

"Really, I think it's waiting for us."

"Guess there's no harm in following it for a second. There's no sign of Beesha anyway."

They turned and followed Tepin's glowie. It led them into the jungle away from the river. A short distance later, Necalli thought his vision was blurring up. He couldn't focus right.

"Do you see that, Tepin?"

"I do. The jungle looks fuzzy."

They walked up to the fuzziness and the air seemed to ripple like the surface of a pond but standing sideways. Tepin stuck her hand into it.

"Wow, did you see that?"

"Amazing."

"What is it?"

"I don't know, but I'm thinking your little glowie just showed us the way to Beesha."

They pressed through the fuzziness. Their bodies tingled and there was pressure resisting their advance. Once they pushed through to the other side, the canopy opened up to a beautiful blue sky. They were surrounded by incredible shades of color. Beautiful flowers and blankets of plush green vegetation flowed along the ground. Many little flowing balls and sprinkles of light floated through the air. Strange little creatures walked on tree branches and stared at them as they walked by as if they were intelligent beings.

One little creature looked like a colorful lizard but with a little head like a penguin. Necalli and Tepin looked in amazement with their eyes wide open and their eyebrows lifted high on their foreheads. A nearby tree uprooted itself and moved away with crashing and swaying cracks into the woods, startling them. Tepin jumped and then grabbed her side in pain when a tiny little monkey climbed down a vine and jumped onto her shoulder.

"You okay, Tepin?"

"Yeah, it's just a little monkey bunny."

Necalli laughed. "Monkey bunny?"

"Yeah, that's what my father called them. The little monkeys."

Necalli continued to laugh. All of a sudden, all the little lights and sparkles spun around and drew together into one bright spot. Necalli and Tepin had to cover their eyes with their arms to block out the light. They both felt warmth and a tingling all over. Their muscles just seemed to relax and a sensation of something approaching came over them. There was a little snap and a young girl appeared out of the light with oddly-shaped red ears and wide, aqua-green eyebrows. She had silver hair with colorful glowing ends like tiny strands of fiber optics. She had little colorful glowing decorations on her face, arms, and sides, not covered by her thin, transparent garment that was not of this world. It was almost as a layer of partially translucent skin, silky and flexible, flowing in the breeze.

"Welcome Necalli," she said in a soft, warm voice.

"Are you Beesha?"

"Necalli, come lay Tepin here on the chaise."

"How do you know our names?"

"Come now, she is in pain."

Necalli took Tepin down from his horse and carried her to the chaise and laid her down gently. The little girl held her hands over her wounds. A warm amber light surrounded Tepin's chest and she let out a little squeal from the tickle. Little specs of light radiated out and into her side. She took a deep breath and felt the need to stretch and yawn.

"How's that, Tepin?"

She sat up and felt her side. "It's healed. Necalli, it's completely healed. Not even a scar. Thank you, Beesha." Tepin reached out and hugged her. She felt an electrical tingling all over her body. "Oh, that tickles."

"So, you're Beesha?"

"You've taken too long, Necalli. The kingdom is in chaos."

"What of Allusshia?"

"I am grieved. I no longer feel her presence."

"So she's dead?"

"Or Malinche is blocking her powers. You must return. Tepin will remain with me. Here she will be safe."

"No, Necalli, I will go with you." Tepin's eyes started to water and she shuddered in panic.

"Tepin, hatsuts, Beesha's right. Here you will be safe and I will be able to travel much faster alone."

Tepin sniffled and wiped her eyes and nose. Necalli felt bad. He hugged her tightly. "Everything will be okay. You'll see."

"Necalli, take the stones from your bag and bring them to me."

"How did you know about them?"

"No time for questions, just bring them."

Necalli opened his saddlebag. The stones were glowing bright green in the presence of Beesha and felt very warm to his touch. He took them and placed them in front of her. She held her hand above them and squinted her eyes shut. Fiery beams of light emitted from her hands and went into the stones. They turned translucent blue and glowed brightly. Something was turning inside them like little black and gold glimmering threads.

"Amazing."

Beesha strung the stones together into a necklace. She placed it around Necalli's neck. "This will protect you. You must get close enough to Malinche to place this around her neck before you end her."

"Couldn't you come with me, Beesha? You could heal my father as you healed Tepin."

"I wish I could, Necalli. That would be wonderful, but if I leave my realm, I will perish."

"Necalli, the green-eyed, hooded man may be able to help if you can find him," Tepin said.

"What green-eyed man?" Beesha asked with a raised voice.

"There was a cloaked man with glowing green eyes who saved us several times."

Beesha's eyes got really big and her mouth hung slightly open. "Oh no." She bowed her head and closed her eyes. "Malinche must have sent him to discover my realm. I didn't realize…"

"Who is he?" Necalli asked.

"Necalli, he's a priest of the ancient Tezcatlipoca, as is Malinche. I didn't realize any had survived."

"Survived what?"

"Necalli, did not your father ever tell you how he became king?"

"He is the son of the great King Caracol, my grandfather."

"No Necalli, your grandfather adopted Ah-Cacaw, for he had no sons. He gave his daughter, Nelli, to your father for a wife."

"I never knew," he said with sadness and wonder.

"Necalli, your father was a great general in Caracol's army. There was a time of great war when Caracol sought to bring the lands together into one kingdom, free from the influence of the powerful Tezcatlipoca priests. Your father and I devised a plan to lure all of the priests into one place to destroy them."

"You and my father?"

"Yes, Necalli. I was King Caracol's moormit before Allusshia ever entered this world from the Otherworld."

"I'm guessing it worked and you destroyed the priests?"

"We were successful in luring them together, but something unexpected happened."

CHAPTER 8

Necalli's eyebrows lifted and his chest tightened. "Tell me, Beesha, what happened?"

"We buried a line of huge Ispus stones under the ground, around a small aquifer, but the priests were still able to use their powers. Somehow their combined strength must have been much greater than I expected. They cast ancient artifice against us, but their power was deflected by the Ispus and redirected down into the spring. Your father's men were able to destroy them and the Ispus absorbed their energy."

"The spring—"

"Yes, the forbidden spring was fortuitously begotten on that day. Ever since, the spring has granted long life to all who drink from its waters. After all, a human's body is mostly water."

"Hold on. I don't understand. Why would Malinche seek the spring if she could simply create her own?"

"Now you understand, Necalli. Malinche never knew what happened that day. Your father, his men, and I were sworn to secrecy by the king. All books and writings concerning the Tezcatlipoca were ordered destroyed by your father. Malinche was to never know of the spring or how it was conceived. How she learned of its existence is now a mystery, as is the existence of yet another Tezcatlipoca priest. Beware of him, Necalli. The Ispus will protect you, but they are cunning and have learned much in their thousand-year lifespan."

"How old are you, Beesha?" Tepin asked.

"I am two thousand three hundred and seven—I think—but I can no longer live in the realm of men and I can't make it back to the well of the Otherworld. I can draw power from my realm to sustain myself, but here I must stay, as it will be also for my sister, Allusshia, when she grows smaller."

"How old is Allusshia?" Necalli asked.

"My sister is relatively young. She is only three hundred and forty-five Earth years."

Necalli stared into space, deep in thought.

"Necalli, you okay?" Tepin asked as she hugged him around the waist. He broke from his trance and put his arm around her.

"Yes, I'm okay. How about you?"

"I feel well but…"

"What?"

"Nothing…"

"Tepin?"

Tepin smiled at him. "Noting, I'm great. I'm just going to really miss you."

"Necalli, come and have something to eat. You will need all your strength to face Malinche."

Necalli ate until he felt stuffed. He and Tepin were famished. Afterwards they walked outside and prepared for Necalli to depart.

"Necalli, please be careful."

Tepin hugged him tightly. She started to well up inside, but Beesha rubbed her back, which had a calming effect and made Tepin feel at peace and rather sleepy.

"Don't worry, Tepin, we will prevail and put Malinche to rest for good." Necalli climbed upon his horse and took the reins. Tepin and Beesha walked alongside him until he walked through the fuzzy barrier of the realm. He looked back and waved at Tepin as he pushed through to the other side.

ℂ◌

Necalli made good time and stopped well short of the pass where they last encountered the dazhidegou. He quietly snuck up and peered around the bend. The dazhidegou lay in the pass facing away from him, sleeping. The wind was blowing toward him and the odor was quite pungent. It smelled like manure mixed with stinky red clay. The beast lay breathing heavily. Each breath expanded its belly to the size of a horse.

Necalli decided that the best strategy was to get a running start and ride right over him in an attempt to outrun him down the trail.

"YAH!"

He held tight to the reins and his horse galloped as fast as he could. Just as they rounded the pass the dazhidegou stood and charged at a hooded figure further down the path. Necalli traversed the ravine in the trail and rode up the other side. A bright blue light shone from the stela in the man's staff and seemed to stun the dazhidegou but only for a moment. It swung its head from side to side and caught the Tezcatlipoca with his horn, throwing him against the cliff. Necalli's horse whinnied out of fear. The dazhidegou heard him, turned, and charged. Necalli's horse panicked and threw him to the ground. Necalli tried to find a place to take cover, but it was of no use. The dazhidegou thundered down the pass and was right upon him. The ground quaked with each stomp of its huge hooves. Necalli ducked down and covered his face with his arm waiting for the impact, but when the beast felt the power of the Ispus around his neck, it slid to a halt only inches from Necalli's face and bowed down his head and front legs in submission. Its huge armored head just inches before him trembled. It made the strangest gargling sounds as its whole body trembled so that Necalli could feel the ground vibrate. The Ispus around Necalli's neck became so hot that he had to pull it from under his shirt. The stones were glowing very brightly, he couldn't look directly at them.

Necalli reached out and touched the dazhidegou with his hand. It felt like rough stone scales. The beast opened its eyes widely and moved its head away. It slowly backed up with its front legs bent in submission. It kept its head bowed down close to the ground. As the beast moved away the Ispus began to cool. Necalli called his horse. He was hesitant but eventually walked closer with some coaxing. Necalli mounted up and rode down the path. He looked back to see the dazhidegou retreat to its ravine and hide its head from view like a scared puppy dog. Necalli drew his sword and dismounted when he reached the Tezcatlipoca priest still lying on the ground. He placed the Ispus around the man's neck and raised his sword in the air. The priest opened his eyes.

"Wait, Necalli! Don't! I'm here to help you."

Necalli's face turned blood-red. "You serve Malinche and you will die!"

"No! I serve your father. Necalli, you must believe me. I saved you several times and helped you to reach Beesha. Did I not?"

"For what purpose?"

"I owe your father a great debt. He saved me many years ago when the Tezcatlipoca were all but destroyed. I helped him to deceive them to rid our world of their evil. Your father and I are friends, Necalli. Together, you and I can destroy Malinche."

Necalli lowered his sword but kept up his guard. He stared into the priest's brown eyes. "Why do your eyes not glow green as they have done in the past?"

"Because the Ispus has taken my powers from me."

"Why would you want to destroy your own kind?"

"Malinche deceived me. I trained with your father. We fought in the wars, side by side. One day, after a great battle, we went to a small town where I met a beautiful woman. We grew close and spent much time together. She told me that I was a great warrior and had not realized my full potential. She enticed me into following her. She took me down into a deep chasm where there was a thick pool of green goo that glowed brightly. She said that all I had to do was to enter the pool and I would become greater than I could ever imagine. Necalli, she tricked me, just as she tried to trick your father before he married. The pool changed me from the inside. I could feel the change but there was nothing I could do to stop it. I ceased to be a man. I don't know what I am now. The cost of power has taken my life from me. I hoped to find Beesha one day in a desire for her to change me back, but I feared that she would only destroy me from fear for her kind."

"Wait, I thought the moormits came from the Otherworld?"

"Yes, but so do the Tezcatlipoca."

"They do?"

"It's more confusing than that, but for that you only have my word."

"If this is true, then why wouldn't my father have had Allusshia mend you?"

"Because no one beside your father knew that I lived. He had deceived his king in letting me live. I only hoped that one day he would allow me to return so that Beesha could mend me." He took a deep breath and sighed. "Necalli, there's something else."

"What?"

"Malinche has taken the capital. We must return before she gains power over the whole kingdom."

"And before she finds the forbidden spring."

"I'm afraid to say she already has."

"I wish I could trust you," Necalli said with a huff.

The priest reached out and took the tip of Necalli's blade and put it above his heart.

"If you don't trust me then there is no hope for me. Just kill me now and be done with me." He frowned and his eyes teared up. His breathing became very heavy. "Do it! Quickly, please."

CHAPTER 9

Necalli was moved in his heart. He reached down and removed the Ispus from the priest's neck and offered his hand to help him stand. His leg was hurt and he stumbled, but Necalli caught him.

"What's your name, priest?"

"Gasha."

"Wait, I remember you. I met you in the plaza when I was training."

"Yes, I remember. I suggested that Moctezuma was being rather harsh in your training. Remember what you said?"

Necalli laughed. "Yes, I said, 'Fear is final but courage is only as strong as the man himself.'"

"Intelligent words for a lad of only eight."

"I just hope Allusshia is okay. She would stop at nothing to defend the kingdom. If Malinche is free then I fear the worst."

"Don't give up hope, Necalli. Allusshia is cunning and powerful."

Necalli mounted his horse. "I need to move quickly and we only have one horse."

"That won't be a problem."

Gasha closed his eyes and tilted his head back. He tapped his staff on the ground and the stela-stone on the hilt illuminated with a soft blue glow. His body levitated up above the ground. They rode down the pass and under the canopy deep in the jungle.

After a while their pace slowed. They passed the field where the previous battle took place, but the dead soldiers and overturned wagons were gone. They couldn't figure out why. They stopped at the stream just past the clearing to rest and fill their water flasks. Necalli thought it was rather strange that the animals of the jungle kept their distance even more so than usual. *Is it because of Gasha?*

He leaned over the stream and his thoughts were of Tepin and the last time they were there. He felt a hollowness inside and frowned. So many questions raced through his mind. *What will I find when I reach home? What happened to Allusshia? Is my father still alive?* He stood up and rubbed his temple with both of his hands.

"Are you well, Necalli?"

"I'm fine, just a headache."

They continued on for a few miles then up a path climbing a large hill until they could see the top of the great temple through the trees, only a few miles away. They paused and Necalli dismounted. His horse jumped, pulling away as a full band of men emerged from the forest with swords and pikes poised to attack. Two of the man charged at Gasha.

"STOP! Stop I command you! He is with me," Necalli said.

"It's the prince!"

The men fell to their knees and bowed their heads to the ground.

"Prince Necalli, we thought you were dead," one of the captains proclaimed.

"You, arise. Tell me what has happened and where can I find Moctezuma."

The soldier stood and spoke. "My prince, Malinche has taken the city and stands at your father's side. Her armies have taken hold and are everywhere. Your father is not himself. He ordered us to kill Moctezuma so we fled."

"My father lives?"

"Yes, my prince."

"Is he well?"

"He's just not himself. He does Malinche's bidding."

"Where is Moctezuma, is he alive?"

"Yes. I will take you to him just over the rise."

The soldier and his men led Necalli and Gasha through the treeline and over the rise. There were soldiers scattered about making camp but they were in disarray. They walked into a clearing where Necalli could see Moctezuma and his captains standing over a makeshift bamboo table.

"General!" one of the soldiers called out.

Moctezuma looked over at Necalli and fell to his knees as if he was faint. He leaned to the ground with his hands stretched out in front of him. All the men around him fell to the ground with their heads bowed. Many moments passed and the general remained still. Necalli walked over to him and put his hand on his head.

"General."

Moctezuma looked up at Necalli with tearing eyes. "I thought you were dead and all was lost. Malinche, she—"

"My father, what happened? Where is Allusshia?"

"Necalli, I don't know what happened. I made sure the guards were rotated out to help keep Allusshia awake, but somehow Malinche managed to get free. The next thing I knew I was summoned before your father. He looked well, but his mind was lost. Malinche had a hold on him. He commanded me to attack Copan."

"Copan? Why on earth would he ask you to attack Copan?"

"Exactly! And when I questioned him about it, he ordered me to be put to death. So I fled."

"And the army?"

"About half the troops fled, some with me and the rest scattered into the jungle."

"And the half that stayed in command of my father?"

"Since they believed you were dead they stayed out of fear. Malinche has been interrogating them and threatening their families. She has put many to death. She has struck fear into their hearts."

"So is it true that Malinche has her own army?"

"Yes, a very large army."

"How many men could she have? We annihilated her entire army."

"Necalli, we never faced her real army. I believe this has been her plan all along, to gain control of your father, then there would be little resistance so that her real army could occupy the city. And there's something else."

"What?"

"These men. They're like nothing I've ever seen before. They're highly trained and heavily armored. Malinche must have been creating this army for years. There's no way we can beat them in open battle. If we had more horses we could try to run them down, but we have so few. "

"We need to find another way to free my father and kill Malinche."

"Did you obtain the Ispus?"

Necalli pulled the necklace from under his shirt. The stones were cool and clear.

"All we have to do is get it around Malinche's neck, and then we can end her for good."

"That's going to be a problem with so many soldiers occupying the city."

"I need to get a closer look. Maybe there's a way I can get into the palace without being seen."

"We can't take that chance. With you I can rally the troops together, but if you are killed there will be no hope and the kingdom will be lost forever."

"Either way I need to get down there and see for myself. Maybe

I can find a weakness or use one of the hidden passageways under the city."

"I would advise against it. It's too risky. Let me just send a few men to spy on them, men who know the city well and have friends among our remaining troops."

"Moctezuma, you worry too much. I will be fine."

"And if Malinche captures you and takes the Ispus?"

"Good point. Send your loyalist men. They need to go in at twilight and report back by morning."

CHAPTER 10

Moctezuma set a large contingent of men to guard Necalli during the night. He himself kept a watchful eye. Come morning he gently shook Necalli to wake him.

"Our spies have returned with news."

Necalli put on his leather armor and wore his sword at his side. They walked out to meet with the spies.

"What news have you?" Moctezuma asked.

"As you expected, there is a huge contingent of soldiers stationed within the city. All hidden entrances into the palace have either been sealed or are heavily guarded. We see no possible way to enter the palace unnoticed. Also, the king's personal guard has been put to death. Malinche is guarded by her own men. She won't let any of our soldiers inside the palace, but I was told her personal guard is not very large."

"How many men?" Moctezuma inquired.

"We don't know. There was no way to find out without giving away our presence."

Necalli seemed to drift, staring out toward the high temple.

"Necalli?"

"General, we need to draw them out of the city. Then a small band of man can accompany me to remove the guards and enter the palace.

Maybe our men in the city will join us when they see me."

The general thought for a few seconds and studied the maps laid out on the bamboo table. "I have a plan, but it will mean facing her troops. Even if you are successful and Malinche is killed we still have to defeat her soldiers. Many will die."

"I can help there," Gasha said.

"This is a daring plan, Necalli. If you're captured or killed it's all over."

"Wait. You said they think that I'm dead, right?"

"Yes."

"I can go in disguised as one of Malinche's men. We just need to kill one so I can use his armor. Do you think we can get our men to fight with us if they know I'm alive?"

Moctezuma's eyes widened and his eyebrows furrowed. "That's a good idea. This could actually work."

The general had no problem getting volunteers for two secret missions. The first group was to try to convince the king's men to fight against Malinche's troops, once led out of the city. The second group was to capture or kill an enemy soldier and return his armor for Necalli's disguise. The plan was set into motion.

⫷⫸

Evening had come and the soldiers returned with enemy armor.

"Nice fit! Good job, men," Necalli said.

Three of the general's men ran swiftly up the hill yelling. As they approached they could see the men's faces were bright red and they were so out of breath they could hardly stand. One man tried to speak but bent over gasping for air.

"General, they're coming!"

"Who's coming?"

"All of them. The entire garrison including our own men leading the way. They captured our spies and killed them. They must know Necalli is alive."

"How far off?" Moctezuma asked.

"Maybe fifteen minutes at most."

"There goes our surprise."

"Bring some horses; we need to see what we're up against."

Necalli, Moctezuma, and the general's personal guard rode out to see the army for themselves. When they drew close, they tied up their horses and hid out of sight on top of a rise. They could see the army keeping in close formation. They marched five abreast with their black shields held firmly in front of them, swords drawn and black helmets with the eye guards down. Their strange metal armor was black with wild golden markings of skulls and fire. They marched with short steps, without drums, but let out an ominous "Hauh" on every fourth step. Their stomping feet kept the beat.

Step – Step – Step – "Hauh!"

Step – Step – Step – "Hauh!"

Step – Step – Step – "Hauh!"

"I must say, that is the most intimidating army I've ever seen."

The sky filled with dark clouds and there were distant lightning strikes. They mounted up and rode for the encampment. The smell of rain was in the air.

"Necalli, I doubt this is a fight we can win. They must have two thousand men and we have about what? Four hundred at most, and we don't know if our men will turn and fight with us."

"General, I have a plan."

"What is it?"

"Ummmm. You trust me, right?"

"Necalli?"

"Just hold them off until I return. Hold as long as you can. We can only hope that our men will join us and fight with us."

"Necalli, where are you going? We stand a much better chance of our men joining us if they see you at the head of the battle."

"Just trust me, General."

Moctezuma had the men bring Necalli the fastest horse they could find that was well fed and rested. Necalli mounted and rode away from the camp as fast as the horse would run. Many of the men watched him gallop away causing questions in their minds. Moctezuma commanded the men to form up and prepared for battle. Small groups of soldiers periodically ran from the jungle and joined up to fight as they heard that Necalli was still alive. Many of their families were trapped within the city, unable to flee.

They stood there waiting and watching. The sound of the approaching enemy soldiers grew louder as their heavy footsteps and ominous chant echoed off the hillside. Moctezuma looked around. The men's faces were pale and vacant.

"Men, stand strong and have no fear," Moctezuma said.

He slammed his sword mightily against his shield and yelled, psyching up the men. All his soldiers began to pound their shields and chant at the approaching massive enemy.

Rat – tat – tat

Rat – tat – tat

Rat – tat – tat

When the enemy soldiers grew close, Gasha waved his staff in the air. The stela began to glow blood-red. Misty reddish vapors emerged upon the ground like a cloud. The vapor became so thick that the two armies could no longer see each other. Gasha waved his arms forward directing the cloud toward the enemy. They were engulfed in the mist that surrounded them and flowed down the hillside. Touched by the mist, all the soldiers became confused. They dropped their shields and swords and held their hands to their heads while their worst fears played out in their minds. Many tried to hold their breath when they saw the mist approaching, but all that was needed was a simple touch of the skin.

All of a sudden a lightning bolt struck the ground startling everyone. The wind gusted forcefully down the hillside and rain poured from the sky. The mist was diluted and washed away. The confused soldiers shook off the enchantment and picked up their weapons. Some of the king's men at the front of the line ran to join Moctezuma's ranks. Moctezuma led his warriors in a charge down the hill and collided with the enemy. It was total chaos. The king's men were fighting each other, not knowing who was loyal and who was following Malinche in the king's name. Malinche's hardened soldiers started attacking everyone no matter whose side they were on. The Tenochcan Army had never before fought against an army of armored men. With each swing of the sword they were pushed back up the hill.

Gasha bowed his head and concentrated. His eyes glowed with an evil green luminance under his dark hood. The stela in his staff lit up bright blue with beams reaching out touching the ground. The clouds in the sky darkened and swirled around violently. The wind gusted and blew around like a hurricane. The air became thick restricting the soldiers' movements. The stela-stone glowed immensely bright so that they had to cover their eyes. Thin strands of lightning started to form on the ground, glittering about and flowing with the wind. Specs of light shot up from the soil and stones lifted up and floated in the air. There was a huge clap of thunder and all the soldiers bent their knees trying to keep balance on the hillside. Everything became deathly silent.

The lighting flowed passed the king's men and began piercing through the front line enemy soldiers. Each hole in their armor was bright molten red, flaming up their undergarments and burning their skin. One after another they fell to the ground dead.

CHAPTER 11

Out of nowhere, a translucent ball of flowing eleamus, about the size of a man, flew rapidly over the heads of the remaining enemy soldiers and struck Gasha. It swallowed him up and lifted him into the air. It spun him around violently until he tore in half, flung out in two pieces landing on the ground. The eleamus exploded, sending out shock waves that sliced though the tops of the trees in the forest. Gasha's artifice was kaput and the remaining enemy soldiers charged up the hill. The Tenochcan Army was no match for them and was being annihilated. Moctezuma was stabbed in the arm and was pulled back by his men.

The air carried the sound of a distant roar that had never been heard before. SNAP! Trees were being snapped in half and falling to the ground within the jungle. Tree after tree fell from the canopy. The men looked back behind them to see the trees swaying and snapping. The ground trembled under the feet of the battling soldiers. With a deep, bellowing roar the beast busted through the outer treeline with trees flying through the air as it swung it enormous head to the left and right. Their ears rang from the immense sound waves.

Necalli sat upon the great dazhidegou and charged down the hill. His men barely cleared a path in time. The beast trampled through the enemy soldiers, swinging his armored head, throwing soldiers a hundred feet in the air in all directions. The charging dazhidegou quickly trampled most of the enemy forces, but Necalli knew he wouldn't fit through the gates of the city. Moctezuma commanded the army to advance and attack the remaining frightened enemy soldiers.

Necalli dismounted the beast and shooed it away. He had a few burn marks on his neck from the heated Ispus stones. Still wearing his enemy soldier disguise, he snuck into the city and walked toward the palace.

"You there! Stop! Where do you think you're going?"

"I must deliver a message to Malinche concerning the battle."

"No one is to enter the palace for any reason."

A few of the soldiers heard the commotion and surrounded Necalli. *Here we go!* He pulled his sword from its sheath ready to fight, even though the odds were impossibly against him. He turned when he heard shouts and screaming to see Moctezuma and his men fighting off the city garrison. They were using the enemy shields and some of his men had on their armor. They pressed forward and bashed their way into the palace. One of Malinche's guards ran at Moctezuma. He punched him in the face though his open eye guard. The soldier fell to the ground. Moctezuma started laughing. The king stood to his feet.

"You! Moctezuma, fall to your knees."

"Sorry, my ahau, but I cannot."

Necalli removed his helmet. When the king saw him, he was stunned. Malinche felt him slipping away from her grasp. Her face turned blood-red and her eyes beamed at Necalli as if she was piercing him through. She screamed an eerie loud cry stretching forth her hands. She conjured up a swirling mist of eleamus that swirled all around them. They couldn't move or even speak. Chairs and books and everything not held down was picked up and dissolved in the eleamus. They could feel a great pressure pulling at them as the doors of the throne room imploded into the elements. The walls began to crack and some of the pillars holding the ceiling cracked in two and were sucked in. All of the soldiers outside could see swirling black clouds above the palace with tremendous lightning bolts striking the top of the great temple.

The eleamus became so powerful that even Malinche couldn't control it. The room became black so that they could only see each other as if the earth had passed away and there was nothing. Malinche threw her hands forward and the eleamus imploded into a single pulsating speck for a fraction of a second then burst out like a bomb colliding with the Ispus around Necalli's neck. The eleamus rebounded and exploded out in all directions. Necalli, Malinche, the ahau, and all of the Mayan people disappeared from the face of the planet.

The cities lay silent. Time and seasons passed and eroded at the great temples. The jungle overtook the roads and pathways. One of the greatest peoples to have ever lived had all but vanished from existence.

CHAPTER 12

Jennifer opened her eyes and stretched her arms above her head then just lay there thinking about silly Cammy, how she would bounce around the house making up silly make-believe words and acting like a real gigglebox. She smiled and licked her finger and stuck it above her head to feel the direction of the wind. Not that there was any wind in the house, mind you, but Cammy did that all the time. If only she could go over to her house and play, but that would be kind of hard being that she was like a million miles away now, Jennifer thought.

She turned sideways and slid off the side of the bed with her feet dangling, reaching for the floor. Tiptoeing past her older sisters, Stacey and Crystal, she breathed quietly so as not to wake them or they would wake up and yell at her to go back to bed. She pranced downstairs with her long, light brown hair bouncing and floating in the air. Quietly, she walked through a maze of boxes to get to the kitchen. She looked around and found a box cutter lying on the table and ran the blade down the center of a box to cut the packing tape. Dish after dish she pulled from the boxes, unwrapping them and throwing the paper on the floor. After searching through several boxes, she found what she was looking for. "Yes!" She put a cereal bowl on one small open spot on the table then went back to opening boxes again.

She heard a gasp. "Jennifer! What are you doing?"

Jennifer jittered. "Mom! You scared me."

"Give me that box cutter, you know better than that."

"But I have to find my cereal."

Jennifer's dad walked in and laughed. "You know she has to have her cereal first thing every morning."

"I don't think we even have milk. I think I threw it out because the cooler was full and you already closed up the moving truck," Lily said, still in her pajamas.

"Why don't you start unpacking and I'll go get some milk and donuts?"

"Sure Lee, leave me with all the work."

Lee laughed at Lily. "I'll be right back." He kissed her on the cheek and grabbed his keys.

"Jenn, go wake your sisters so they can help with unpacking."

"Okay, Daddy."

Jennifer ran up the stairs and into the large bedroom over the garage. "Wake up!"

"Go away, Jennifer," Crystal said.

"Get up, right now! Dad said so!"

"Girl! Take a chill pill, would ya?"

She shook Stacey. "STOP!"

Jennifer's nostrils flared. "Get up now!"

"Shush, you little lemming," Stacey said.

"Jennifer, go downstairs, we'll be down in a minute," Crystal said.

"You better hurry. You have to help Mom unpack."

Jennifer ran back downstairs.

"She's so spoiled."

"She's such a brat. I'm sure she's downstairs telling on us right now. The little lemming."

"I can't wait to go to the beach. Do you think there will be waves?"

"How should I know, Crystal?"

"I'm sure we'll be unpacking all day anyway."

"Well, at least you get your own room after everything's done. I'm stuck here with the little lemming."

"So? I'm the oldest."

Stacey stuck her tongue out at Crystal then took off running downstairs.

Crystal chased after her. "You better run!"

"Okay, girls, calm down. We have a lot of unpacking to do."

"When do we get to go to the beach?"

"Later, Crystal, we have to get some of this done first."

"I thought the whole reason for moving to Virginia Beach was so we could have fun at the ocean?"

Lily laughed. "We will, we will. Be patient."

"Yeah, Crystal, you have to unpack first."

Crystal laughed. "Jennifer be quiet."

"You would not believe what I caught your sister doing this morning."

"I don't know, eating dog food?"

"Ha! Ha! Stacey. Very funny!"

"She was trying to open boxes with a box cutter looking for cereal."

"Aww, Jenn, you are so cute," Crystal said.

"Feisty is more like it," Stacey added.

"Crystal, start washing the dishes and putting them into the cabinets. Stacey, put all the paper on the floor in the trash and get the dishes out of those open boxes. Just set them on the table."

"Who wants donuts?"

"Daddy's home, Daddy's home!" Jennifer said. She ran into the living room and hugged him with her little arms then everyone sat down to eat their donuts.

"It's really hot out. Girls, guess what I got at the store?"

"What, Daddy?"

"I got a little pool for the back yard."

"How big?"

"It's just a little kiddy pool for now."

"I thought we were going to the beach," Crystal said.

"We will. This is just something to play with in the back yard."

"Oh, can I swim in it now, Daddy?"

"In a little bit. Let me find the boxes with the garage stuff so I can get a hose."

After several hours of unpacking they finally had a chance to fill up the little pool in the back yard. Jennifer jumped out of the back door, already wearing her bathing suit. Lily started laughing at her. Crystal giggled and went and picked her up. "You're such a cute little thing."

"I'm ready to swim!"

"Okay, jump in," Lee said with a gleaming smile.

Crystal walked over to the pool and bent over, but Jennifer held her feet up out of the water so she dropped her. Jennifer screamed and gasped heavily as she scurried quickly out of the pool. Everyone was laughing at her. She wrapped her arms around herself, shivering.

"That's freezing!" she said and ran into the house to dry off.

"She is so silly," Lily said.

"Well girls, you'll just have to wait a day or so for the water to warm up."

"Dad! Can't we go to the beach now?"

"Okay, yes, I give up. Let's go to the beach."

"Yay!"

Crystal and Stacey ran upstairs.

"Jen, put your bathing suit back on, we're going to the beach."

Lee and Lily went into their room to try to find the box with their swimwear.

"Lee, don't you think it's a little too late to go to the beach now? It'll be dark soon."

"Nah, it's okay. I used to swim in the moonlight all the time, it's fun."

"If you say so."

"Just make sure the girls stay near the beach. They'll be fine."

CHAPTER 13

The family loaded up into the Bronco and drove the twenty minutes to the beach.

As they turned onto 5th Street they could see the ocean between the buildings with amber glowing surf as the small waves surged onto the sand. The sun was setting behind them and the last shades of yellow and orange illuminated small, puffy clouds floating out over the ocean.

"I so can't wait," Crystal said.

"Daddy, are there sharks in there?" Jennifer asked.

Lee laughed. "No sweetie, not where you'll be swimming. You'll be fine."

Stacey started laughing.

"You liar! Why'd you have to tell me that, Stacey?"

"Shut up, little lemming."

They found a free parking space near Rudee's Inlet and walked to the concrete boardwalk. The breeze off the ocean was brisk and smelled of sea water. The girls ran down on the sand toward the ocean with the wind in their faces and hair. Crystal ran into the waves up to her knees while Jennifer and Stacey ran away from the surf.

"Come on, you chickens," Crystal said just as a big wave smashed into her from behind. She closed her eyes and tried to hold her nose, but the wave twirled her around and up onto the sand. She ended up with a mouth full of seawater and sand in her bathing suit. "Eww, yuck." She spit it out and kept spitting.

Lee and Lily laughed. "That's right, you girls never tasted salty seawater before."

Crystal reached up and felt her long, blonde hair. It was wet and matted and full of sand. She dipped it in the surf to try to rinse it out.

"This stuff feels sticky," Jennifer said.

"Come on, let's walk up the beach some," Lily said.

They all walked along the edge of the surf for a while. The girls would run after the receding waves then run away when the next wave came in. The sun tucked in behind the horizon, barely tickling the sky as it started to get dark. Some of the hotels along the boardwalk turned on bright spotlights mounted high up on the rooftops that lit up the beach.

A little farther out, the sea looked white because many seagulls had landed on the water and were bobbing up and down with the swells. Many were flying around making use of the breeze blowing in from the ocean with a "Caw, caw, caw."

Stacey and Crystal played in the shallow surf, but Jennifer just stood up on the beach.

"Come on, Jenn!"

"Go ahead, Jennifer," Lily said. She took her by the hand and led her down into the shallow surf. The water was warm and felt tingly on Jennifer's fingers. She sat down and put her hands into the water to pull up some sand. Very dim streaks of light shimmered through the waves.

"Lily, look at that."

"Oh, that's pretty. What is that?"

"I don't know. I've never seen anything like it. It looks like the northern lights reflecting off the water."

"There are no lights in the sky except the ones on the buildings."

"That's so strange." Lee stood relaxed with his fist under his chin gazing at the wonderful patterns.

"It's quite beautiful," Lily said. She tilted her head like she was a bit mesmerized. "It's getting late, girls, we need to start heading back now."

"Aww, Mom!" Crystal said.

"No argument, let's go, girls."

They all got up and started walking down the beach toward 5th Street.

"Hey, Lily, look. The lights in the water, they're gone."

"Hmm. That was so strange, wonder what they were."

Lee just looked on down the beach. The girls ran up ahead through the water as the waves washed up the shore. About half way back Jennifer stopped and was tapping her toes on something.

"What's that, Jenn?" Crystal asked.

"I don't know. It's squishy. Watch."

Jennifer tapped her toe on a round, translucent clump of goo that lit up with little lightning bolts inside with each tap.

"Sweet! Let me try," Crystal said.

Lee and Lily caught up with the girls.

"What'd you find?" Lily asked.

"Hey, don't touch that. It's a jellyfish," Lee said. "It can sting you."

"No Daddy, it's dead. See." Jennifer kept tapping it with her toes.

"It can still sting you. Leave it. We need to get going."

They all continued walking but Jennifer lagged behind and ran back to the jellyfish. She kneeled down in the sand next to it with her long, light brown hair blowing in the wind. She went to pick up the side of the jellyfish, to try to look under it, but as soon as she touched it, it moved and glowed brightly. It was somewhat translucent except for deep red shades all around the outer circumference. She carefully picked it up with its long tentacles hanging down below, blowing in the wind.

She lifted the tentacles gently with her hand and held it at the bottom.

"You wouldn't sting me, would you, baby?" she whispered. The soft glow lit up her face as she walked down into the shallow surf. She set it free in the waves. The glow faded when her little fingers parted; then it gracefully fluttered out into the ocean currents.

"Jennifer, what are you doing?" Lee yelled from a distance.

"Nothing!" She ran up the beach to catch up with everyone.

"What were you doing over there?"

"Nothing, Daddy."

"Stay with us now."

She reached up and took Lily's hand as they walked. After a few seconds Lily felt a little tingle in her fingers and let go, wiping at her hands. It felt like little hot cobwebs were stuck on her palm.

"Mommy, I'm hungry."

"Well, if you would eat more at dinner time you wouldn't be hungry every hour. Lee, did you bring the Jennifer snacks?"

"Yelp, right here." He gave Jennifer a cookie that she devoured in a couple seconds. The last time they forgot Jennifer snacks she started crying with stomach pains so they always made sure to bring plenty of Jennifer snacks wherever they went. They loaded up into the Bronco and headed for home.

Crystal had moved into her own room and Jennifer's bed was moved next to the window looking outside above the garage. The sun was peeking over the horizon amidst a clear blue sky and shining right into her face. She rolled over and put a pillow over her head, but then it got too hot so she hopped off the bed and tiptoed past her sister. She started her morning ritual with cereal and cartoons while sitting at the kitchen island on a high stool.

The rest of the family got up and ate to prepare for another day of unpacking.

"Stacey, go see what your sister's up to," Lily said.

"Fine."

Stacey started laughing when she walked into the living room.

"What's so funny?" Crystal asked.

"Jenn's already got her bathing suit on."

"Aww, she's such a cutie." Crystal turned to talk to Lily. "Mom, I think she's already unpacking."

Lily laughed and walked into the living room. "What ya doing?"

"Unpacking so we can get into the pool."

She laughed at her because she looked so cute, but Jennifer didn't mind; she just smiled and tried to look cute with her hand on her hip.

"Yelp, she's a ham," Stacey said as she stuck her tongue out at her. Jennifer replied in kind.

A few hours later, with a huge mess in the living room, Jennifer took in a deep breath and let it out.

"What's with you, little girl?" Crystal asked.

"Can't we go swimming in the pool now?"

"That pool's tiny, I want to go back to the beach."

"But we can swim in the pool first."

"Dad! Jennifer wants to go swimming in the kid pool."

Lee walked downstairs. "I guess you can take a break for a while."

"Woo Hoo." Jennifer jumped up and down and ran for the back door.

"Not so fast, Jenn. Wait for your sisters," Lily said.

"But Mom!"

"Don't look at me with those cute blue eyes. You heard me."

The girls went out back to the little pool to see if it was still freezing.

The sun was hot, but the air was sweet and not too humid. The back yard smelled slightly of cedar due to the many cedar trees along the edge of the property.

"Eww! There's a huge, ugly toad in the pool!" Crystal said.

Jennifer kneeled down to take a closer look. She stepped into the pool and bent down at the knees.

"Aww, come here, little baby." She reached out with her little hands together and scooped up the frog. It was quite large and bigger than her two hands together, but it just rested there with its long legs hanging down over each side. The frog looked right at her. Its voice sack in the neck was just lightly pulsing in and out as it breathed. Jennifer moved it to the left then to the right and its eyes followed her. She giggled and moved it around to hold it with one hand so she could pet its head.

"Kiss it," Stacey said. "Maybe it'll turn into a prince."

"Eww, shut up, Stacey. Don't tell her that, she might do it," Crystal said. "That's gross."

Jennifer leaned in and kissed the frog on the nostril. It started making faint croaking sounds that almost sounded like a kitten purring.

"Eww! Mom, Jennifer kissed a frog!" Crystal said as she ran into the kitchen though the sliding door.

"What?"

"Jennifer kissed a huge, ugly toad."

Lee and Lily went out back to see. Lily laughed and held her hand to her lips. Lee said, "That's my little tomboy."

"Jennifer, that thing's going to give you warts on your face," Crystal said.

"No, he's not. He's nice! His name's Jacob."

Lily and Lee laughed.

"Where's my camera? You're just too cute," Lily said.

"You need to take him and let him go over there by the fence."

"But Daddy, can't I play with him for a little while?"

Lee laughed. "Okay, but only for a little while, he needs to get back to his family."

Jennifer played with her frog all afternoon and let it swim with her in the little pool. The big toad climbed on her shoulder and just sat there for a while.

"Jennifer, you're so weird," Stacey said. "Why don't you let that thing go?"

"I like him. He's my friend," Jennifer said while petting the frog. "And anyways, he likes me too."

"He's gonna pee on you. You know that, right?"

"He wouldn't do that."

"Time to eat! Jennifer, let that frog go now, down by the back fence, then come and eat."

"But Daddy—"

"Now, Jennifer."

Jennifer took a deep breath and let it out with a huff. She took the frog and stomped down to the far corner of the back yard and put him down in some fluffy pine needles at the base of a big pine tree.

"Jacob, you stay right here till I get back. Okay? You're my new best friend." She petted the toad then walked back to the house to eat dinner. The family sat down to eat but, as usual, Jennifer ate like a bird picking at her food.

"Jennifer, you need to eat," Lily said.

"But I'm full."

"You better eat, girl. You're too skinny," Stacey said.

"I can't eat any more."

"Well, just try to eat a few more bites."

"She ate all her green beans." Crystal laughed.

"Never met a child who loved green beans so much," Lily commented.

Jennifer just picked at her food until they lost interest in her eating habits then she creeped down from the table and sneaked towards the back door. She slowly reached for the handle on the sliding door when she heard, "Jennifer, where do you think you're going?" She turned around slowly with a fake grin on her face.

"Nowhere, Mommy."

"Go upstairs and put your pajamas on."

"Mom!" she said, dragging out the letters. "Can't I say goodnight to Jacob? Please!"

Lily took a deep breath. "I'm sure he's gone by now."

"No, he's not. I told him to wait."

Crystal laughed. "You're so cute. Come on." She took Jennifer by the hand and led her outside. They walked down to the fence and there Jacob sat, right where she'd left him.

"Hmm. I guess he did stay," Crystal said.

"Told you. Good night, baby," Jennifer gently whispered and petted his head.

CHAPTER 14

Jennifer lay in bed looking out the front window at the stars. She wrestled around trying to fall asleep and lost most of her covers on the floor. Finally, she grew drowsy and her eyelids slowly shut.

She walked through a clearing next to a body of water. The blades of grass were very tall and felt sharp on her legs and hands. The sky was black and twirling. The air was thick, humid, and it was hard to breathe. *Jacob, where are you?* There was a clap of thunder across the way. She ducked down and her heart beat like a humming bird in her chest. She looked all around for a place to hide, but the dense forest felt as if it were watching her. The trees bent and yawed, yet there was no wind. The water was still but for a line of ripples coming at her as she stood on the shore.

"Jennifer. Jennifer. Wake up."

Jennifer opened her eyes wide and sat straight up. She looked around in a daze. Lily was standing over her. "You going to wake up some time today, sleepy head? It's almost noon."

"Jacob," Jennifer whispered under her breath as she jumped out of bed and hurriedly dressed. She ran downstairs and toward the back door.

"Jennifer, not until you eat lunch."

"But, Mom, I just need to check on Jacob."

"Come over here and eat first."

Jennifer ate so quickly her tummy hurt; then she ran to the back fence by the big tree and looked around. "Jacob, Jacob, where are you?" She felt around the pine needles and through the grass growing around the fence posts but no Jacob. Her heart fluttered. A cold, hollow feeling welled up inside her. Her eyes watered as she looked all around. "My friend." She shrugged her shoulders and walked along the fence gazing at the ground. She sniffled and wiped her nose with her arm.

"Hi!"

Jennifer jumped and put her hand to her chest. She looked up.

"I'm Allie," a young voice called out from the other side of the fence. Jennifer looked up to see a girl about her age but much taller with reddish hair and a big smile. She had freckles on her face and rather red lips. She was wearing a blue baseball cap.

"Hi, I'm Jennifer Varnick," she said in a sad tone.

"Did you lose something?"

"Yes, Jacob."

"Who's that?"

"He's a toad."

Allie giggled and said in a high-pitched voice, "A toad! Why would you want to find a toad?"

"He's my friend."

"I'll be your friend."

"Okay, can you look over there for Jacob?"

"He wouldn't be over here. I know where frogs go."

"You do?"

"Yep, I know where there's lots of 'em."

"Can you take me?"

"Okay, come on."

Jennifer found a gap under the fence and squeezed through. She followed Allie through a gate at the back of her yard that led to a protected wildlife area where no one was allowed to build homes or cut down any trees, just behind the neighborhood. She followed Allie for about a quarter of a mile through the woods until she saw a huge body of water. There were several sailboats backed up waiting for a drawbridge to open.

"Allie, what's this place?"

"It's a water where boats float."

"Oh."

They walked out into a clearing with tall grass and muddy areas. The sun was high and hot, but a cool breeze blew from the woodline. Jennifer looked around at the beautiful flowers growing at the shore and listened to small waves splashing up against the bank. The air smelled slightly like a musty swamp. They stepped carefully to stay out of the mud while Jennifer searched for Jacob. A shallow little stream cut through the marshy area and had rocks the girls could step on to get across. They stopped and kneeled down next to the clear stream.

"Jacob, here boy. Jacob!"

"Guess he's hiding," Allie said. "I love finding pretty smooth rocks." She sifted through the creek bed with her long fingers. Jennifer ran her little finger through the top of the water. Small swirls of illumination followed her movement in the water radiating outward as they dimed off. She just watched as she moved her hand back and forth.

"How do you do that?"

"Do what?"

"Make that light?"

"I don't know. I never did that before."

Allie swished her fingers across the water, but nothing happened. Jennifer stood up and adjusted her balance a bit so she put her hand on Allie's bare shoulder for a moment to steady herself. When she did, the water lit up around Allie's fingers.

"Oh, look! I'm doing it now," Allie said. But then it stopped when Jennifer took her hand away. "Aww, now it's gone."

The girls followed the waterway for a while until Jennifer heard some frogs croaking. The closer they walked the louder the noise became. More and more frogs joined in. Allie held her hands to her ears to stop them from ringing. Jennifer kneeled down and a small, noisy green frog jumped right into her hand. She and Allie sat down in the leaves at the edge of the forest and petted the little thing. Two more frogs jumped up on Jennifer's shoe and leg. The frogs quieted down but seemed to gather around the area hidden in the brush and leaves.

"I think they like you, Jennifer."

"They're so sweet."

"I think they're kind of sticky."

Allie held one in her hand and turned her hand upside down. The frog just hung there, handing upside down from her palm for a bit, then crawled around to the top of her hand. She giggled. "That tickles."

"See, they like you too."

"Are you starting school next month?"

"I don't know."

"Maybe we'll be in the same class."

"Yes, we should be." Jennifer giggled.

"I'll ask my mom about it. She works at school," Allie said.

By the time the girls decided to head home, Jennifer had at least ten frogs sitting or climbing on her. They felt tingly to the touch as they walked around on her skin. She kept two, one sitting on her shoulder and the other in her open hand as they walked. When they reached the trail leading through the woods, they could hear talking. They pretended to be ninjas and snuck up on two boys by hiding behind some trees along the path.

"Jennifer," Allie whispered, "that's Sean and Roy. They live down the street."

"Let's scare them."

"Okay," Allie said while holding her nose, trying not to laugh.

They snuck as close as they could, but Allie stepped on a twig. SNAP! The girls hid and tried not to laugh. The boys looked around and started to get spooked. Jennifer threw a rock away from them. When the boys tuned their heads toward the sound, the girls ran at them and screamed. Sean jumped and took a few steps back. Roy dropped the logs he was holding and let out a girly scream. The girls laughed so hard they turned red.

"Allie, you are so gonna get it!" Sean said.

"Roy, you scream like a girl," Allie said, giggling.

"Who's this?"

"She's Jennifer. She just moved in next door."

"You should help us build our fort. We have to watch out for aliens."

"What aliens?"

"You can hear them at night. Just listen." Jennifer looked at Allie and they laughed. "What's so funny?"

"That's frogs, silly," Jennifer said. "See." She held out her hand and showed him the green tree frog. He tried to take it, but she pulled her hand back. "Don't touch him. He's mine."

"I wasn't going to keep him. I just wanted to see him for a second."

"Okay, just don't hurt him."

"We have to go home now. My mom will be looking for me," Allie said.

"Come back and help us with the fort tomorrow," Sean said.

The girls walked up to the fence in Allie's back yard.

"I like Sean. He seems nice," Jennifer said.

Allie laughed. "My mom calls him a silly dirt ball."

"I think he's cute."

They walked in through the back gate. Allie's mom called her inside.

"See you tomorrow, Jennifer."

"Bye!"

Jennifer crawled under the fence and into her back yard. She opened the sliding glass door.

"Jennifer! Where have you been? We've called the police and everything."

"I was looking for Jacob."

"You are in so much trouble, girl. Don't you ever leave this yard without telling me again. You hear me? I was scared to death!"

"Okay," Jennifer said as tears dripped from her cheeks.

"Where were you anyway?"

"I was with Allie. We walked to the water to find Jacob."

Lee ran in, took a deep breath and let out a sigh.

"Lee, don't say anything. I already yelled at her. So who's Allie?"

"She lives next door."

"Lee, she said she was with this girl and walked to some water back behind the house."

"Yeah, I heard someone talking today about the Intracoastal Waterway. I hear it's very deep and wide enough for ships. I think it runs through the protected wildlife area behind the house. I'd like to go see it tomorrow. Jennifer, you are way too young to go running off on your own. Don't ever do that again."

"But, Daddy, I wasn't alone, I was with Allie and Sean."

"Who's Sean?"

"He lives down the street. He wants us to help him build a fort."

"Upstairs and get ready for bed."

Jennifer stomped off and ran upstairs.

"Lily, I think we need to go meet this Allie's parents tomorrow. I don't see how they would just allow her to take off into the woods like that."

"Yeah, I was thinking the same thing. And we'll ask about this Sean fella."

"Girls. Why'd we only have girls?"

"Hey, that's your fault."

Lee laughed. "Don't get technical on me."

Lily giggled and walked away.

CHAPTER 15

Lee tossed and turned in bed. He put a pillow over his head, but it just wasn't enough.

"Lee, what is that?"

He took a deep breath and let it out all at once. "Frogs. It's got to be frogs."

"That loud?"

"Evidently so. What time is it?"

"Shesh, it's four a.m."

Lee got up out of bed in a snit and walked downstairs. There was a musty draft flowing up the steps. He walked to the back of the house and saw something moving out of the corner of his eye. He ducked down and turned on the dining room light to reveal Jennifer sitting at an open window facing the back yard with three tree frogs climbing on her arm.

"Girl! What are you doing?"

"Daddy, Jacob's back."

She held up her hands holding the huge bullfrog. As Lee walked to the window the frogs quieted down.

"How did you get the screen out of the window?"

"It just fell out."

There were several small green tree frogs climbing on the window sash.

"Jennifer"—Lee put his hand to his head—"you need to get upstairs. You don't do this anymore and don't be opening windows or doors at night. You hear me?"

"But they were calling me, Daddy."

Lee laughed. "Jennifer, they're frogs. That's what they do, make a lot of noise and drive me crazy. Now, up to bed."

He put the screen back in and closed the window. He let Jacob out the back door and gave him a little nudge to make him hop away. He walked upstairs and got back into bed.

"Who were you talking to?"

"Jennifer. She had the back window open with frogs climbing all over her and that big toad in her hands."

"Are you kidding me? That girl! She's driving me nuts."

Lee closed his eyes for about three seconds.

Croak! Croak! Ribbit! Croak! They started back up even louder than before. Lee scurried out of bed and stomped down the steps and across the hardwood floors. He opened the back door and walked outside on the deck. The sound was so loud that his ears rung. He held his hands to his ears and stomped on the deck. He jumped up and down and the frogs finally stopped. He went back to bed, but as soon as he pulled up the covers they started up again.

"You've got to be kidding me!" Lee rubbed his temple with both of his palms.

"What are we going to do?" Lily asked.

Lee got up and turned on the computer. He read up about ways to quieten the frogs then he got dressed and put his shoes on.

"What did it say?"

"It says that their skin is very sensitive. I'm going to pour gasoline on them."

"What? Lee, no. You'll end up burning the house down."

"I'm not going to light it. I'm just going to coat them with it. Maybe they'll leave."

Lee went to the garage and got the lawnmower gas can. He walked out back and threw cups full of gas all around the bushes. The frogs kept croaking. He got a branch and smashed it down into the bushes. The frogs quieted down for a few moments but then started back up again. After emptying the entire gas can and beating the bushes to death he gave up and went back upstairs. He walked into the bedroom with his head down, totally defeated.

"No luck?"

"I tried everything. I think we'll have to move."

Lily laughed. "I don't think we're moving just because of frogs."

"Don't you hear them?"

"Of course, but they won't be there forever."

"I don't know. I think they followed Jennifer home from the woods or something. She had them crawling all over her."

Lily laughed. "They do seem to be attracted to her and she actually likes them. Eww. She's so strange."

"Maybe she should have been a boy," Lee laughingly said.

"Yep, she's a little tomboy between the frogs and her obsession with tree climbing. Maybe she's part frog." Lily giggled.

"She does seem to have rather sticky skin."

Jennifer walked through the tall blades of grass. She pushed them out of her way so she could see the lake. The air smelled like rain and she could hear distant thunder. She watched for snakes as she struggled through the underbrush. She reached the lake where Jacob was sitting on a lily pad. "Here Jacob! Come here, baby," Jennifer said from the edge of the bank. She waded down into the water and swam over to him. She picked him up as she noticed a long, flowing ripple just under the surface of the water. She swam for the shore as fast as she could, but it was too late.

She screamed as the crocodile opened its huge jaws. She tried to climb the bank but kept slipping on the mud. The crocodile was upon her; she leaned back against the bank as far as she could and closed her eyes. She reached out with her hand right in front of the crocodile and there was a bright flash. She screamed and sat up in bed. Lily, still being awake, ran into her room. Jennifer was crying and her heart beat rapidly. He body was all sweaty.

"Jennifer, it's okay, sweetie."

Jennifer cried and her body was shaking. Lily held her and put her hand on her head, rocking forward and back slightly.

"Shhh, it's okay now, I got ya."

"Mom, he was going to eat Jacob. I had to save him."

"It's okay, it's okay. It's just a bad dream."

She held Jennifer for a while until she calmed down.

"Go back to sleep, sweetie," Lily said as she stroked her daughter's long, light brown hair. She covered her up and tucked her in tight under the covers. Jennifer grabbed Fruity, her favorite teddy bear, and held on tight. He was hot to the touch and kind of smoking a little bit. Jennifer could see a thread of smoke rising up in the moonlight shining through her window. There was a brown spot at the back and a small fading red ember that was smoking. She looked at it, confused, then brushed off the burnt fibers with her hand.

❧

Lee and Lily slept in after the frogs finally stopped croaking. They didn't get up until about eleven a.m. Lee walked downstairs and heard the girls talking in the kitchen. Jennifer was talking about frogs.

"Jennifer, what are you yapping about?"

"Dude, I'm talking here."

Lily stepped into the kitchen behind Lee and started laughing. She turned red and almost fell over. Lee's eyes widened and he took a step back. Everyone was laughing harder because Lily was laughing to the point where she couldn't breathe.

"Okay, miss ornery. I'm your dad not some dude."

"You're still a dude, Dad," Crystal said.

"That's beside the point."

"Dad, what did you do to the back yard last night?" Stacey asked.

"Yeah, there are pieces of bushes all over the place," Crystal said.

Lily opened the sliding glass door and looked outside. She started laughing again.

"Um, Lee. What did you do?"

There were uprooted parts of bushes and weeds strewn all over the back yard.

"Well, I had to try something to shut them up."

"Daddy, you didn't hurt them, did you?" Jennifer asked.

"Evidently not."

"Good, cuz I have to go find Jacob so I can show him to Allie."

Lee, Lily, and Jennifer went next door and met Allie and her parents. Jennifer had found Jacob near the back door so she introduced him to Allie.

"Whoa! He's so big."

"Pet him."

"That's okay."

Lee, Lily, and Allie's mom laughed at her.

They all became good friends and shared some good times together over the years. Allie and Jennifer were in the same classroom in grade school and shared as many classes as they could in middle school, but Jennifer desired Sean's attention. Anywhere Sean was there you would find Jennifer and Allie.

Jennifer had had grown to about five foot three inches by high school. She hardly ate at mealtimes and was quite skinny but very beautiful with her long, light brown hair, blue eyes and shapely round butt. Every morning, she would wait at the bus stop with Allie, impatiently, for Sean to arrive. She would kind of bounce on her toes a little and smile widely at him when he approached. They would always sit near the back of the bus just behind Allie and Roy, who had also become rather close. Sometimes one of Sean's many friends would sit at the end of the seat, but Jennifer didn't mind being squished between Sean and the side of the bus. She liked feeling the heat from his body, it made her feel warm and safe. She was always cold with such a slender build. Sometimes Sean would rest his head on Jennifer's and she could feel the warmth of his breath, and on occasion he would let her take his hand. She sat next to him in home room and gave him her full attention whilst most of the other girls played with their phones until class started. She would text him throughout the day when she could get away with it and follow him closely between classes.

Sean would reach out and squeeze her shoulder with his hand. She would bend her head down trapping his hand between her shoulder and her neck to keep it there while she stared at him with her twinkling eyes. Sean never really committed to a relationship with Jennifer, but most of the time he didn't mind her clinging on to him or following him around. She and Allie would stay after school to watch Sean and Roy practice track and field. Jennifer wanted to go to the away track meets with him so she tried out for the track team, but they said she was too skinny and had to gain some weight first.

It was about halfway through ninth grade, just after Christmas break, when there was an interruption during home room. A sweet looking young lady with blonde hair, a cute smile, and a voluptuous body, standing about five feet six inches was escorted to the door by the school secretary. Everyone watched as she talked to their teacher, Mrs. J, for a few moments who then walked her over in front of the class.

"Everyone, this is Vicky Doutic. She will be joining our class for the rest of the year so I hope everyone will give her a nice welcome."

There wasn't a young man in the room whose eyes weren't affixed on her. She smiled and spoke confidently with a heavy French accent. "Good morning to everyone. I am very happy to meet you."

Mrs. J guided her to a seat over on the left, near the door. Vicky looked Sean's way and he winked at her. She smiled and winked back. Jennifer's face turned red and she looked down at the newly sharpened pencil on her cold, smooth desktop and thought about jabbing Sean in the side with it. She gave him the dirtiest look she could with big eyes and raised eyebrows and a furrowed forehead. Sean kind of rolled his eyes and looked away. He kept looking at Vicky during class so Jennifer smacked him on the shoulder when the teacher wasn't looking. He gave her a snarling look with crossed eyes.

After class Vicky stood across the hallway from the classroom door. She smiled at Sean when he walked up. Jennifer tried to stake her claim by putting her arm around Sean's waist, but he pushed her away by the shoulder. "Give me a little space, would ya?"

Jennifer covered her quivering chin with her hand. She couldn't swallow and held her breath in her throat. She had a tight feeling in her nose. She rammed her way between Sean and Vicky, knocking both of them back a bit. She could hear Vicky speaking with her French accent as she hurried away. "Whew, somebody has a crush on you, I think."

"No, she's just a friend."

By the time Jennifer met up with Allie by the lockers her face was soaked with tears.

"Jennifer, what's wrong?" Allie asked with great concern as she rubbed her friend's back.

"I think Sean just broke up with me."

"Wait, what?"

"He likes the new girl that just started today."

Allie gave Jennifer a tissue and she wiped her eyes.

"Come with me." Allie took Jennifer by the hand and led her to the ladies' room. They sat on a little red-cushioned bench back from the door.

"I can't believe Sean. How can he push me away, right in front of her?"

"Jenn, I don't know. I don't get what happened." "This stupid new French girl started today. Sean was winking at her right next to me."

"What a jerk. What did you do?"

"After class he went to talk to her so I tried to hug him and he just pushed me away. He said he needed space."

"Oh, damn! I can't believe he did that! What a jerk."

"I really love him, ya know?"

"I know, I feel so bad for you." Allie hugged her and gently patted her head.

"We need to get ready for class. You going to be okay?"

"No, I'm not going."

"Jenn, you have to or you're going to get into trouble."

"Allie, I don't want him to see me this way."

"I'll stay with you then."

"No, you don't need to get in trouble for me."

"Really?"

Jennifer hugged her and cried, "Thank you."

"What are best friends for?"

The two girls sat out of a few classes until lunchtime. During lunch they walked around outside the school, just to get away and breathe some fresh air.

Jennifer sat next to Allie in science class. They were partners and graded together on their work. The teacher started giving instructions for their next assignment. "Pass around the handouts and prepare for the lab. Today, you and your partners will be dissecting a frog. Make sure you record your results."

Allie looked at Jennifer. She looked back with her lip sticking out and her mouth curved down. She started to tear up again.

"Jenn, it's okay."

"This day just keeps getting better and better." Jennifer got up and ran out of class.

"What's wrong with Miss Varnick?" the teacher asked.

"I think she's going to be sick. Can I please go check on her?"

"Yes, please."

Allie met up with her in the ladies' room again.

She hugged Jennifer tight.

"Allie, this is the worst day of my entire life."

Allie's eyes glossed over and she rested her head against Jennifer's.

"It will be okay. Somehow it will be okay, I promise."

"I wish we could just run away and never come back."

When Jennifer finally went back to class, her eyes were swollen and red. Her face was a pouty grimace. She couldn't wait for the bus ride home to have some time to talk to Sean alone because it seemed everywhere he went Vicky was right there with him.

In her last class she sat at the back of the room under the wall clock. The room was silent during the test except for the tick, tick, tick of the second hand. She wiped away a few tears that had fallen on her test paper and had hardly answered any questions. When the bell rang, she ran to the lockers to put away her books. Allie was already there with the locker opened that they'd decided to share when school first started.

"Hey Jenn, how are you feeling?"

"I can't talk now, I need to get to the bus before anyone tries to sit with Sean."

"Jenn wait! Dangit! I tried to warn her."

Jennifer quickly stepped up on the bus and headed for the back, but when she looked up, there sat Sean and Vicky in Jennifer and Sean's usual seat. They both looked at her standing there. She ducked into one of the seats on the middle left and tilted her head down so that her hair covered her face. After a few moments, Allie sat next to her.

"I tried to warn you. Vicky's family moved into the Creag house one street over from us. She rides our bus."

"Of course she does," Jennifer said as she wiped away her tears with her long sleeve.

"Hey Jenn, why aren't you sitting with Sean?" Stacey said.

"He seems to be into the new girl," Allie said.

"Oh shit! Seriously? Want me to kick his ass, little Sis?"

"Don't you dare say anything," Jennifer said in a deep voice.

"He's a bum anyway, Jenn, just move on. Lots of fish in the sea, ya know."

"Just shut up, Stacey, okay?"

"Whatever!"

Jennifer went straight to her room when she got home. Stacey went and told Lily that Jennifer was upstairs crying, so Lily hurried up to her room.

"Jennifer?"

"I don't want to talk about it."

"It might make you feel better."

"Why are guys such jerks?"

"Did something happen between you and Sean?"

"Yeah, Vicky Doutic."

"Aww, baby, I'm so sorry. I know you really liked him."

"No, I hate him. Why can't he like me? I tried so hard. What's wrong with me?"

"Sweetie, there's nothing wrong with you."

"I'm too skinny."

"Well, you'll be happy about that when you get older, trust me. So I was thinking, maybe we should get away this weekend. Go camping down by the lake or something. What do you think?"

"As long as I don't have to think about Sean with her."

"Maybe you can invite Allie to come with us."

"No, she's going to the dance at school with Roy. Guess I don't get to go to the dance either."

Jennifer started sobbing again.

After dinner Allie came over to try to comfort her. They sat on the couch in the dimly lit family room and watched television. The room was very homey with brown paneling and a stone surround wood burning fireplace on the far wall. Jennifer pulled up a throw to cover her body. She toggled through the channels but couldn't find anything to watch.

"You'd think there would be at least something on with five hundred channels," she said.

"I know, right?"

Allie took the remote and opened the channel guide. She put on a documentary about frogs and the biologists that study them.

"Here, you should like this."

The two girls watched the program. The biologists were studding frogs to try to find cures for various diseases. Of special interest were the rare poisonous frogs of South America. They trekked through the jungle in search of the many varieties of amphibians. They had footage of underdeveloped tribesmen hunting with poisonous darts made from the oils secreted by certain frogs on their skin. The hunter shot a marsh deer called *Blastocerus Dichotomus*. Only seconds after striking the animal it fell to the ground in anaphylactic shock with its legs lunging and shaking violently. In less than a minute the animal died. They showed very colorful images of the many types of poisonous frogs.

"Oh, look at that blue one. It's so pretty."

Allie laughed. "Only you would say a frog is pretty, but I will admit they are a lot nicer to look at than the frogs here."

The documentary talked about ancient myths of frogs with powers to heal. The biologists believed that these myths were actually based on fact due to the natural healing remedies created by extracting oils from the skin of frogs and certain types of lizards.

"I know what I want to do now."

"About what?"

"School, the future. I want to be a biologist. I want to catch and study frogs."

"You know in biology class you'll have to dissect one."

"Well, that's never gonna happen."

"Of course, if you dissect one then you can learn more about them and how they live."

"I guess. Still not happy about cutting open one of my babies."

Allie laughed. "Hey, are you sure you don't want me to blow off the dance and go with you on the camping trip?"

"Yes, go be with your boyfriend. I'm sure he wants to go to the dance."

"You could come with us."

"Ah, no. That's okay."

CHAPTER 16

Jennifer and Stacey helped hold the tent poles while Lee banged in the stakes and tightened the ropes.

"Stacey, you and Jennifer can share this tent."

"Why do I have to be in with Jennifer?"

"Well, it's either that or you sleep out under the stars because you're not sleeping in our tent," Lily said.

"Why does Crystal get out of camping anyway?"

"When you're as old as Crystal you can make your own decisions, but until then you will do as you're told!"

"Ugh!"

Jennifer lay back against a tree looking down through the colorful trees at the lake. The air smelled of dried and musty leaves. The occasional cold snap would bite at her nose when the wind blew gently from the north. She felt a shiver and pulled her sweater closed. Easy ripples across the lake fractured the mirror image of the autumn leaves still cleaving to the maple branches along the far shoreline. Jennifer closed her eyes. She could smell the wood smoke from the fire her Dad had made in the middle of the campsite.

She ducked down in the woods before the clearing as a clap of thunder rang in her ears. The sky was dark as night and spun around as if the world had turned on its edge. She made her way through the thick brush while watching for snakes. She followed the waterline walking faster and faster. There was Jacob croaking loudly. The water surface was broken with a ripple, parting like an arrowhead in the water. Jennifer jumped into the lake and grabbed Jacob in her hand. The crocodile's teeth were like a thousand small knives ready to chomp down on her arm. She reached out her hand…

"Jennifer, hey! Wake up." Her mom gently nudged her and she awoke with a gasp.

"Oh, Mom."

"Having that same nightmare again?"

"No, I'm okay."

"You sure? You look pale."

"Mom, I'm fine."

She got up off the log and they ate dinner at the picnic table as the sun began to set beyond the trees of the lake. It was quite faint at first, but then it grew louder and louder.

"Really?" Lee said.

"Dad, it's not that bad."

"If those frogs keep this up all night I will never get any sleep. I hate frogs."

Jennifer got up and walked down to the lake by herself.

"Lee, you know she's already upset."

"Why is it that I'm the only one that can't stand all that croaking?"

"I don't get why Jennifer gets all the attention anyway," Stacey said.

"Stacey, she just broke up with her boyfriend. Show a little concern," Lily said as she got up to follow Jennifer down to the lake.

∞

Jennifer stood at the edge of the water watching the moon reflecting off the glassy surface of the perfectly still lake. She waved her arm in the air and said, "Be still, my babies." The hundreds of frogs around the lake went silent. Footsteps in the dead leaves rustled behind her.

"Jennifer, you okay?"

She turned to her mom. "I quieted the frogs for Dad."

"They heard you walking and it scared them."

"No, I told them to be silent and they listened."

Lily put her arms around Jennifer and hugged her tight. "It makes us feel good to think we have power over something, but in the end none of us really have power over anything."

"Mom, I really did. I made them be quiet."

"Let's get back up to the warm fire, silly."

They started to walk back up the hill. Jennifer lagged a step or two behind and turned toward the lake. She waved her arm in the air and mouthed the word "speak" and every frog at the lake croaked loudly as she turned to walk beside her mom who turned and said, "See, Jennifer. As soon as we walked away they started back up again."

Jennifer just smiled. "Okay, Mom, I see what you mean."

Jennifer looked down and shook her head.

Jennifer was not looking forward to going back to school Sunday night. She tried to prepare herself but ended up sleepless, tossing and turning. Her mind was racing thinking about Sean and Vicky together. She already missed him so much and kept going over that one moment in her head over and over and over again. *How could he just push me away like that after giving him so many years?* She went from excitedly getting up for school every morning to dreading falling asleep because the sooner she fell asleep the sooner she had to get up and deal with humiliation and heartache. Her chest was tight and hurt from all the stress.

She got up out of bed and took her sheet and covers with her to lie on the couch to watch some television. She toggled through the channels and stopped on an old relaxing show that she watched with her mom when she was just a tiny thing. It was soothing with a calming effect that put her at ease.

Her eyes grew heavy and...

She walked through the sharp blades of grass scraping at her ankles and arms as she walked. She could feel the cuts in her skin that burned and itched. The sky was angry and black, spinning around like a hurricane above her. She could feel the eyes of the forest watching her intently, so many shadows, so many eyes. The trees bent over and a cold burst of wind threw her off balance. CRACK! THUD! A huge tree snapped in half and came crashing down to the ground nearby. The air was too thick to breathe, she grasped at her chest. A snap of thunder burst out as a huge bolt of lightning struck the ground a hundred yards away. Jennifer ducked down and screamed. She could feel every hair on her body stand up on end as the air was electrified.

She crawled to the edge of the lake alone, needing someone, hopeless. A cold hollowness welled up inside her like a hard stone in her stomach. *Jacob!* Jennifer desperately scurried for the water. She could see Jacob sitting on a lily pad croaking loudly.

Hurriedly, she picked him up and tried to climb out, but the mud on the bank just pulled away and it was no use. She was afraid to turn. Maybe it wouldn't be there. But it was! She leaned back against the bank and reached out to stop the crocodile from chomping down, so many sharp teeth. It was so close she could see down its throat. She closed her eyes tightly and waited for the bite... It was like lightning, it just flowed from her hand like a warm cream striking the crocodile and burning it completely through, blowing out its tail, which flew across the lake and landed in the water. Jennifer could feel a great heat on her side.

She sat up on the couch and screamed. She quickly covered her mouth with her hands. Her sheets and blanket were on fire and filling the living room with smoke. Her pajamas were singed and filled with glowing embers. She quickly pulled the sheets and covers outside to the back yard and stomped out the flames. She frantically brushed the burning embers from her clothes with her hands. Breathing very heavily, her heart beat fast. *What the heck is going on?*

She went into the house and got a few trash bags and put the sheets and blankets into them. She took off her pajama top and stuck it in one of the bags, tied them shut, then put them out into a big metal trashcan. She hurried back into the house hoping no one saw her. She picked up a throw to cover her chest and back. She sat for a minute to try to calm herself, but her heart wouldn't stop racing. She looked at the clock and it was almost time to get up for school. She lay down for just a minute.

"Jennifer."

She opened her eyes. "Mom."

"What are you doing down here?"

"I couldn't sleep."

"Well, you'd better hurry up, the bus will be here soon."

When Jennifer got to school, she was completely out of it. Everything seemed to happen in slow motion as if she were in a dream. She just ignored Sean and didn't even make eye contact, not even once. The day dragged on forever.

CHAPTER 17

Jennifer tried to harden her heart, but every time she saw Sean with Vicky she felt a hollowness in her chest, like a piece of her was missing, like Sean had stolen it and would never give it back. The hardest part was seeing them kissing each other in between classes in the hallway. Sean would never do that with her, but he seemed to have no problem doing it with Vicky. *The wicked boyfriend-stealing bitch.*

Jennifer and Allie took an art class elective in tenth grade. During the second half of the year the class was given an assignment. Each student was supplied with a full-size canvas and easel. They were told to take their time and sketch an image then paint it in detail.

"Jennifer, have you decided what you're going to paint yet?"

She looked at Allie as they walked to the bus to ride home.

"I think I'm going to paint Jacob sitting on a lily pad on a pond."

"Seriously? Like your dream?"

"I think so."

After several days of class Allie walked over behind Jennifer while she was working on her painting.

"Hey!" Allie put her hand on Jennifer's shoulder.

"Hey."

"I thought you were painting Jacob?"

"I did too."

"So what's this?"

"I don't know. It's just something I was thinking about."

"Did you see it in a magazine or on TV or something?"

"I don't think so."

"Umm, Jennifer…"

"What?"

"Seriously, what is this?"

"I just told you, I don't know."

Allie walked closer to the unfinished painting and stared at it for a while.

"What do you think?"

Allie turned her head and gazed at her for a few awkward moments with her head tilted a bit.

"It's amazing, the detail is just amazing."

"Thanks."

"Jennifer, what is it?" Allie asked with a puzzled look.

"It's just a thought I had."

"Jennifer, this is not just a thought. It's like a professional masterpiece. I just don't get it. How can you even imagine this?"

"It's kind of more like a memory than imagination."

"But you said you've never seen this anywhere."

"Gees girl, it's not that big of a deal."

"Is this real?"

Jennifer had fully sketched out what looked like an ancient hall, temple or burial tomb of some kind, but the fascinating part was that the detail was exemplary and realistic. The colors she used for the sandy-tone stones were spot-on. The front of the structure had two large statues to each side that were actually carved out of the same stones that made up the front wall. They looked like two strangely dressed men looking toward the door with evil expressions on their faces. The stones were pitted and weathered as though they had been standing for many centuries. There were steps leading up a stone walkway to a closed double door with hieroglyphs engraved into the flat surface. Pictographs extruded from the stones surrounding the double doors working their way outward across the front wall. There was a stone transom above the door with chiseled stone decorative patterns laid out in small squares, which met up on either end with several protruding stone pillars that ran from top to bottom with layers of detail around the front circumference, almost like what the Greeks used in their ancient structures, but this was more like an Egyptian style building or something similar. Jennifer even captured the shadows cast from the sun at a particular angle.

"Well, you're certainly going to get an A in this class."

Jennifer stuck her tongue out at Allie and went back to work. The exercise felt therapeutic to her. When she was working on the painting, it was like nothing else in the world mattered. It put her at ease and relaxed her, until she glanced at the hieroglyphics she painted into the doorway. She had no idea what they were, but for some reason they threw her off guard and she felt a cold shiver run up her back making her get down off her stool and take a step back for a second.

The room seemed to spin around and she felt dizzy. Her heart rate increased and her breathing became heavy. She shook her head to shake off the feeling then went back to work, paying no mind to the strange feeling.

CHAPTER 18

Twelfth grade career day, a full day of persuading undecided students to select a career path for their future. Jennifer sat behind Sean and Vicky with her arms crossed and rolled her eyes every time Vicky spoke to him, shaking her head at Allie with squinting eyes. Anytime Sean would look back at her she would look away as if staring out the window, pretending to ignore him. Visiting liaisons for various careers showed clever films to incite interest from the students. Jennifer and Allie just whispered and passed notes while listening until an archaeologist showed a film about uncovering ancient artifacts from dig sites around the globe. Of interest to Jennifer was the near-death experience of an archaeologist visiting a primitive site in South America near the great Ziggurat of the Moon at Teotihuacán in central Mexico. He was poisoned in his sleep by a local using oils from indigenous frogs.

At the end of the presentation the archaeologist asked for a raise of hands from those interested in receiving additional information. Sean raised his hand but Vicky did not, so Jennifer quickly threw her hand in the air. Sean looked back at her and she stared right at him with glossy eyes never breaking eye contact. Allie, being undecided, also raised her hand. After receiving a collage packet about archaeology the students were free to leave.

Sean was standing in the hallway without Vicky. Jennifer walked up to him and was ready with an insult about Vicky, but Sean looked intensely at her and stepped closer until he was only inches away.

"Jennifer, Vicky and I just broke up."

"It's about time, don't you think?"

"You know she's really not as bad as you make her out to be."

Jennifer turned her head back toward Allie and stuck her finger in her open mouth. Allie giggled.

"To each his own, I guess."

"We have more similar interests than Vicky and myself."

"I could have told you that four years ago."

"Don't be mad."

"What do you want?"

"Jennifer, you don't have to answer now, but will you think about going to the prom with me?"

Jennifer's whole body quaked and her face turned red. She tried not to smile. She wanted to be like ice but she couldn't help it. She looked up at Sean with a big smile and said, "I would love to go to the prom with you."

Sean smiled while clenching his jaw. "Okay great."

Jennifer leaned in and he hugged her quickly then turned to walk away. Jennifer jumped up and down then clinched her fists together and put them to her lips to contain her wide smile. She turned to Allie.

"Jennifer, I don't think you should have done that."

"What do you mean?"

"Something's not right. He wouldn't just break up with her and immediately ask you to the prom."

"Why not? She's not right for him. You said it yourself."

"True, but I don't trust him."

"Allie, I know what you're going to say and I don't wanna hear it."

"Jennifer, I know you've loved him since middle school, but you're blinded to the truth, something's not right. He still loves Vicky. She has him wrapped around her finger and you're just gonna get hurt."

"Allie, just shut up! What do you want me to do? If I have a chance to go to the prom with Sean, I'm taking it."

Jennifer walked away with a huff, breathing heavily. Allie just stood there taking a deep breath and letting it out. She looked down at the floor and shook her head.

Jennifer, being so excited about the prom, thought everything through in her head. How wonderful it would be to dance all night with Sean and stick her tongue out at Vicky while she had to stand by and watch. And, afterwards, she planned to give herself fully to him. It was all she could think about for days. Lily took her shopping for the perfect dress, but after visiting twenty stores Jennifer had still not found her perfect dress. Since Sean had taken an interest in Vicky, Jennifer had lost interest in eating. She'd lost even more weight and was not happy with her appearance.

Lee searched the internet looking for the perfect dress for his daughter and was determined to find something she would love. After a couple hours of searching, he and Stacey found an elegant purple dress that they just knew would please her.

"Lily, what do you think?"

"Umm, Lee, did you look at the price?"

"I know it's a bit much, but you know how much this means to her. She's finally happy after years of being irritable and a pain to be around. I like her much better this way. I'm willing to pay the price if it means she'll be happy for a change."

"It's your call, but I just hope everything works out after spending this much on a dress she'll only wear once."

"There, it's done. It will be here in two days. Plenty of time to make any adjustments."

CHAPTER 19

Roy had talked secretly with Allie about Sean and his plans for the prom. Allie stood outside waiting for Jennifer so they could catch the bus to school. She kept biting her fingernails and putting her hand to her head. She closed her eyes and could feel her heartbeat. Jennifer came bouncing out of the house and stopped in front of Allie, smiling widely, just like old times.

"Hey!"

Allie jumped and breathed in heavily. "Hey."

"You ready?"

"Jennifer, I have to tell you something."

"Me first. My dad bought me a beautiful dress for the prom. It's purple and pleated with open shoulders. I love it so much."

"That sounds amazing, Jennifer."

"I know. I can't wait." They walked toward the bus stop.

"What were you going to tell me?"

"Oh, nothing. I can't remember now."

Allie frowned and kept playing with her necklace all the way to school.

❧

Jennifer caught up with Sean and hugged him around the waist. He looked down at her and patted her back for a second. She leaned in on him as they were walking.

"Hey Sean. I can't wait for the prom." She looked him deeply in the eyes. "We are going to have so much fun, if you know what I mean," she said with a wink.

Sean shook his head as if to say yes, but he didn't say a word. Jennifer took his hand on the way to home room. Vicky sat on the other side of the room on the same row. She was smiling and kept peering over at Sean thinking she was unnoticed.

Allie sat behind them and gave Vicky a nasty look. She couldn't concentrate and kept taping her fingers on the desktop. She decided to write Jennifer a note but dared not pass it in class. The teacher would always make the students read their notes out loud to the whole class. Allie couldn't live with herself if that happened. Not now with what was going on. Her hands started to shake as they got up at the end of the period. Jennifer and Sean walked out first holding hands. Allie thought about slipping the note into Jennifer's back pocket, but Sean was keeping an unusually fast pace. Lunchtime came and went but she couldn't say anything. She started justifying it in her mind. *Maybe it's not really true.* She sought out Roy for some comfort.

"Roy, are you sure about what you told me?"

"Why?"

"I just can't see Sean being so cruel. He knows how much Jennifer loves him. I just can't see it."

"You know Sean does nothing without Vicky."

"This just seems too cruel, even for her. What does Vicky hope to gain by this?"

"Put yourself in her shoes. What would you do if your boyfriend's old girlfriend was constantly seeking after him?"

"I guess I can see that, but does she even love Sean?"

"Vicky loves Vicky, but as long as Sean gets what he wants from her I don't think anything will change."

Allie's face turned a bit red and her breathing was heavy. She hurried to their locker and stopped Jennifer before she could try to meet up with Sean. She handed her the note.

"What's this?"

"Jennifer, I have been trying to tell you something all day, but there's no good way to say it."

"To say what?"

Sean walked up to Jennifer. She smiled and hugged him. Allie motioned for her to put the note into her pocket. Jennifer complied but gave her a funny look. They climbed onto the school bus home and Jennifer leaned her head against Sean's shoulder.

Just like old times, the way things were meant to be.

She remembered the note and pulled it from her pocket. As she read her face became blood-red. The vein on her forehead pulsed as her blood pressure raised considerably. She crunched down hard on her teeth, looking up at Sean between sentences. She stared down at the floor. She could smell that tainted mix of dirt and clay from everyone's shoes. It was a dry, heinous smell that stuck in the nostrils. She crinkled up her nose and furrowed her brow. As her mind raced her breathing became so heavy that her whole body flexed with each breath. Her eyes glossed over and her chin quivered.

The ride home seemed to take forever and the longer she thought about it the harder it was to catch her breath. She felt a pain in her stomach that couldn't be eased and felt hot inside. She turned her head to look back at Allie a few seats back. Allie couldn't believe the look on her face. She had never seen Jennifer look so mad.

As soon as the doors opened Jennifer flew out of her seat and off the bus; her long, light brown hair blew back behind her in the air. Sean tried to catch up and run after her with Allie trailing swiftly behind.

"Jennifer, wait!"

She kept walking away until it was only the three of them on the street. Sean grabbed her arm to turn her around. She jerked her arm loose.

"Get off me! Asshole!"

"What the hell's with you?"

"You! That's what's wrong with me!"

"What did I do?"

"You never planned on taking me to the prom, did you?"

"Who told you that?"

"It doesn't matter."

Jennifer ran at him and shoved him hard, pushing him back. "You're such an asshole!" Her eyes teared up and her voice became broken. "You never loved me, did you?" Sean stood silent. "Answer me! You're such an asshole! Were you really going to pick me up just to break up with me in front of everyone at the prom? Really? Even after my dad spent a fortune on my dress and everything. You want to embarrass me in front of the whole school?"

Sean smirked an evil grin. "What can I say? Shit happens!"

Jennifer clinched her fists tightly and yelled, "No! Shit doesn't just happen! It comes from ASSHOLES! And you're the biggest one I know!"

Her face strained to the point where her blood vessels appeared black and her eyes turned dark red. Her chest, neck, and forehead were wet with sweat. Sean jerked his head and was totally taken aback. Then, suddenly, Allie and Sean spread out their arms and bent at the knees to try to keep their balance. The ground was shaking under their feet.

Jennifer clinched her fists even tighter and loose gravel and stones floated up into the air. A gust of wind struck them hard and blew their hair with a hot breeze. A crack formed across the road and up the sidewalk between them. Allie ran to Jennifer and took hold of her arm. She seemed taller, but when she looked down, Jennifer's feet weren't even touching the ground, she was floating several inches in the air with her head tilted back and her arms out to her sides.

"Jennifer! Jennifer!" Allie pulled at her arm and was shocked with energy. She backed up with wide eyes looking up at her friend while rubbing her arm and chest.

Sean stood still, shaking all over. The sky darkened with swirly back clouds blocking the sun. Lightning struck the ground about a hundred feet away with a huge clap. Sean and Allie jumped and ducked down, terrified.

Jennifer opened her eyes; they were solid red with catlike irises. Allie cringed and took a few steps back. Sean turned and ran away. Jennifer landed on her feet and the stones and rubbish floating in the air fell to the ground. Allie was hesitant to speak.

"Jennifer, you okay?" she finally said with terror in her voice.

Jennifer's body went limp and she fell to the ground. Allie tried to catch her but only lessened her fall. Jennifer lay unconscious. Allie tried to wake her but couldn't. She panicked and ran to get Lily. When they returned, Jennifer was breathing rapidly but still unconscious lying in the neighbor's yard. They carried her home and laid her on the couch.

"Allie, what happened?"

Allie told Lily about the note and what Sean had planned to do. She told her that Jennifer fainted when she read it. Lily was about to call an ambulance when her daughter finally opened her beautiful blue eyes.

"Jennifer, you okay?"

"Ugh, what happened? How did I get here?"

"Shhhh, I'll tell you later." Allie held her finger to her lips.

"You feeling alright, sweetie?"

"Yes, Mom."

"You scared me."

"Blame that on Sean."

"I'm so sorry, sweetie. I know how much you like him."

"Mom, I loved him. How could he?"

"I don't know, sweetie."

"I'm sorry about the dress, Mom."

"Don't worry about that. I'm sure your dad will have a little talk with Sean's father when he gets home."

"No, Mom, no. I don't want anything to do with Sean or his family anymore. That will just make things worse."

Jennifer and Allie went up to her room and shut the door.

"Allie, what the heck happened?"

"What do you remember?"

"I remember yelling at Sean. I wanted to cry, but instead I just got really mad. Then I don't know … something strange. It felt like a hard hot ember in my stomach, burning me from inside, and I couldn't stop it; then I woke up downstairs. What happened?"

"Jennifer, you floated in the air. I mean rocks were floating up, the wind was blowing with dark clouds out of nowhere then a huge burst of lightning. The air smelled funny, almost like burning, then the ground was shaking. It shook so bad the road cracked."

"What do you mean? You're saying I did that?" Jennifer started breathing heavily and her lips turned down. Her eyes teared up.

"Come with me, I'll show you."

Jennifer and Allie went outside. Allie pointed at the cracks in the sidewalk and the road.

"I did that?"

"Yes!"

"But how?"

"I don't know, Jennifer, but you scared the crap out of me and Sean."

Jennifer giggled. "Really? Sean was scared?"

"You should have seen his face before he took off running."

"What do you think he'll say?"

"I don't think he'll say anything. After all, who would believe him?"

"Why didn't you run away too?"

"Umm. Trust me, the thought crossed my mind more than once, but I couldn't leave you. I was so scared though. You actually made lightning."

Jennifer stood staring into space.

"Say something, Jennifer."

She looked at Allie with teary eyes. "I'm some kind of freak, aren't I? It's no wonder he likes Vicky."

క్రా

The following days at school Sean stayed as far away from Jennifer and Allie as he could. Whenever he saw them heading his way he would duck into a hallway or the men's room. Jennifer would stare at him in class, knowing he knew she was looking his way, but he just looked straight forward without ever glancing. He could feel her eyes upon him like they were burning a hole through him. He would dart out the door after class for any subjects they shared.

Jennifer felt it was quite comical and enjoyed tormenting him. She was thinking about going to the prom to get back at him somehow, but the thought of it hurt too much. At night, when alone in her room, she would try to make things move with her mind. If she could make stones float why couldn't she wiggle a lamp shade or knock over a picture? She felt strange inside and couldn't sleep.

CHAPTER 20

Jennifer and Allie were standing at their locker when Charlie, a stocky, blond-haired football player, walked up.

"Hi girls."

"Hey," Allie said.

"Mind if talk to Jennifer for a second?"

Allie smiled at Jennifer and said, "See you back in class."

"Hey, Jenn, I was wondering if you might want to go to the prom with me." Jennifer hesitated to answer. "You don't have to tell me now, just think about it, okay?"

"Sure, I'll let you know."

"Cool."

Jennifer walked to class and sat down next to Allie.

"So, what'd he say?"

"He asked me to the prom."

"Really? What'd you say?"

"I said I'd think about it."

"You should totally go. Please?" Allie clamped her hands together in front of her face. "Please go, Jennifer, please."

"Sheesh, okay, okay."

"Goodie, I'm so excited and now you can wear your pretty new dress."

&⟋○

Crystal and Stacey both helped Jennifer get ready. They curled her normally straight hair to poof it up a lot and decorated her face in beautiful shades to match her natural tan complexion.

"You're really pretty, Jenn. You should wear makeup more often," Stacey said as she reached over to apply some black eyeliner.

The doorbell rang.

"I think he's here," Crystal said. "Let me run downstairs and then you can make the grand entrance down the staircase."

"Okay, just don't make a big deal about everything, okay?"

Crystal and Stacey walked down the steps and met Charlie, who was talking with Lee. Stacey shook his sweaty hand. He seemed a bit jumpy and kept playing with his shirt collar like it was choking him.

"Relax Charlie," Crystal said. "You're gonna give yourself a heart attack." She giggled.

"Here she is," Stacey said.

Jennifer slowly stepped down the stairs. Charlie looked up and started sweating. She was so beautiful. A gust of air blew in through the open doorway and blew her slinky, purple dress about. Her hair was full and curly. She smiled at Charlie and extended her hand. He took it and helped her down the last step. He held her hand up as she stepped off the last step such that she was about a foot shorter, even with her high heels. He was a tall fella, taller than Sean.

&⟋○

The prom was held in a fancy meeting hall across town. There were a lot of students and the prom committee did a fabulous job with the decorations. It was a tropical theme with faux palm trees, large leafy plants, and a couple real colorful parrots. The lighting was dim and inviting. The walls had muslin murals of sandy beaches and blue waters hanging all around the room. A platform had been erected for the band at the far side. Each table had decorative sandy-colored tablecloths, seashells, and balloons.

Allie was waiting with Roy when Jennifer and Charlie arrived. She grabbed Jennifer's hand and led her to the bathroom.

"Girl, you are so pretty."

"You too. Sexy!"

"Roy was scared to touch me," Allie said, giggling. "We're going to have some fun later tonight. Wink, wink. What about you and Charlie? He's cute."

"No, no, no. He's just my prom date. Not like I'm in love with him or anything."

"It's your prom, girl, let loose a little."

"It is exciting. And I'm going to pester Sean all night. I hope he has a horrible time." She giggled.

The girls met up with the guys and danced a while. Jennifer was actually enjoying herself. Charlie gave her his full attention. He stood behind her chair and slid her in when she went to sit down. He went with Roy to fetch her some snacks and something to drink.

Allie patted Jennifer on the shoulder. "So how do you like Charlie?"

"He's sweet and nice. I like him."

"See, not all guys are like—"

"Don't even say it."

Jennifer looked over at Sean and Vicky, slow dancing. They were holding each other close. Sean felt her eyes upon him giving him dirty looks. He quickly looked away and slowly swayed through the other dancers to get out of her view. He was hot and started sweating.

The prom was winding up and Allie left with Roy to place unknown. Jennifer stood outside at the top of the steps leading down to the parking lot. She watched as Sean hurriedly walked past with Vicky scurrying away without a word. He looked up the steps at Jennifer as he drove off. She turned angry, knowing what they were going to be doing. *He's such scum!*

"Here's your jacket, beautiful."

"Thanks Charlie."

She looked up at him with her cute blue eyes. Charlie tried to speak, but his words came out in a stutter. "Jenn, you want to go to the park?"

"What?"

"Do you think you would like to go to Bellflower Park with me?"

Bellflower was simply a nickname the students used to describe the park, the place the fellas would take their southern bells to make out. Jennifer looked up at him in his handsome but rather snug suit and smiled. She had never been there with a guy and there were no lights in the woods there at night. The place was both spooky and romantic at the same time.

"Yeah, why not?" she said, being all bubbly.

Charlie had a grin on his face that just didn't quit. His cheeks turned blush and his heart rate increased with anticipation. They drove through a narrow gate at the rear, unofficial entrance to the park and hit a few ruts bouncing up in their seats.

"Dang, Charlie, slow down. You're going to jerk my neck off."

Charlie let out a little laugh. "Sorry sweetie." He quickly found a place to park and turned off the car. He left the key on and played some soft music he'd downloaded onto his flash drive for the occasion. The original CD was titled, "Sex mood music."

He put his arm around her and reached down to her butt to scoot her closer. He didn't waste any time and leaned over to kiss her. They shared a short kiss, but Jennifer wrinkled her nose when she sensed his stinky breath.

She turned her face away a little so Charlie kissed and licked down her neck. She felt tingles and it tickled a little bit. Charlie felt a strange sensation in his hands and his lips as he touched her. It was a warm, electrical, tingly feeling that made him throb and start to lose control. His body felt electrified. He pulled up Jennifer's dress and ran his fingers down into her underwear and stroked her. Jennifer kind of liked it and really started breathing heavily. Charlie pulled at her underwear to try to take them off, but Jennifer held them on.

"Alright." She pulled his hand away, but he wouldn't stop. "Charlie, stop!"

"Just enjoy it, you'll like it."

Charlie grabbed her hands together and forced her down onto the seat, holding her down. He rubbed his hand between her legs. Jennifer bucked to try to force him to stop, but her skinny little arms were no match for his strength and bulk.

"Get off me!"

"Just shut up!"

Charlie pushed down hard on her arms holding them over her head.

"You're hurting me, get off!"

Jennifer fought as best she could. She started crying and her body tensed all over. Her heart raced out of control. She reached her leg up and kicked Charlie hard against the steering wheel. He got mad and struck her across the face hard. He pulled down his pants and lay on her using his weight to pin her down while trying to pry her legs apart. Jennifer screamed and her body got hot; she could feel that ember heating up inside her. It burned hot; her eyes turned fire-red and glowed brightly. Charlie looked at her face while holding her hands over her head.

"What the hell?"

With a deep, dark voice Jennifer spoke. "I said get off me!"

Electrical current flowed across her body and into Charlie's hands, shocking him such that he felt it in his chest. He sat up for a moment. Jennifer reached up and a shock wave exploded from her hands, hitting him, thrusting him hard into the car door. His head cracked up against the glass with a thud and he fell unconscious onto her. She could feel the ember taking control of her emotions and got scared. She tried to relax, but it was so hard. She closed her eyes and calmed her breathing. She could feel the ember within her start to cool. She reached up behind her and pulled the handle to open the door. Her head hung out over the seat as she tried to inch herself from under him. At first she couldn't move. She squirmed and squeezed until she finally got free from under him, squeezing out onto the ground on her back.

She looked down and noticed her dress had blood on it and was ripped. She looked at Charlie and his head was bleeding from hitting the window. She checked to make sure he was still breathing. She got her purse off the floor and ran off into the black night of the woods. It was half a mile to the main road. She got her cell out and texted Stacey.

"Stacey, can you come get me?"

"Where are you?"

"At Bellflower."

"Way to go, girl!"

Jennifer felt like she couldn't breathe. Everything just hit her all at once. Her heart rate increased. She stopped and bent over with her hands on her knees. She teared up and her nose started running.

"Jenn, you there?"

"Just come get me."

"What happened?"

"He tried to rape me."

"Oh, God! On my way, Sis."

Jennifer sat and waited at the end of the dirt road. The more she thought about it the madder she got. She wanted to go back and beat the crap out of him. Then she got scared. *What if he bleeds to death?* She could feel that burning in her stomach again. She tried to calm her mind, but then her head started pounding with a severe headache. Stacey pulled up and let her in.

"Where is he?"

"He's back in his car unconscious with his head bleeding."

"Really? How'd that happen?"

"When he was trying to hold me down, I kicked him into the door and he hit his head."

"Dang girl." Stacey picked up her cell and started to dial 911. Jennifer grabbed the phone away.

"What are you doing? We need to call the police."

"No."

"What do you mean no? He just tried to rape you."

"I mean no. I don't want anybody to know about this."

"Jennifer."

"I mean it, just take me home."

"What are you going to tell Allie?"

"Nothing, she doesn't need to know and don't you say anything to anybody. Not even Mom and Dad."

"I don't get you. I really don't."

"I'm fine. Trust me."

"And what if you don't say anything and he comes after you again?"

Jennifer couldn't help it and started laughing.

"Did I miss something?"

"I kicked his ass; you really think he wants everyone to know that?"

"I'm lost, girl. Seriously. You can't even kick a ball across the street and you're saying you kicked that huge football player's butt."

Jennifer smiled. "Yep! Trust me when I say he won't ever mess with me again."

ℰ∂

Allie didn't get home until much later so Jennifer didn't have a chance to talk to her until the next morning.

"Soooo?"

"So what?"

"So how was Charlie? Did you guys do it?"

"No, I just had him take me home."

"Sorry Jennifer. I know you're still crazy about Sean."

"No, not anymore. I'm done with guys."

ℰ∂

Jennifer was excited about going to college. While she and Allie were standing at their lockers, Allie said, "Jennifer, what are you going to wear to graduation?"

"Nothing, I'm not going."

"You have to go, please. You're my best friend. I want you there."

"I'm just done with Sean and guys in general. Over it."

"But what about collage? We both elected archaeology because that's what Sean was doing."

"I don't care about what Sean is doing anymore, but I'm looking forward to studying archaeology and biology."

"Except he will be at the same college as us."

"Who cares?"

"You know there's going to be a lot of cute guys there?"

"Guys are just assholes, you know? I'm done with all that ridiculousness."

"You know all guys are not like Sean."

"I have a pretty good idea they are."

"Roy wasn't like him at all."

"Wait, then why'd you break up with him?"

"I wanted to be free. I want to enjoy college and experience life. Plus, I'm free to date anyone I want. I'm going to find the guy of my dreams and have a lot of fun along the way then make lots of babies and buy a house."

Jennifer laughed.

"If you're nice I know you can find a great guy too."

"Hey, I'm nice."

Allie laughed out loud.

"You're nice to me, true, but I think you enjoy biting the head off any guy who even tries to talk to you."

"I don't know. Maybe my heart's gone. Just a big empty hole there where Sean used to be."

"Weren't you just saying you're over him?"

Jennifer looked down with her lips curled downward. Allie hugged her tight.

"What is life about if not love? You just have to make a change. Besides, it'll be okay by the time you're married. "

Jennifer looked up and smiled.

"Now you sound like Mom."

Chapter 21

Jennifer stepped lively, skipping, as she and Allie headed for their first class.

"What are you so happy about?" Allie asked.

"Isn't it exciting? We finally get to learn something interesting. And no parents telling us what to do. I love college!"

"Shesh, I don't know how I let you talk me into this, never in a million years would I have thought about taking biology."

"Just relax, it'll be fun and we get to learn about all kinds of living things."

"Even archaeology class will be better than this."

"How do you know? You may love it, and it was your idea to take double majors anyway."

Allie looked at Jennifer with tired eyes. Jennifer hugged her while they walked. "It's gonna be fun, I promise!"

Allie yawned with her hand over her mouth. "It would be better if you weren't up all night talking."

"You were laughing and talking, too, ya know? We have the best dorm mates, don't you think?"

"I think they're both silly like you."

Jennifer stuck her tongue out at Allie. Allie shook her head and let out a silly half-giggle and cleared her throat.

They were the first to arrive at the early morning biology class. The room was arranged similar to a science lab with a bunch of metal-topped tables and two high metal stools behind each one facing the front desk and whiteboards. The walls were a light bluish-gray with posters and world maps hanging at various locations. One was a jungle poster with the slogan, "Save the Rainforest," and a second portrayed two large whales in the ocean with one ejecting water from its blowhole. Next to that was a shiny picture of dolphins at a public aquarium with a biologist in a wetsuit at feeding time. Jennifer particularly liked the large picture of several biologists on a boat at sea with scuba gear on their backs. She set her backpack book bag down on a table next to Allie's and looked around. The second-floor windows overlooked the courtyard and student square, with stone benches and a water fountain.

She looked down. "Aww, Allie, look at all my babies."

Jennifer bent down next to the aquariums and put her face by the glass.

"You and your frogs," Allie said suggestively, shaking her head.

"There're so pretty. Look at them! They're amazing. I've never seen frogs like this before. I love them! Oooooh, look at the pretty blue one."

The frogs gathered at the edge of the tank near her face and started croaking. Jennifer reached up with her skinny arms to remove a large, gray rock holding down a graded metal cover.

"I don't think you're supposed to be doing that, Jennifer," Allie said with caution. "The sign says don't touch."

"It's okay, I just want to hold him for a second."

She reached into the tank and the blue frog jumped onto the side of her hand. He used his sticky toes to climb up the rest of the way onto her palm. She lifted him out of the tank and he crawled up her forearm. She wiggled and laughed. "Hey, he's really ticklish." A few other students had come in and were watching her being silly and smiling.

"He's so sticky, I bet he's a great climber." She put her face closer to him. "Aren't you, baby?"

"How do you know he's a boy?"

Jennifer looked up at Allie with a serious look and tilted her head. Allie giggled.

The teacher, Miss Janet, walked through the door in the back of the class next to where Jennifer stood with the frog.

With a gasp she dropped her leather briefcase and the box in her arms, spilling her stuff.

"WHAT ARE YOU DOING?" she exclaimed loudly with huge eyes and raised eyebrows, her neck stretched and head high. She hurriedly grabbed two napkins and pulled the frog off Jennifer's arm, putting him back into the tank.

"Stay right there!"

"I'm sorry, I wasn't hurting him, I promise," Jennifer said sadly.

The teacher swallowed hard and took a deep breath. "Are you okay?"

"I'm fine. What's wrong?"

She grabbed Jennifer by the arm. "Come with me."

Miss Janet pulled her along by the arm and ran down the hallway. They hurried down the steps and stopped at the nurses' station. Miss Janet felt a little tingling sensation in her hand. She flung open the door and called out, "Nurse Amber, quick! This young lady was handling one of the poisonous dart frogs in my lab."

"Oh crap!"

Nurse Amber grabbed a pair of latex gloves while asking, "Where did it make contact?"

Miss Janet said, "It was along here," as she ran her finger down Jennifer's arm.

"How do you feel?" Amber asked.

"I'm fine really."

"I don't see any redness or swelling."

Miss Janet started flinging her wrist about some.

"Janet, you okay?"

Janet's eyes rolled back in her head and her head rocked backwards as she fell back to the floor. Her whole body started convulsing violently. Jennifer stepped back and screamed, putting her hand over her lips. The nurse tried to hold Janet still and called out to Jennifer, "Call 911!"

Jennifer dialed and asked for an ambulance with broken shrieky speech. Miss Janet started foaming at the mouth. The nurse gave her a shot of something for emergency anaphylactic shock treatment.

Jennifer got really hot and stepped further back. She held up her hand holding her phone and it was shaking dramatically. She tried not to cry. "This can't be happening."

She stood watching, not moving a muscle, wishing the ambulance would hurry up and get there. Nurse Amber screamed, "Get me that case, right over there!"

"This one?" Jennifer asked while rushing over.

"Yes, the defibrillator."

Miss Janet was no longer having seizures and her body lay still on the hard floor. Amber prepared the paddles and cut Janet's blouse and bra open to expose her chest. She turned on the unit and let it charge with a high-pitched hum.

"CLEAR!" SNAP! Janet's whole body lifted at the center, arching upward. Nurse Amber put her stethoscope to Janet's chest. No heartbeat.

"Ooooh, please," Jennifer cried out.

Amber shocked her again. SNAP! Again, Janet's body arched up in the middle. Amber listened again, still no heartbeat. Jennifer's body tensed up tight. Every muscle stressed in tension. Her heart beat so rapidly that she couldn't catch her breath. She reached out for the counter and thought she was going to have a heart attack. She almost fainted, falling to her knees, but she caught herself, placing her arm against the lifeless Janet. She tried to get up, accidentally placing her hand on Janet's chest and Janet's eyes glowed brightly. Her chest rose as she gasped in a deep breath. Her eyes opened and she held out her arms to sit up, coughing. Nurse Amber helped her to sit up and held her for a few seconds.

Jennifer got down on her knees in front of her and held her hand. She started to cry, saying, "I'm so, so, sorry."

Amber pulled her hand way. "Stay back until we can clean your arms and hands!"

The ambulance arrived and transported Janet to the hospital. Nurse Amber frantically scrubbed Jennifer's hands and arms until she was all red from the bristles. It took her a few minutes to calm down a bit enough to realize what she was doing.

"I don't know what happened, one minute she was dead then—I don't know."

Jennifer stuck out her lower lip and her mouth turned down. Amber hugged her for a second.

"It's okay, sweetie. It wasn't your fault."

"No, it's my fault. I'm so stupid."

"No sweetie, I've told them having those things around is dangerous. They need to be destroyed."

"No, please. They can let them go or give them to a zoo or something."

"Or something," Amber said with a stern tone. "How are you feeling?"

"I don't know, I'm scared."

"It's going to be okay. Why don't you head back to the dorms and take it easy for a while?"

"Why didn't the poison bother me?"

"Everyone reacts differently, some people are immune."

Amber let her go and handed her a tissue to wipe her tear-soaked face.

"If you need to talk about it I'm here, okay?"

"Okay, thank you."

Jennifer left and walked outside, she was still shaking all over and walked very slowly. Allie ran up to her and hugged her very tight.

"I thought it was you in the ambulance," Allie said tearfully. "I was so scared." She looked at Jennifer and saw that her eyes were bloodshot and her face was all red. "Are you okay?"

"She was dead. She fell down and her whole body was flopping around on the floor, it was so horrible."

"What happened?"

"I guess she got poison on her from my arm."

"Shesh, you and your frogs. What am I going to do with you?"

"Good thing I didn't kiss it."

"Ya think?"

Allie took Jennifer back to their dorm room.

"Great first day of college," Jennifer said. "I should have listened to you and left them alone."

"Don't worry about that right now. Just try to put it out of your mind."

Miss Janet never returned for the semester. Another instructor had to take her class. His first act was to have the frogs removed from the classroom. After a few weeks Jennifer was able to open up again to start enjoying the college experience. She just wanted to forget the whole incident. It all happened so fast that it seemed like a big blur in her mind, and anytime someone would try to bring it up she would change the subject.

Sean actually came around and was of some comfort. It was a

little awkward being at the same college with him and Jennifer was still uncomfortable being anywhere near him, but her mood softened a bit without Vicky around. To her surprise, Allie really enjoyed studying biology, but Jennifer tended to like archaeology classes better. Plus, Sean was in those classes. One day she even looked back and smiled at him.

CHAPTER 22

Second semester, Jennifer, Sean, and Allie were in the same class titled "The Study of Ancient Mayan Cultures." Jennifer really got into it and looked forward to class every Monday, Wednesday, and Friday. Actually, she enjoyed any subject to do with archaeology.

One particular day, the teacher said, "Turn to page thirty-two in your textbook, 'The Great Kings of the Forest'. From your assigned reading can anyone tell me when the first King of the Maya emerged? Yes, Ron?"

"About two hundred B.C."

"That is incorrect. Remember that the early Mayan provinces were individually ruled by their own chieftains, not kings; so, can anyone tell me when the provinces started to unite into various kingdoms and who was the first king?"

Jennifer raised her hand.

"Yes, Jennifer?"

"It wasn't until about two hundred nineteen A.D. that the first kingdom started to form under king Yax-Moch-Xoc."

"Correct. Can anyone tell me when the last Mayan king ruled? This was around nine hundred A.D."

A student raised his hand and asked, "Weren't there kings in the

Yucatan Peninsula at much later dates like King Moctezuma who died at the hands of the Spanish conquistadors?"

"King Moctezuma was an Aztec ruler and not a Mayan. The Mayans died off well before Moctezuma's time; however, the Mayan civilization did span for over a total of a thousand years. The last great king of the Mayans was the Ahau or god king, Ah-Cacaw, and he is believed to have ruled around nine hundred A.D.

"After that time the Maya seemed to have disappeared as there is no archaeological evidence of their existence after that time period. Actually, it wasn't until explorers found the ancient Mayan temples, overgrown by the jungle, that the existence of the Maya was made known in our day and age. They were clearly very advanced for their time and if they had survived to this day it could be conceivable that they could have been one of the greatest superpowers of our time.

"There is speculation that the demise of the Mayan people was due to deforestation. There is evidence of a great decline in vegetation around the massive city of Tikal, possibly due to poor management by the king over the environment. At some point all vegetation was stripped away from around the city for hundreds of miles. They could have had an excessively cold winter and used the trees for warmth or maybe their advancement and building of structures required more wood than was locally available. In any case, the entire people seemed to have simply vanished by all known evidence."

Jennifer inquired, "But being so advanced, how could they have simply died out from a decline in vegetation? That just doesn't make sense to me."

"You make a great point. Many predominant archaeologists in the field have contemplated the mystery of their race being lost in the vagaries of time for many years," replied the teacher.

"The Maya were the most advanced, even more so than their Egyptian counterparts on the other side of the world. They even had developed their own two-hundred-and-sixty-day calendar marked by cycles of twenty days each. Their civil calendar was over a full three hundred and sixty days known as the Haab with month signs or pictographs representing the days of each cycle.

"There have been those who have believed that the Maya calendar even predicts the future; however, that belief was abandoned when the earth didn't end in December 2012." The students giggled a bit.

"Although others believe that the 2012 date was simply misinterpreted and off by several years and that the prediction that all life on Earth will end will still come true in the near future. Did the Ancient Mayans know something we didn't?"

A student stated, "It all sounds like a bunch of hocus pocus to me."

The students laughed and the teacher smiled.

"Well, the people of that period believed very strongly that their god kings had supernatural powers and could predict the future. They fashioned various items out of stela-stones, which were nothing more than crystallized meteorites that fell from the sky. They believed that these 'gifts from heaven' had unnatural powers that the kings could use to battle their enemies. They even used them in the creation of some of the tree-stones, or stone totem poles, that commemorated their major achievements and victories over rival kings. Most of these tree-stones have survived for over a thousand years and still stand today. It may all seem like a lot of hocus pocus, but there are more than a few unexplained phenomena."

"Like what?" a student asked.

"Yeah," several more students expressed.

"Tell us more."

The students were very still and really took interest. Except for the gentle shush of the cooling system, the room was very still and quiet.

"Take, for instance, the Valley of the Monkey. The dig site resembled that of a massive grave intermixed with weapons, wagon parts, and clasps from leather battle armor. Evidently there was a great battle that took place on that site where over a hundred thousand lost their lives; yet a tree-stone commemorating that event has never been found. The Maya kings of the last dynasty were quite fanatical about memorializing their achievements so it's very odd that an event of this magnitude was never recorded."

Jennifer sat with a confused look on her face. She slowly slipped her hand in the air.

"Yes Jennifer?"

"That does sound odd, but it's not like it's magical or anything."

The teacher smiled and snickered a little bit.

"I wasn't finished. The most interesting and baffling thing about the dig site was that all of the remains of the fallen warriors were at the same level of sediment, meaning that they all died in the same relative time frame, the great battle; but when the bones of the soldiers were analyzed and carbon dated, the remains varied in age from twelve hundred to five thousand years old."

Most of the students sat up with interest and a few with puzzled looks on their faces. The room was very quiet as all the students listened intently. All of a sudden the silence was broken when Sean blurted out, "I love archaeology!"

The other students jumped a little and giggled. Jennifer looked over at Sean and smiled. Allie leaned up against Jennifer to get her attention and said to the teacher, "Tell us more."

"Yeah, tell us more," several of the other students asked, shaking their heads, urging the teacher to continue.

"Well, there is this." The teacher put a slide on the screen depicting the front wall of an ancient temple. "This was nicknamed 'The Temple of the Jaguar', not far from the great Temple of Naranjo. No one has ever been able to translate the text written on the entrance and the construction of the temple is unlike anything of this period anywhere in the world. The pictographs are Mayan, but the writings on the door don't match any known dialect. Linguistic experts have tried to decipher the text for over fifty years and they are no closer to understanding it today than when they first started. So the question is who built it?"

Jennifer looked at Allie who sat with her mouth hanging open and wide eyes. "Isn't that the temple in your art painting from high school?"

"Shhh." Jennifer put her finger to her lips.

Allie squirmed in her seat and stared at Jennifer. "I can't believe you drew that. What does it mean?" she whispered.

"I don't know," Jennifer said quietly, shaking her head. "I think I'm in shock."

"You said you never saw that temple before, but your painting looks exactly like it."

"I don't know how I drew it, it was just in my head. Like I was remembering it."

The teacher said, "By the way, this is not something we normally offer to freshmen, but there are a few openings for our summer archae-ological expedition, which will include visiting this temple. It's worth six credits and we have limited spaces. I do have to warn you, though, there is some risk involved. We will travel deep into the jungle; there are deadly reptiles, animals, and local politics to deal with, but that's all part of archaeology, is it not? Would anyone have an interest in attending?"

Sean's and Jennifer's hands were the first to go up.

"Allie, raise your hand," Jennifer said and turned her head to look directly at her.

"I don't really want to go."

"Come on, it'll be fun."

"Did you not hear what he just said? It's dangerous."

"Aww, come on. It's exciting and I want to go."

"Aren't you worried you might get bitten by a snake or kidnapped or something?"

"Are you kidding? We're standing on the precipice of the greatest adventure of our lives!"

"Sorry, Jennifer, I can't see myself trekking through the jungle with deadly stuff ready to bite me. I can see you doing it. I feel sorry for anyone going with you though."

"What do you mean?"

"I'm sure all the poisonous frogs in the jungle will be climbing all over you."

"Hey, I thought we agreed not to bring that up again."

"I'm just saying..."

"Well, at least Sean's going," Jennifer said and looked over at him and smiled.

For the next two days, Jennifer nagged Allie until she finally agreed to go on the trip. Jennifer was so excited; she couldn't wait until the end of the semester.

CHAPTER 23

The girls were all packed and pretty excited. They said their goodbyes then Allie's dad drove them to the airport. Allie and Jennifer sat together and made themselves comfortable for the long flight to South America. They didn't bump into any other students going on the summer excursion, but then it was a large aircraft and they were all scattered about in different seats. Jennifer thought she caught a glimpse of Sean in the aisle near the front, but she wasn't sure.

She had never flown before and had the jitters. She was a total chatterbox talking a mile a minute. She had a little shortness of breath and thought about the time she rode her first, only, and last rollercoaster. It wasn't a pleasant experience. She gripped the armrests tightly when the jet accelerated down the runway. She could feel her body being pushed back into the seat cushions. Then the nose of the aircraft seemed like it was pointing straight up toward the heavens. Jennifer looked at Allie with huge eyes and fright on her face.

"Jenn, just relax. It's only the landing gear," Allie laughingly said. "Breathe girl, breathe."

"What was I thinking?"

"It's fine. We're all good. Relax, there's nothing to worry about."

The flight attendant started the food and beverage service. By the time Jennifer finished picking at her food she was a little more relaxed, but the ceaseless anxiety of being thirty thousand feet up never strayed far from her mind. She tried to nap, leaning her head on Allie.

The landing was smooth, but the flight was late and they had to take a connecting flight on a small turboprop airplane. They ran through the small airport trying to find the terminal, but it was hard because the signs were not in English. They just had to guess based on the terminal numbers at the bottom.

The plane was sitting out on the tarmac such that they had to walk outside. When they exited the door, a down sloping ramp led them onto the hot asphalt. The intense heat and high humidity hit them like a hot wall of sticky sweat. Jennifer opened a few buttons on her shirt as sweat dripped down her chest.

They walked with lively steps up onto the small plane. Jennifer smiled and thought it felt small and cozy. "This is more my style." She looked down at the narrow aisle with seats on both sides. It was like a high school flashback of getting on the bus to go home. She took another step and froze; her shoulders dropped like she was trying to make herself small and unnoticed. She stood with her mouth hanging open.

Allie bumped into the back of her. "What are you doing?"

Jennifer quickly slipped into a seat. Allie looked back and saw that only a few seats away sat Sean with Vicky. Allie stowed her carry-on while looking over at them a few times then sat down.

"What's she doing here?" Allie asked.

"I don't know, I mean she's not even in our class or even in our school," Jennifer said with a nasty tone.

"You okay?"

Jennifer peered over her seat behind her and Vicky was staring directly at her with a nasty look. She sat back down hard in her seat with her arms crossed.

"You gotta be freaking kidding me!" She took a deep breath and heavily exhaled. "Why'd she have to be here? I mean really! She's gonna ruin everything!"

"I thought you were over Sean."

"It doesn't matter whether I still love him or not. She's just evil and this … was … my … trip. I can't … freaking … believe this!"

Allie put her hand on the back of Jennifer's neck and lightly massaged it.

"Just try to forget—"

Jennifer interrupted. "She's such a nasty bitch, you know?"

She took another deep breath and held it for a second. Her nostrils flared and her body tensed up. The more she thought about it the more her blood pressure pulsed; her face was very red and heated. Allie sat back and let Jennifer sulk for a while. She knew there was no comforting her when she got like this.

The plane took to the air for their short flight over the jungles of the Yucatan Peninsula flying at only a few thousand feet. Jennifer breathed heavily, glaring out the window at the green, flowing canopy below, wishing she could be somewhere else—anywhere else, as long as she wasn't there. The longer she sat the more she fidgeted in her seat. She kept huffing and crossing her arms, unable to sit still.

The plane hit some rough turbulence and yawed sideways, jarring the passengers. The sky grew dark and a black fog covered the windows to where it was impossible to see anything. The plane thrust left then right. The turbulence increased several fold until it became extreme, knocking the plane all around. Jennifer grabbed tightly on to her armrests. A huge gust hit the aircraft and the floor under their feet flexed and creaked. Several baggage bins popped open, spilling out luggage onto the floor. Several students screamed. Magazines and tablets fell off their tray tables into the aisles. Everyone was holding on tight as the plane was battered all around. The flight attendant unbuckled her belt to try to gather the bags on the floor, but the plane dropped in altitude very quickly and she flew up into the ceiling, hitting her head, then fell hard to the floor while the passengers screamed.

Allie took rasping breaths with her eyes squeezed shut and her head back against the seat. She turned her head and looked over at Jennifer. Her whole body cringed when she saw the look on her face. She had seen that look once before. Jennifer's eyes were flaming red and reptile like with vertical irises. A tremble ran up Allie's spine and her body quaked. She leaned over and whispered harshly in Jennifer's ear, "ARE YOU DOING THIS?"

Jennifer kind of stared at her for a moment then shook her head to snap out of it. She didn't even notice the burning ember deep within her, trying to get out. She breathed so heavily that she couldn't catch her breath and tried to relax, but it was so hard to calm herself. Her eyes watered and her skin felt freezing cold to the touch, but she burned from within. She put her head back and let her mind drift. Her thoughts strayed and she thought about all the fun times she and Sean had growing up, his playful antics that made her laugh. His cute smile that made her insides melt, leaving her pining over him at night. That first day when they met when she scared the crap out of him, hiding in the woods with her frogs. She breathed and her eyes faded back to normal and she started to smile.

The fog lifted and sky calmed as if there was never a storm, everything was still and quiet. No one made a sound. A few of the passengers got up to help the flight attendant to her feet. She had blood all over her face from a small gash in her forehead. Allie tried not to cry, but it was hard and she welled up inside. Jennifer hugged her tight.

"I'm so, so, sorry."

"I should never have come on this trip."

"Allie, it'll be okay."

"We could have died."

"It's Vicky's fault. You know?"

"I've never been so scared in all my life."

"I'm sorry. Please forgive me." Jennifer started tearing up.

"I just need some time to process, Jen. I can't believe that just happened."

"Don't be mad at me, please, you're all I have. I can't lose you too."

"Jen..."

Allie wiped her eyes with a tissue. The pilot said to prepare for a landing over the intercom system so everyone picked up their items as best they could. All the passengers tried to get up at the same time to rush off the plane when it landed. Several of them had red faces and had the jitters, hands shaking, and weak knees.

The students collected their baggage and were met by a guide who took them to several Land Rovers waiting outside the airport to take them to their hotel. The drive took about an hour on a dirt road and most of the students were tired and burned out. The heat made them all very sleepy. By the time they arrived at the hotel, most of them were sleeping, leaning up against each other, except Jennifer. She sat awake looking into the jungle while they drove. She felt strangely content and smiled when they drove past a little monkey hanging on a vine near the side of the narrow track, the two ruts that served as an unimproved road to the hotel.

It felt good to finally arrive. The hotel was deep in the jungle, completely surrounded by trees, vines, and wild animals. The sun was low in the sky and a yellow tint collocated against the green vegetation with beams of light shooting down to create light spots on the ground through the canopy. Monkeys howled from the tops of the trees waiting for someone to drop some food on the ground. The hotel was seven stories high and looked new. The outside was fancy with jaguar statues and white pillars by the front entrance. The dirt road led up to the courtyard that was paved black and was kept very clean. The roof was high with a steep slope and had large leaves of the canopy draping over it. Thick vines hung down from the trees and swung in the breeze. There was a side parking lot filled with four-wheel drive vehicles. The hotel was an oasis of freedom for those who desired to escape reality for a while, but it was also in a perfect location for the archaeology expedition to begin.

They walked into the large lobby and waited at the front desk. The floors were made of beautiful polished bamboo and the walls were maroon with natural wood trim. There were large vases or planters made of patterned glass but rather than holding plants they were lit up in both the square base and the round planter top. The decorative patterns on the floor were very eye appealing and soothing. Jennifer had never seen such a fancy and beautiful hotel lobby. She smiled and took a deep breath. She felt strangely odd and content.

The students were informed of their itinerary and that they would be visiting the Temple of the Jaguar the next day, which was where the Hotel Jaguar got its name.

CHAPTER 24

First thing in the morning there was a knock at the door. Jennifer excitedly climbed out of bed in her pajamas and looked through the peephole. It was Sean. She opened the door and he just reached out and hugged her. She didn't even have time to hug him back.

"You okay?"

Jennifer answered, a bit in shock. "Umm, I guess so."

"I was worried about you after what happened on the plane."

"No, we're okay," she quickly blurted out. "How about you?"

"Vicky and I are doing okay."

Of course you have to mention her.

Jennifer's expression was neutral.

"Well, they said everyone needs to get downstairs and eat soon so we can hike to the temple," Sean said.

"Okay, we'll be down in a few minutes."

The girls rushed to get ready. Jennifer put on some cute blue shorts and a blue and white plaid looking formal wear bikini top and hiking boots. Allie put on a long-sleeved shirt, jeans, and high dress boots.

"Allie, what are you wearing?"

"Me, what about you?"

"Okay, it's really hot out."

"Well, I'm not getting bitten by anything. You know there are bad bugs, snakes, lizards, and other deadly things in the jungle."

Jennifer laughed. "You are going to die out there. Put some shorts on and take off those boots. You just look silly."

"Fine," Allie said with an attitude.

"Come on, Allie, relax and have some fun. Where's your sense of adventure?"

"I would be just fine at home by the pool."

"You're such a baby," Jennifer said then ran out of the room with Allie chasing her down the hallway. They almost ran into a maid running to the elevator. When it opened, they hurried in and pressed the button for the door to shut.

Allie caught her breath and started laughing. "I can't believe we're doing this. You know we could die out there, right?"

"Shesh, shut up!" Jennifer semi-jokingly said.

The girls caught up to the rear of the group on the far side of the hotel parking lot. They all filled up their canteens and prepared for their trek through the jungle. Jennifer stood next to Sean on one side and Vicky was on the other. Vicky looked over at her with her nasty gaze so she stuck her tongue out at her then looked forward and smiled with an ornery grin. Vicky flung her hair back and curled up her nose with narrow, smirking, puckered lips. She swatted away a gnat buzzing around her ear then took in a deep inhale rocking her head back and forth like, *Let's get this over with.*

Jennifer leaned over to Allie's ear and whispered, "Maybe I should find her a poisonous frog."

Allie smiled back and shook her head. Sean looked down at Jennifer with her bikini top on and her nice tanned skin. He reached out and patted her back for a few seconds. She looked up at him with her gleaming blue eyes. Vicky gave him a look of death with her head cocked back and her lips tightened together. Jennifer noticed so she winked at him, just to aggravate her. Vicky grabbed Sean by the arm and pulled him to the front of the group huffing and puffing while they walked.

Allie giggled and said, "Jen, you are so ornery."

"So? She deserves it."

The archaeology professor in charge of the expedition spoke up. "Everybody please gather around for a minute. This is the first time out for a few of you and you need to be aware that there are many deadly things in the jungle you may come in contact with like poisonous snakes, deadly spiders, and a whole array of wildlife. You need to pay attention to your surroundings at all times and don't touch anything you're unsure of.

"Please stay with the group and don't wander off. There have been recent sightings of jaguars in the area. If we come in contact with them, stay calm. Avoid any sudden or abrupt movements. Whatever you do, don't run. They are smart and powerful creatures and they need to be respected because they can be extremely deadly. I can't express that enough. Don't make any sudden moves if you come into contact with one. Jaguars, in legend, are the protectors of the jungle, from an archaeology standpoint."

The group walked along a well-traveled path with the professor leading the way with his impressive walking stick. It had engravings running the length that looked like a Mayan tree-stone. It was cherry-red and glossy, except for the grip, which was bare wood, the paint rubbed off from continuous use.

There were twenty in all with Jennifer and Allie bringing up the rear. The jungle had grown over the trail further up so the men started taking turns with machetes to clear the overgrowth. Some of the girls were getting eaten up by bugs and their bug spray didn't seem to help at all. Allie was smacking and swatting at them constantly.

"I shouldn't have listened to you and wore my long-sleeved shirt. Shesh, this is crazy. Aren't they biting you?"

"No," Jennifer said as she looked up high in the canopy with wide eyes. She looked through the forest all around her.

"Why aren't they bothering you? All that exposed skin and they're tearing me up."

"I guess I just don't taste good. Awww, Allie, look at that."

"What?"

"Over there in that tree."

Jennifer walked off the trail while Allie watched.

"What are you doing?"

"Looking at my little baby."

There was an emerald-green boa coiled around a tree branch sunning itself. Jennifer got close and watched it for a few seconds, it lay perfectly still as if it were sleeping. Its skin glistened in the sun, its long body slowly expanding and contracting with each breath.

"Allie, come look, he's so beautiful."

"No, I can see it just fine from here. You need to leave that thing alone before it bites you. Jennifer, come on!"

"You wouldn't bite me, would you, baby?"

She reached her hand out to touch its head and it perked up, coiling back. It followed her movements, its tongue tasting the air with every flicker.

"Jennifer, you're scaring the crap out of me right now. He's going to bite you. Everyone's leaving us."

Jennifer hesitated for a second with her hand in the air above the snake then she slowly stretched out, and when she touched it, she felt a little tingle in her fingertips, kind of the same feeling as when she touched a nine-volt battery to her tongue at the coaxing of her sisters as a child. At her touch the snake relaxed. It felt silky and moist. It slithered closer and worked its way up her arm. Jennifer giggled at its tickle and petted its head.

Allie cringed and her whole body tensed up, she sucked in air through her gritted teeth. She put her hands up to her face.

"Jen!"

The snake slowly wrapped itself around Jennifer's skinny arm with its big head up on her shoulder from behind, looking ahead as she walked back toward the trail. The snake smelled like grass after it had been mowed on a hot day. She reached Allie about the same time as the professor yelled back to the girls.

"What are you girls doing? You were told to stay with the group."

"Were coming," Jennifer yelled.

Allie stepped back a few steps.

"Jennifer! Put it down before it bites you!"

"He's my baby, see."

She petted its head.

"You're crazy, you know that?"

They were some distance away from the group so they hurried to catch up with them. Everyone stood waiting and staring back at them.

"Isn't he beautiful, Allie?"

"You mean deadly."

"He's not poisonous."

"How do you know?"

"Okay, you're the straight A biology student. You tell me what kind of snake it is."

Allie looked at it for a second while they walked.

"I guess it looks like a boa constrictor, which isn't poisonous."

"See, he's harmless."

"I didn't say he's harmless. You know he kills his food by strangling it with his body and he's wrapped around your arm. He does have a very painful bite also. "

A huge jaguar walked out on the path, right in front of the two girls, between them and the group. Several of the girls in the group cried out. "*Oh no!*" The professor put his hand up on top of his hat, not sure what to do.

The jaguar looked right into Jennifer's deep blue eyes. She held her breath, afraid to move a muscle. His nose was only half an inch from hers as he sniffed her. She could smell his putrid breath and almost taste it with each exhale he made, blowing her hair into her face. He sniffed her hair and put his nose against her face. She felt that tingle again like an electrostatic shock but it was continuous. The snake coiled back ready to strike in her defense. Jennifer closed her eyes shut, taking in a breath of air. The jaguar gently sniffed around her body. It lifted its paw and extended a little bit of its nails, grabbing her waist and pulling her closer. It ran its wet nose across her exposed belly tickling her. She couldn't help but giggle.

Allie slowly stepped backward, her hair standing straight up on the back of her neck; she held out her hand, shaking heavily. The jaguar looked at her and she froze, but her knees were weak and it was hard to remain standing. Some of the students were recording the whole incident on their phones. The jaguar released Jennifer, leaving tiny claw marks on her sides, and glanced their way and then back at Jennifer. His eyes turned to see the snake coiled around her arm. Jennifer felt relieved. She could sense he was of no threat to her. She slowly reached out and petted the side of its head. One of the students yelled, "Are you crazy?"

CHAPTER 25

The jaguar slowly turned and walked off into the jungle. Allie about collapsed, falling to her knees with gasping breaths, and her whole body trembled. The group hurried back to them and the professor stopped short of Jennifer when he saw the snake coiled back, ready to strike at him.

"Hold still, Jennifer, I'll try to distract him so they can cut off its head."

She stepped back.

"No!" She held up her hand. "He's mine, don't you hurt him. He's just a baby."

"How did it get wrapped around your arm?"

"I picked him up. He's just so pretty, I couldn't resist."

Several of the students helped Allie to her feet and tried to calm her.

"Jennifer, I think you need to let it go before it hurts you."

"He likes me, I'll let him go later. I'm gonna hold him for a while."

"You're such a freak," Vicky said.

"I think it's cool," Sean said.

Another student, a senior, said, "What was it like? Weren't you scared?"

"Are you kidding? I was terrified. At least at first. I just held my breath and didn't move. But then he … like … touched my face and I knew he wasn't gonna hurt me."

"I can't believe you touched him."

"Yeah," several other students said. "That was so cool."

Allie finally found her footing and calmed down, but she was out of her element and not liking life just then. Jennifer, on the other hand, felt right at home, like the jungle accepted her and wanted her there, a sense of belonging. It was like something awakened inside her and it was exhilarating and scary, like it was bigger than her. She breathed it all in, in utter AWE of everything.

They continued hiking and chopping at the overgrowth to make their way through to the temple. It took longer than expected but at least there was now a clear path back to the hotel. The professor absolutely did not want to be caught out on the trail at night with all the nocturnal predators, he urged them to move faster.

Jennifer's skinny arm was aching trying to hold up the weight of the boa constrictor so she let her arm lower down to her side. With her bringing up the rear, no one noticed when the snake slithered up across her shoulders and coiled a few times around her neck, it's head next to her cheek. A little later, Allie looked back and her eyes opened wide; she began to speak, but Jennifer put her finger to her lips, not wanting everyone to freak out.

They arrived at the site of the Temple of the Jaguar. It looked just like Jennifer's painting except for several statues along the path. One statue was of a short, skinny, young woman with strangely shaped ears holding a staff in one hand and pointing at the temple with the other. She had a snake coiled around her neck with its flat head flexed back looking in the direction of the temple. The staff had a stone inserted at the top that was bright green and reflected the sunlight on the ground. The statue itself was light sand-colored.

A cold shiver ran down the professor's spine when he looked back at Jennifer noticing the snake had coiled around her neck. Everyone was quite shocked and speechless, staring at her. "What?" Jennifer said, putting her arms in the air with her palms facing upward.

Vicky put her hands to Sean's ears and whispered something. He turned his head to her with an irritable glance. The professor thought intently for a few seconds but then just shook his head, ignoring the strange coincidence. He cleared his throat and said, "The temple was believed to have been discovered in 1912; however, the indigenous people of the area claim to have known of its existence for many generations prior to its discovery. There are many myths about the temple, passed on from generation to generation. One of such myths is the existence of powerful beings that came from inside the earth and had power over the jungle. The indigenous people opposed outsiders visiting this site, believing it to be sacred or maybe even cursed. It is only in recent years that they've been more receptive to outsiders. Please be careful not to disturb anything or give them any cause to deny our presence in the future. This temple has never been opened. Not in a thousand years. All requests to excavate the site or open the temple have been denied."

The students walked around and examined everything, making sketches and renderings of the pictographs and the strange unknown writings on the huge sealed door and taking pictures with their cell phones, which didn't have signal in the jungle but at least they could record video and pictures.

Jennifer stood next to the statue of the woman with the snake around her neck. She stood up on the base and hugged it, she was about the same height. She handed her cell to Allie.

"Allie, take a picture."

Allie walked around and took a few pictures from different angles. Then she stood up next to Jennifer.

"Let's do a selfie together."

Allie clicked a few pictures until she looked at the image and saw the snake right next to her head.

"Whew!" She giggled and stepped down quickly, her heart beating fast.

"He's not going to hurt you."

"Okay, but I'm not really a fan of frogs, snakes or bugs, you know."

"Aww, baby, she doesn't like you," Jennifer said as she kissed her snake.

"Isn't he heavy? You've been carrying him around all day."

"A little, but I love him."

"Are you going to take notes or make some sketches?"

Jennifer giggled and said, "Why? I have a painting at home just like it."

"Yeah, true."

Allie walked up the few stone steps to the huge doorway. She took individual photos of each of the strange symbols making up the unknown text. Jennifer stood next to her and ran her fingers along the chiseled stone letters, feeling the indentations and edges. They were smooth and filled with dirt and some mossy sections from years of weathering. She took a step back and started mouthing the words. Allie took notice and said with a whisper, "Jennifer, what are you doing?"

"Looking at the writings," she said quietly.

"You can read this?"

"I think so."

"How?"

"I don't know. I just can."

"So what's it say?"

"Umm… It's kind of hard to say, but it seems like it says something like, 'Only a guardian,' and something about 'another world'."

Jennifer followed down to the next section with her finger.

"I think this is a warning. It sounds like, 'guarded in time or locked in time,' then here it says, 'don't wake the rest.'"

"Spoooooky!" Allie said with a giggle. "Wonder what that means, 'Don't wake the rest.'"

"Wait, there's more; it says something about, 'trapped in the shadows,' and, 'the scourge will awaken.'"

Allie grabbed Jennifer by the waist and said, "Boo!"

Jennifer jumped and screamed. She put her hand on her chest, breathing fast. "Oh, you scared the crap out of me."

Jennifer's snake coiled back, ready to strike.

"Oh, easy, baby. It's okay." She petted its head.

Allie tilted her head and laughed; she walked down the steps to look at some of the statues. Jennifer studied the remaining text on the door, but Allie urged her to keep quiet about it because everyone, especially Vicky, would think she was a weirdo and not believe her anyway.

&O

The group started back to the hotel, being that it was late and the professor worried a lot about getting stuck out in the jungle at night. He told Jennifer to find a nice place to let her snake go, but she had no intentions of letting it go. She really loved the feeling of it around her neck, like it made her feel safe or something, like a hug. Allie and Jennifer talked and laughed along the walk back and felt comfortable walking a few paces behind.

When they reached the hotel, the professor waited for Jennifer to catch up and said, "You really need to release the snake now. They won't allow it into the hotel."

Jennifer looked at him and her eyes glistened over.

"I don't think I can."

"I'm afraid I must insist."

Jennifer put her hand up to hug the snake close to her head and kissed him. She wiped away a tear with her hand.

"Just let it go, you sick freak! We're all tired of your crap."

"Shut up, Vicky! You skaggy, boyfriend-stealing bitch."

"Wooow," a few of the students said.

"Vicky, calm down," Sean said.

"No, I've had enough of her," she said harshly. "She's such a freak. Walking around with a snake wrapped around her neck. I mean who does that anyway? Really, am I the only one who thinks she's a freak?"

The professor said, "Okay. Okay." He motioned Jennifer over to a tree. "Time to release it."

Jennifer could feel the ember start to warm inside her. She took a deep breath to try to calm herself. She thought for a second.

"No! He's mine and you don't own me or him. You have no right to tell me I have to let him go."

"I'm telling you, you can't take him into the hotel."

"Well then, let them tell me that."

Jennifer stomped past the other students and stormed through the front doors of the hotel, her hair blowing all around due to the gust of wind entering with her. The ground under her feet shuddered slightly with each step. She could hear a few of the guests in the lobby gasp as she walked briskly toward the front desk. The hotel manager, standing behind the desk, looked up at her with the professor walking right on her heels, worried she would put him in a precarious position with the authorities. As soon as the manager saw her he rapidly blinked his eyes a few times. His neck bending forward and hands shaking, he stretched out his palms to her and bowed his head with tears in his eyes. Jennifer stopped in puzzlement. Everyone had seemingly frozen in time, staring at her. She stepped back when an attendant ran from behind the desk whimpering. He fell on his knees before her. "Ahau - la!"

The man, with his face to the ground and palms facing upward, was shaking profusely, like he was seeing a ghost.

CHAPTER 26

Quickly, the other guests and workers, all the locals, fell to the ground.

They said, "Ahau - la, Ahau - la!"

The bartender in the adjoining room heard them and ran toward Jennifer with uncertain steps, his palms facing upward. He, too, fell on his face before her. The other students filled the open doorway, wind to their backs. Jennifer's long, light brown hair floated about and her snake swayed from side to side.

She stood with her mouth hanging open thinking, *What in the world?*

The professor had never seen anything like it in all his travels around the world as an archaeologist; he and the other students stood there confused. Allie stepped up next to Jennifer and asked, "What's going on?"

"I've no idea. I'm freaking out right now."

The hotel manager looked up at her with teary eyes and held up his palm. "Ahau - la."

Jennifer looked at him with concerned eyes, her heart softened and the ember inside her went cold. She had the strangest feeling, a tingling all over her body like soft, little butterflies flapping their wings all over her. She reached out and touched the man's hand and felt that same tingle like when she touched her snake for the first time, like the feeling when the jaguar touched her belly. The man felt it so strongly it made his whole body tremor; then he knew. He quickly withdrew his hand and turned his face back toward the floor. Jennifer looked around and everyone who wasn't bowing before her was staring at her waiting to see what she would do. She knelt down and patted the man on the back.

"It's okay," she said with a soft voice.

He looked up at her with the snake looking down at him. He tilted his head away.

"Sir, it's alright, really, you can get up."

The man pushed himself up to his knees.

"Ahau - la?"

She reached out and took his hand with the electrical stimulation tickling her fingers even stronger than before. She helped to pull him to his feet. He stood and stared at her, his hands still shaking.

One of the students whispered to the professor, "What does Ahau - la mean?"

"I think it means goddess of the jungle in this context."

The hotel manager motioned for Jennifer to follow him. He led her out back to a courtyard between the two wings of the hotel. The denizens got up off the floor and followed as did the other students. It was dark as the sun had finally set beyond the canopy. It was hard to see anything, but there were distinct shapes out in the plaza.

The manager opened a small external fuse box and reached in to toggle a large, heavy duty switch.

CLICK!

Lights illuminated all around a beautiful tropical garden with large, sacred Yaaxche trees wrapped in lights. A fountain sat in the center of the garden with three tiers of waterfalls lit up with alternating purple and red lights. There was statue on top resembling the one at the temple except it had colorful polished marble stone rather than the dual sand-colored and weathered stone of the temple. It depicted the same young woman holding a brown staff with a green, shiny stone at the hilt. She had a smooth, green boa constrictor wrapped around her neck.

The manager pointed to the statue and said, "Ahau - la." The denizens followed Jennifer at a short distance and watched her every move. When she stopped, they stopped; when she walked, they walked. She roamed around the fountain admiring the delicate detail of the workmanship and looked up at the girl with the snake around her neck. There were small pictographs chiseled into the stone basin that looked quite old. She reached out her hand to touch it and the denizens gasped. It was forbidden for anyone to touch the sacred fountain and it was believed that anyone who did would die at the very touch or be struck down.

Jennifer hesitated for a second and looked back at them; they stood with wide eyes, some with their hands to their lips. Jennifer slowly reached out her hand. She could feel their eyes upon her, she could hear their swift breathing as their hearts beat fast in their chests. She touched the fountain thinking nothing would happen.

SNAP!

All the decorative bulbs around the courtyard burned super bright and several popped with sparks; then the power went out. Everyone instinctively ducked down and a few of the ladies screamed. The denizens fell to the ground, fearful in the dark; their eyes began to adjust, and then they saw it. The fountain started to glow with an amber-green brilliance. It grew brighter and brighter. Jennifer swished her fingers around in the water and rainbows of red, green, and amber followed her motion, fading off into ambient. The green stone in the hilt of the staff high on top of the statue was radiant, creating diamond patterns on the ground and on their bodies. Some of the denizens with their faces to the ground started squealing and fanning themselves; their blood rushed and coursed in their veins and their bodies tingled. Some slowly crawled on their hands and knees to reach out and touch her. When they did, they could feel electrical stimulation on their fingertips, which made their bodies tingle. They quickly backed away on all fours with their heads bowed. Vicky, for the first time, had nothing to say. She stood back with one knee to the ground, holding on to a low branch of a tree. The students definitely looked at Jennifer in a different light. It was no longer just a neurotic coincidence that she resembled the statues.

Even the professor was in total disbelief at the events unfolding before him. Did they unlock some ancient curse? Was there something special about this petite young woman or was this all just some crazy coincidence? He walked to the fountain and reached out his hand to touch it, but the denizens sprung to their feet shoving him violently, gasping and speaking in their language with raspy vigor. Jennifer touched them and tried to calm them and they stepped away. The other students gasped and stepped back. They were totally perplexed, except for Sean and Allie.

Jennifer felt exhilarated. She petted her snake and smiled at the denizens, motioning for them to rise. She urged them to return to the hotel, but they were reluctant to go in without her. She led them inside and hugged a few. She couldn't understand them and most didn't know English, but they made her feel loved and appreciated in a way she'd never experienced before.

As they left the garden Jennifer could hear the hotel manager whisper to one of the denizens, "She's the one," in English.

She wanted to turn around and ask him, "The one what?" but she was already overwhelmed and trying to make sense of everything so she kept walking in silence.

All of the students turned in for the night being emotionally drained and confused. All but Jennifer, who lay wide awake, petting her snake. Her mind raced trying to understand everything that happened.

How is it that I can do these strange things? Is Vicky right? Am I just a freak?

She lay still and thought about the temple and what it said about a guardian. *Could I be the guardian?*

Then it came to her. She grinned widely and jumped up out of bed and started getting dressed. She gently shook Allie.

"Allie, wake up."

"What is it? Is it morning already?"

"No, silly. Guess what."

"Geeze, what?" Allie said, half asleep.

"I know how to open the temple door."

"How do you know that?"

"I was thinking about the writing on the door and it just came to me. Come on, we need to go."

"What? Where?"

"To the temple."

"You're crazy. I'm not going out into the jungle at night."

"Come on, Allie, where's your sense of adventure?"

"I'm here, aren't I?"

"Come on, get dressed. We have to get back before everyone wakes up."

"We can do it tomorrow."

"No, we can't, we're all hiking into the jungle tomorrow and camping halfway to the next dig site. And, besides, there's no way the professor would let me open the temple if he knew about it."

Allie got very stern. "Jennifer, I'm not going into the jungle at night. That's stupid. Seriously, we were almost killed by a jaguar yesterday and that was with the whole group, which, by the way, wouldn't have happened had you not stopped to pick up the killer snake."

Jennifer teared up and her lips sagged and curled down. She sat on the edge of her bed and wiped her eyes.

"Jennifer, I'm sorry, but you know we can't go there in the middle of the night."

"But it's our only chance and maybe there's something in the temple that will explain why I can do these things. Everyone thinks I'm some kind of freak or something."

Allie rolled over to face her friend. "Jennifer, you know I love you, but there's just no way."

Jennifer stood up and huffed. "Fine! I'll go myself."

She continued dressing and put on her boots. Allie got up out of bed and grabbed her arm. "Jen, stop! I'm not letting you do this. I'll get the professor if I have to."

Jennifer started crying. "Please, Allie. Come with me. I have to do this. I know I was meant to be here. Can't you see that?"

Tears were streaming down her face and her heart hurt in her chest like it was beating too slowly. She sat on the side of the bed with her head down and her shoulders slumping.

"Okay, fine! But if I die I'm going to kill you!"

Jennifer wiped her face and nose on her sleeve and giggled.

"How are you going to kill me if you're dead?"

"Believe me, I'll find a way. You know I didn't really want to come on this trip in the first place. Now you want me to get eaten by a tiger or something."

"Or kidnapped and eaten by cannibals."

Allie cocked her head and put her hand on her hip, staring at her.

"Very funny!

"We'll be fine. I promise."

"Is that like a get your money back if you're not completely alive guarantee?"

CHAPTER 27

Jennifer and Allie walked outside the hotel. They looked up at the clear sky through the canopy. The moon was full and the sky was riddled with bright stars. Monkeys were screaming in the distance and the jungle was surprisingly noisy for the middle of the night.

"Jen, are you hearing this?"

"Uh-huh."

"This is so crazy, you sure you want to be doing this?"

"Yes, absolutely."

"Jen, we don't even have flashlights."

"I've been thinking about that. Come with me, I think I saw some torches over by the fire pit over there."

They walked to an outside guest seating area with a fire pit and lounge chairs. Jennifer grabbed two Tiki torches and lit them. They moved fast down the trail toward the temple. After a few minutes Jennifer stopped to get her snake to move up to her neck because he was weighting her arm down.

"We really shouldn't be doing this."

"Shhhh."

Allie kept slapping at mosquitoes that were biting her arms, legs and neck. They kept buzzing around her ears as they quickly moved through the jungle. They were able to move very fast with the trail already cut back.

"Ouch!"

"What?"

"Stupid mosquitoes. It burns."

"Just keep walking."

"Aren't they bugging you at all?"

"No."

"Ugh!"

Allie bumped into Jennifer as they walked. Jennifer looked back at her with her eyebrows pulled downward. The moon cast scary silhouettes on the ground and Allie got the willies. Something fell hard on the ground nearby and they could hear the underbrush as it walked. It sounded like the footsteps were coming up from behind. Allie pushed past Jennifer on the narrow trail to get in front of her.

"What are you doing?"

"There's something back there."

Just then they heard a slow, low-pitched growl.

"It's probably a jaguar."

Allie stopped for a second.

"Don't stop, keep going."

"Aren't you afraid?"

"Just keep going, we'll be there soon."

Another animal was making noise swinging on branches in the trees.

"What was that?"

"Allie, just relax. Keep going."

"We shouldn't be doing this. Ouch! Damn!"

"What now?"

"It burns. Every time they bite me it burns."

Allie stopped and whipped at her arms and started tearing up.

"It hurts real bad. It feels like my skin is on fire. Look at this, my arm's swollen."

Jennifer held the underside of Allie's arm to look at the bug bites. As soon as she touched her, Allie felt a tingling sensation in her arm, a static electricity sensation like when someone rubs a balloon in their hair and then it sticks to the wall. Allie's whole body started to tickle with goose bumps. She squirmed and pulled her arm away.

"That tickles. What is that? It feels so weird."

Jennifer giggled. "I know, right? It was like that whenever I touched those people at the hotel too."

"Hey, my arm feels better now."

"Let me see."

Allie held up her arm and the redness was gone as well as the swelling.

"I don't think they're biting me anymore either. What'd you do?"

"I didn't do anything. Maybe they got tired of hearing you complaining about everything."

"Ha, ha, very funny."

Something big walked across the path in front of them and stood there. Allie stopped and stood perfectly still, holding her breath. She could see a large shape in the moonlight like it was watching her. She could hear Jennifer breathing behind her and leaned back into her, ready to turn and run. Allie's heart beat faster and faster. Finally, she had to take a breath and breathed in hard. Whatever was on the trail turned its head. They both stood motionless. Allie could feel something crawling on her ankle. She wanted to brush it off so bad but she was too terrified to move. Jennifer's snake slithered onto Allie's shoulder. She frowned and bent a little at the knees squinting her eyes and turning away.

They both screamed when the dark object took off running fast into the jungle. Allie's thoughts were scattered. She tried to catch her breath.

Her heart nagged at her body.

"Whoa!"

"Aah!"

"Jennifer, I think you're going to get me killed," Allie said, breathing heavily.

"I think we're here though. I think it's right up the trail."

"Yeah, the direction of whatever that was."

"It's gone now."

"You don't know that."

"Allie, it's long gone. We could hear it running away."

"Okay, you go first. And keep that snake off me."

"Okay. Okay."

They walked up the trail about a hundred yards. Allie was extra alert. She walked slowly, looking to both sides. She was so jumpy. She moved the torch and let out a high-pitched scream, seeing a face staring back at her.

"What?"

"Stupid statue. Scared me."

"Allie, relax. We're here."

They walked up to the temple door.

"Can you open it?"

"Give me a second, would ya?"

"Okay, I would much rather be inside than out here."

Jennifer mouthed the words and felt the engravings. She ran her finger along the impressions.

"Darnit! I wish they'd shut up, I can't even think."

"Who?"

"All the stinking animals."

"Oh. I know. It's like a low roar. Guess they're having a lot of fun."

"Ya think?" Jennifer said with a giggle.

"More fun than us, I'm sure."

Jennifer read the last line of text and stepped back to look at the huge stone doorway.

"I really hope this works, it says only a guardian can open the door."

"Wait, you never said that before."

"Give me a break, it's thousand-year-old ancient text. And I believe I told you that this afternoon. Okay, here goes."

Jennifer reached up and pressed on a symbol to the left, but nothing happened.

"Umm."

She put her hand on her chin and thought for a second. She looked down at the text again.

"Maybe…"

She reached up again.

"You have no idea what you're doing, do you?"

"Shhh."

"Stop shushing me. You're always shushing me. Who made you queen anyway?"

"The people at the hotel," Jennifer said with a giggle.

"Yeah, very funny."

Jennifer moved the torch down and looked at Allie's face. They both started to laugh. Jennifer walked to the side of the path and picked up a long, narrow stone.

"Allie, hold my torch for a second."

The moon was shining brightly so she could see the symbol clearly enough. She stood on her tippy toes, reached over her head and tapped the stone against a symbol a few times. It started to move inward a little. She pressed it with her fingers again, but nothing happened. She stretched up against the wall and tapped it harder with the stone. It really started moving inward until they both heard a metallic click. They looked at each other. Jennifer smiled at Allie. Then, all of a sudden, the symbol clicked out again, even with the rest of the text.

"Shesh."

Jennifer huffed and reached up again with her fingers and fully pressed in the symbol. They heard a loud click and stepped back from the door. Nothing happened.

"Okay, now what?" Allie asked.

"Wait for it."

A crash of thunder struck the ground nearby. They both screamed and ducked down low to the ground. The sky darkened with swirly clouds overhead. The jungle was suddenly silent. Not a sound other than the two girls panting and trying to catch their breath. In the darkness they could see four small, glowing white images appear on the face of the stone. Jennifer walked up and pressed on each one in a specific order. Allie looked around them in the darkness. A cold shiver ran up her back. Everything was so quiet, dark, and eerie.

Each of the images Jennifer pressed strongly with the palm of her hand depressed about two inches and each time a green glow appeared above a pictograph on the front wall of the temple brighter than their torches. Two on the left and two on the right. A loud crash came from inside the temple. It was so loud it could be heard for miles in the silent jungle. The ground shook under their feet.

Allie and Jennifer hurriedly stepped back several feet. Jennifer took her torch back and they watched as the huge stone door slowly lifted up into the temple wall, an inch at a time. Stagnant air and dust poured out from under the door like a gusty dark cloud of air escaping. The cloud rose up in the shape of a woman in front of them. The girls grabbed each other, ready to run, but then it dissolved into the air.

Jennifer fanned her face with her hand with her nose and bottom lip crinkled up.

"P-U."

Still, the entire jungle was silent. The one-foot-thick solid stone door had finally risen fully up into the temple leaving an open invitation for the girls to enter.

They both curiously but cautiously walked up to the threshold. Jennifer extended her arm to allow her torch in and peeked inside. It was very dark except for a large, circular object in the floor that slightly glowed and seemed as if it were moving or floating about.

Jennifer stepped inside and looked around.

"Jen, what do you see?"

"Come look."

Allie walked inside. The room was amazing. It was about forty feet wide and fifty feet long. The walls were completely covered with pictographs and full, life-size, stone extrusions of warriors and kings dressed in battle armor. The strange unknown writings were written in various places around the room. Always the same pattern.

In the center of the room was a dim, shimmering circle surrounded by green stones. The inside of the circle looked like a pool of darkness with choppy waves that floated around under what looked like a thin layer of luminescent film that dimly glowed. Jennifer found a place for their torches in the wall. She slid the handles into the holes. Everything they said and every move they made echoed off the walls.

There was a faint whisper. "Over here." Jennifer's snake lurched up and tasted the air.

"What?" asked Jennifer.

"What?"

"You said, 'Over here.'"

"No, I didn't."

"Guess I'm hearing things."

Jennifer looked around the room but saw nothing. Then she heard it again but louder.

"Over here."

"Okay, I heard it that time."

Allie took down her torch and moved it around, but there was still nothing. She felt the hair stand up on the back of her neck. Jennifer could feel her skin prickle, her arms covered in goose bumps.

They stood close to each other.

"Maybe we should go back to the hotel now," Allie suggested. "It will be getting light soon."

Jennifer walked over to the glowing pool and kneeled down to look inside. She could see something in the black stuff.

"Allie, look, there's something moving in there."

Allie walked over and kneeled down next to Jennifer and they both stared into the black pool. Two glowing, green, vertical slits seemed to float about in the blackness. They drew closer and closer and then a face appeared. The girls jumped back and screamed.

"What the hell is that?" Allie screamed.

Jennifer creeped closer, peering over the edge into the blackness. It was the face of a black panther with glowing green eyes. She kneeled back down to where her face was only inches from the surface. It was like staring at a reflection out of the darkness. Allie pulled at Jennifer's shirt.

"Come on, Jen, this is getting too creepy."

"I don't know, I mean what is this? I don't think it's really there."

"What is it then? What's all the blackness?"

CHAPTER 28

Jennifer kneeled and stared at the panther face in the darkness. It stopped moving about and stared back at her only inches beyond the barrier. She felt it pulling at her and reached out her hand, but Allie grabbed her arm.

"What are you doing? Don't touch that stuff."

"Geeze girl, relax. Seriously."

"Jennifer, please, I beg you. Let's go back now."

"Shesh, fine!"

Jennifer went to get up and placed her hand on one of the green stones surrounding the black pool. When she did, all of the surrounding stones shone brightly with a beautiful, greenish-amber light. It lit up the entire temple and shined outside the doorway into the jungle.

The thin, luminescent film slowly dissolved away and the panther sprung up from the well and leaped with a loud roar at Allie and Jennifer with its long claws extended. Allie screamed hysterically. Jennifer put her hand out in front of her to block the blow. With the panther only inches from her face, a surge of energy blasted out with a brilliant flash striking the animal, throwing it across the room and up against the far wall. It let out a horrifying painful screech with its fur smoking.

It looked at Jennifer for a moment with those green glowing eyes then ran from the chamber, out into the twilight of the jungle.

Jennifer lay back on the ground, held up by her elbows, planted into the dusty floor. She let her head lean back and started laughing, exhilarated by what just happened, and her heart beat dramatically.

"Are you okay?"

Ally replied in a whiny, broken, voice, "No, I'm not okay. This isn't okay, nothing about this is okay."

She cried and wiped her eyes.

"Aww." Jennifer reached out to hug her. Allie squirmed back against the stone wall.

"Don't even touch me. Who the hell are you? What the hell are you?"

"Allie, come on."

"No, not this time. Just stay away from me."

Allie got up and wiped her eyes and nose on her sleeve. She was covered in dry dust such that it looked like mud under her nose and across her chin and lips.

"I'm going home."

"Allie, wait!"

Allie ran quickly out the doorway and headed down the path. The sun was about to come up and the sky was light gray.

"Allie, I'll see you back at the hotel."

Allie turned with her crinkled nose, wrinkled forehead, and tightened lips. "I won't be there. I'm going home."

"Allie! Stop! Allie. It's gonna be okay."

Allie walked down the path, stopping for nothing, into the jungle by herself. Jennifer hurried to try to find a way to seal the temple again, but she couldn't figure it out so she said, "Ah, forget it," and ran down the path to try to catch up with Allie. She ran all the way back while the sun slowly lit up the clearing sky. The clouds were orange and red on the horizon. A few patches of fog floated across the trail.

Jennifer made it to the hotel but never ran into Allie. She got scared and ran up to her room but no Allie. Her heart sank, she teared up and walked toward the door when she noticed Allie's things were gone. She took a deep breath and a sigh of relief as she ran downstairs to the lobby by way of the grand staircase.

"I said you were a freak," Vicky said while standing by the front staircase. "Even your best friend thinks you're a freak."

Jennifer looked around for Allie but she wasn't there.

"That's right, she left," Vicky said nastily.

"Vicky, stop—now," Sean said.

"No, I won't. She's a dangerous freak, walking around with that snake around her neck. Thinks she's some kind of jungle queen or something."

Some of the other students laughed at her and took Vicky's side. Jennifer ran up to her room feeling empty inside. She cried and trembled, feeling all alone now. It felt like she had two big holes in her heart, one for Sean and one for Allie.

What have I done? What's wrong with me?

She lay crying on her bed. She kissed her snake while looking up at the fancy hotel ceiling, her pouty lips protruding and chin quivering. She could still hear Allie's screaming in her head when the panther came up out of the well, but she felt so powerful when she slammed the big cat against the wall. Her heart was beating so fast and it actually felt exhilarating. She thought about the ancient text on the walls of the temple but couldn't understand its meaning.

There was a knock at the door. It was the professor asking why she and Allie were up so early and out in the jungle.

Jennifer thought, *Good, she didn't tell him.*

"We were, umm, looking for a good place to let my snake go."

"What happened to Allie that she was so upset?"

"Umm, there was a panther in the jungle."

"That's not possible, there are no panthers in this part of the jungle, only jaguars."

"Are there solid black jaguars?"

"No."

"Well then, what was it?"

The professor thought for a second and said something that he rarely ever said. "I don't know."

☯

The students gathered by the trail for their next excursion into the jungle, a two-day hike to their next dig site. They would have to make camp at the halfway point and had a lot of ground to cover.

Vicky was being a naggy bitch the entire hike. She would look back at Jennifer and then whisper something to Sean and both laugh at her. The more they made fun of her the more she could feel the ember heat up inside her. She felt that she had more control over it and tried to ignore them. She was fascinated by the jungle and loving every step bringing up the rear. She daydreamed about running away and living in the jungle by herself with only her snake and maybe a few frog buddies. She just didn't fit in well with people. Most seemed to constantly annoy her, which was odd for someone who loved to talk so much.

While they were walking with Vicky constantly turning to gawk at her, Jennifer had a pleasant thought. *Maybe the black panther could come back and eat Vicky! My, wouldn't that be wonderful?*

They reached the halfway point and set up camp. Everyone paired up and erected their two-person tents. Jennifer was the odd girl out and tried to set up her tent by herself, but she really needed someone to hold the pole for her so she could bang in the tent stakes. She walked up and timidly whispered to Sean, "Can you help me a second?"

Vicky gave her the nastiest look ever. Sean looked at Vicky the turned to Jennifer.

"Sorry, that's probably not a good idea right now."

Jennifer walked away and tried to hide her tears. She didn't want Vicky to see her crying. She left her tent lying on the ground and sat on a fallen tree just outside camp. She unwound her snake from her neck feeling very hot and sweaty. She sat him down on the log, but he slithered back up her arm, up to her shoulders. That made her smile.

At least somebody loves me.

She played with him, holding him in front of her to admire his beautiful emerald-green skin with white lines, how his body flexed in and out with each breath. He had the prettiest green and red eyes.

"Jennifer! Would you like to join the rest of the group?" the professor asked with a sarcastic attitude.

"Oh, shut up," she said under her breath.

She walked up next to the campfire and ate while staring into the flames. The sun was low on the canopy casting long shadows of the trees and hanging vines.

Vicky immediately started in on her. The other students started laughing at Jennifer's expense.

"There she is, queen of the jungle. Can't even put up a tent. Let's all bow down before her."

Jennifer had had about enough of it.

"Vicky, why don't you grow up? You're acting like a freaking child."

"Why don't you just kill yourself? Nobody likes you, you sick freak."

"Shut the hell up, bitch."

"Why don't you come and make me?"

Sean could see that look on Jennifer's face. That same look he feared. The wind started picking up. Jennifer stood up and walked at Vicky. Vicky jumped up fast and ran a few steps away in fear. She totally didn't expect petite Jennifer to come after her.

Vicky yelled, "Get away from me with your nasty snake. You're so gross. Always kissing that nasty thing."

Sean got up. "Vicky, stop now."

"She's a nasty witch and someone needs to teach her a lesson. Just go sit your nasty ass back down, jungle freak."

Jennifer's eyes turned flame-red with a black reptile looking iris. She could feel the ember inside her burning out of control. The other students freaked out when they saw her eyes, they were glowing red. They got up and moved away from her. The wind picked up stronger and black clouds darkened the sky, spinning around overhead. Lightning struck the ground a few hundred yards away. The students scrambled around in confusion with the sudden storm. Afraid she would hurt someone, Jennifer ran off into the dense jungle.

CHAPTER 29

Jennifer couldn't wait to get away from them. She stomped heavily through the jungle, her insides turning. She mumbled under her breath how much she hated Vicky, how she was sick of being lonely, why she should even go on, she had no one. Utterly alone. Utterly alone. She felt like hurting herself to stop the pain. She walked without care, without purpose, giving no assiduity to her whereabouts.

The wind blew with vigor against the swaying trees. She could feel the breath of the jungle on her face and through her hair. She slogged deeper and deeper into the jungle, devoid of concern.

THUD!

CRASH!

Trees were cracking, popping, and snapping off at the base, crashing to the ground, breaking off branches and limbs as they fell. Vines swung around while the monkeys fled to safety, leaves falling from the trees and blowing in the wind.

Jennifer stopped and looked around. A cold shiver ran down her spine. She had no idea how to get back and an eerie feeling came over her, like she was being watched, eyes in the jungle following her. She looked up at the sky; dark black clouds spun around her.

There was a tall patch of grass and reeds, sharp to the touch, cutting at her ankles and hands. She looked down to make sure there were no snakes, she didn't want to step on any of her little babies. In an instant a huge bolt of lightning struck the ground about fifty yards away. It cracked and sliced through the sky like a fighter jet going supersonic, crashing into the ground. Jennifer screamed and squatted to her knees. She breathed heavily such that her heart beat right out of her chest. The ember inside her burned intently, she couldn't catch her breath. Lightning creeped across the ground in all directions like little electrical spiders. Jennifer stood up and stepped backwards, but the lightning was attracted to her. It arced quickly at her feet and her body absorbed it, taking it all in. She felt like she was on fire and ran toward a pond to find a way to cool off. The tall grass cut at her ankles and arms.

She looked at the lily pads on the pond. They seemed familiar. She knelt down and looked. There he was, Jacob, sitting on a lily pad croaking and watching her. She knew what would happen next so she ripped off her shoes and socks.

She ran and slid down into the murky water, scooped up Jacob into her hands and placed him on the bank. She tried to climb out but the bank was muddy and slippery. She tried to get out, but it was of no use. The rain started pouring down on her face. She turned to see the ripples in the water coming at her fast. The fully grown crocodile surfaced and opened it huge jaws. It came at her quickly, so close she could see its teeth and right down its throat. Her snake coiled back, ready to strike. She reached out her hand and squinted her eyes and focused. An immense bust of energy blast out of her hand as lightning. All her anger, bitterness, hopelessness, all the built-up energy expelled all at once. It seared the crocodile's flesh down to the tail that blew off and flew twenty yards through the air, landing hard into the pond with a big splash. The dead crocodile floated upside down and its momentum caused it to drift into Jennifer.

She pushed the smoking crocodile away from her. She felt so week and her body stressed. Her chest and lower back hurt from being so tense. She leaned back and was finally able to calm herself. The wind slowed and the rain fell steadily. It was dark, cloudy and cold; the sun was at rest beyond the canopy. Jacob croaked while sitting on the bank of the pond. Jennifer dug in the mud and made hand and foot holds so she could climb out. She picked up Jacob and petted his head. Exhausted and no more desire to dwell. Her snake slithered around to her side and looked at Jennifer then the frog.

"Don't you even think about it!"

She giggled. She felt relaxed for the first time that day.

"Poor baby. That mean ol' gator wanted to eat you for dinner. Or maybe he wanted to eat me, I don't know."

She petted the frog's head and puckered her lips, kissing him on the nostrils. A brilliant flash of light—for a brief second an image of a man standing before her—then total darkness. Jennifer felt like she was floating in a cloud, everything still and quiet. Utter darkness. She tried to open her eyes but there was only darkness.

The professor was all a jitter, not understanding what happened or if Jennifer would survive through the night, especially with the powerful storm snapping off trees and pouring rain blowing sideways. He wanted to go after her but didn't want to endanger himself or the other students, after all, the deadly jaguar normally hunts at night. Sean huddled with the professor trying to keep the campfire going in the rain, building a coverlet over the fire pit and adding small twigs that would catch quickly. They hoped that Jennifer would see the light and find her way back. The professor tried to radio the hotel or anyone else who might hear his transmission, but they must all have been asleep.

"I'll have to wait and try again in the morning."

The storm weakened and the wind died down. Sean sat on a big stone, soaking wet, breaking sticks to put on the fire.

"I think I'm going to go looking for her."

"I know how you feel, Sean. I thought about it myself, but it's way too dangerous at night. Jaguars hunt at night and the jungle's full of them."

Vicky walked over wearing leopard skin pattern pajamas with her long, wavy, blonde hair blowing in the breeze. Her top had a few buttons loose revealing a fair amount of cleavage by firefight. She came up to Sean and put her arms around his neck, leaning into him and said, "Come to bed, baby," and gave him a wink.

"No, I have to keep the fire going so she can find her way back."

"Why do you care?"

"Vicky, she could be dead for all we know."

"Who cares?"

The professor gave her a disgusted look. Sean pushed her away. "I can't believe you just said that."

"She's a freak, you saw her eyes."

"You know, before you came along she was the sweetest skinny little thing and she was never mean to me."

"You said she teased you all the time."

"Okay, she was just being playful and witty. Not totally mean. She was never mean to anybody and now she may be dead."

Vicky let out a growling huff.

"Just get away from me."

"What are you saying?"

"I'm saying we're done, Vicky."

"Sean, baby, you don't mean that."

She tried to give him a hug, but he pushed her away again.

"Just get away from me."

Vicky teared up and she felt a knot in her throat. She couldn't swallow. She welled up inside. Her lips turned downward and her lower lip protruded. She took short little breaths trying not to cry.

"Sean," she said in a broken voice, "please, you're all I have here. I had to leave my friends and my life to come here. There's nothing here for me without you."

"Then maybe you shouldn't be so cruel to people."

"I'm sorry."

She slowly put her arm around him and pressed herself nigh unto him.

"Go to bed, Vicky."

"Are you coming?"

"I'm waiting here in case she makes it back."

Vicky turned away and let out an aggravated breath.

"Fine!"

She stomped off to their wet tent. Sean spoke under his breath. "Yeah, stomp off, you heartless bitch."

He walked to the edge of the campsite and called out, "Jennifer!" several times.

CHAPTER 30

Jennifer woke after some time, how long she knew not. Her mind was groggy. Then a faint light. She tried to open her eyes but it was hard, like trying to awaken from a dream. Voices, so many quiet voices. What were they whispering? It wasn't English. She could only make out a few words.

"She's the one," a gentle voice said with exhilaration.

Jennifer slowly opened her eyes and tried to focus while lying on a bed of hay. A man's face stared down at her. She smiled at him, he was beautiful. He had the brownest eyes she had ever seen. He had dark hair, a perfect tan complexion, and his chin was darkened by stubbly facial hair. The hair on his head was a little long but rustic looking, kind of jagged cut. He wore some kind of ancient looking battle costume with a sword at his waist and a lot of leather. His muscular arms and shoulders were exposed except for leather bracers buckled on his forearms and fancy leather pauldrons on top of his shoulders.

He was smiling at her like he was mesmerized by her angel-blue eyes. Only once before had he ever seen a woman with such eyes. But she was an albino woman while Jennifer had light brown hair.

Jennifer's heart started to pummel. He was so cute.

"Are you okay?" he asked softly in perfect English.

Jennifer's head hurt and her mind raced, she tried to clear her throat to speak.

"Ahem… I think so." She rubbed her forehead with her hand. "What happened?"

"You passed out."

"Where am I?"

"I brought you into the realm."

Jennifer looked around curiously at the huge cavern. She was lying in a bed of hay surrounded by lashed logs, her head on an animal skin that felt soft and warm. There were torches and fire boxes illuminating the walls with flickering lights and dancing shadows scattered against jagged stone. Several men sat and kneeled around her, watching her intently. She could hear many distant voices talking in a strange language and sounds of tools chipping and chopping. There was white light coming from behind her, somewhere, that shined brightly and differed from the yellow light of the torches.

"Umm, what's a realm?"

"This is the realm." He motioned around with his arms.

"It looks like a big cave to me."

"It's a lot more than that, it's hidden to the world."

"Who are you?" Jennifer asked as she stretched out her arms and tried to sit up.

"I'm Necalli."

She looked up at him and smiled. "I'm Jennifer."

She offered to shake Necalli's hand, but he thought she wanted help getting up so he gently grabbed her hand. As soon as he touched her he could feel a great tingle across his whole body, it ran down his spine all the way to his toes and make a tickle in his nose. Jennifer felt it too. It was so strong her whole body tingled and tickled. She took in a deep breath all at once. Necalli was stunned for a moment, he wasn't expecting that. He pulled her to her feet, but she was still groggy and started to fall backward. Necalli caught her in his muscular arm around her back and neck. They stood only inches apart. Necalli felt the electrical current running through his arm. She felt warm, soft, and tingly to the touch. He took a deep breath of her perfume. Never before had he smelled something so alluring.

They were both breathing very heavily while looking into one another's eyes. Neither wanted to let go. Jennifer felt safe and was completely content in his strangely strong arms. She sparkled. Necalli blushed a little and made a silly twitch with his nose. Jennifer giggled but then her smile turned into concern and her eyes glistened over. She felt around her neck.

"Jennifer, what's wrong?" Necalli asked softly, still holding her around her waist.

"My snake, he's gone," she said in a trembling voice.

"Aww, hatsuts, he's not gone."

"Then where is he?"

"Well … umm … I mean… He's here."

"Where?"

Jennifer backed up and Necalli let her go.

"Relax, Jennifer, he's here and safe. His name's Akna."

"How do you know my snake?"

"I've known him for many years."

Jennifer tilted her head and looked at him funny.

"It's all right hatsuts, I'll take you to him."

Jennifer looked around and noticed all the men watching her. She felt a cold shiver run up her back and moved closer to Necalli. She whispered, "Why are all these guys staring at me?"

"Because they believe you can free us from the realm."

Necalli spoke in a foreign voice. All but one man got up and left the area.

"How's that, hatsuts?"

"Better," Jennifer said with a smile. "Necalli, I still don't understand where we are."

"Come, walk with me, let me show you."

Necalli held out his hand and held his breath for a second hoping Jennifer would take it in hers. She wrapped her fingers around his and his arm twitched with a tingle. He let out his breath and blushed a little. He looked at her and she at him. Her bright blue eyes fascinated him. Jennifer felt warm and content holding his hand. Her fingers felt tickly. Necalli stared at her as they stepped. He was stimulated by everything about her. Not what he was expecting at all. He wanted to show her everything within the realm. He pretty much forgot about the main factor that led him to bring her into the realm in the first place. She was so much more than a way out for his people, so much more, and he knew it at first touch.

They walked downward on a wide path through the cavern. Jennifer noticed the light changed and there were no more torches. It was a greenish-orange glow that lit the walls. It took a few minutes for her eyes to adjust. They reached another large cavern opening with long stalactites hanging down like huge icicles and stone huts built along the base. Bright, glowing mushrooms and a few campfires provided enough light to see once one's eyes adjusted. There were women watching after young children running and playing. There were so many stone homes running all the way up the side of the cavern walls with wooden walkways. There were looms with colorful cloth patterns woven to make clothes, rugs and blankets. Jennifer thought she was in a dream. *How can this be here, who are these people?* Several of the younger children ran up to her. They wanted to touch her and feel the tingling.

"Aww, you're so cute," she said to a young girl who gave her a strange glowing flower. Jennifer picked her up and held her. The girl laughed as she tickled everywhere they made contact.

"Necalli, how many people live here?"

"Several thousand here and many more in other areas of the realm."

Jennifer scrunched her eyebrows. "Really? How big is this realm?" she asked.

Just then her eyes widened and her head and neck went back with her chin tilted slightly down. Her head turned slowly as she watched a huge silvery-green beetle carrying a stack of lumber on its back. It was taller than a man and its hardened shell was glossy and captured the light. Its legs were long and spindly with huge hooks running downward along the length. It had two interconnecting horn-like armored mandibles that reared up from the mouth to above the head. It walked gracefully, slightly wobbling from side to side with each step.

"Ugh. Necalli, what is that?" she asked as she backed up slowly.

"It's okay. He's just a worker beetle."

"Umm, well, he's freakishly huge! What's up with that?"

"Would you like to touch him?"

"Ugh. Maybe later."

Necalli laughed. "He's harmless."

"You know beetles are not normally bigger than people, right?"

"Not normally, no."

"What is this place?"

"That's hard to explain."

"Where did you come from?"

Necalli took her to a bench and they sat. Jennifer watched as the beetle walked off down a passageway.

"What do you know of the history of Tikal and the Tenochcan kingdom?"

"You mean like the ancient Mayans? I study archaeology in college. That's why I'm here actually. We were on the way to see the great Temple of Naranjo."

"So the ones you call Mayans were the people of Tikal?"

"Yes, this whole area, they were very advanced for their time. Until the last time of the kingdom under the rule of Ah-Cacaw, the great jaguar king."

"Ah-Cacaw was my father."

"You mean like father of your race?"

"No, my actual father."

Jennifer giggled for a second but then saw how serious he was. She looked at the cavern, his clothes, his people, the sword he clasped at the hilt with his left hand. She had that eerie feeling again and felt a cold shiver shake her body and run up her spine that ended in the feeling of a thousand little needles in her back. She looked at Necalli with squinted eyes and wrinkled forehead.

"That's not possible, you would have to be like a thousand years old or something."

"What does your history say happened to my people?"

"They say you died off, everyone at the same time. Your history just stopped. Some say you stripped away the trees and died because of deforestation."

"Would you like to know what really happened?"

"Yes, please, because right now my only explanation is that I'm dreaming and you aren't real. Please tell me you're real, and if not, please don't wake me up."

Necalli snickered. "Yes, I'm real."

He took her hand and placed it on his heart. His whole chest tingled.

"Feel my heartbeat."

Jennifer blushed and smiled at him. He smiled back and kept her hand there whilst he talked.

"We have been trapped within the realm for almost a thousand years. Anyone who tries to leave the realm is transfigured into fog or a snake or something else that I'm not going to mention."

"Um, what?" Jennifer tilted her head and squinted her eyebrows tightly together. "I'm not following you."

"Jennifer, about a thousand years ago, my people ... we fought against a powerful fiend named Malinche. We won the battle, but she used ancient artifice to try to destroy us with eleamus, but it rebounded off my Ispus and we were trapped here."

"Eleamus? Ispus?" she questioned.

"Malinche used the power of the Tezcatlipoca to conjure eleamus, I don't know how to describe it to you, but it's like a thick cloud of green energy that can destroy, move or melt people or things. An Ispus can be used to absorb the power of the Tezcatlipoca or neutralize it, but she was too powerful and somehow we were sent here to the realm where we have been trapped for a thousand years until now."

"Until now?"

"Yes, you have the power to free us."

"I do?"

Necalli smiled. "Yes, you do."

"But how?"

"Just like you freed me before you passed out."

"When did I free you?"

"Outside, just after you saved me from the crocodile."

"You mean—"

"Yes, I was the one you called Jacob."

"This isn't happening."

"It happened. When you held me and kissed me, I was released, but then you fainted and I had to bring you into the realm and make sure you were still alive. It's real. Just ask Akna here." He pointed to the short man who was following them.

"Wait, you said Akna was my snake."

"He is your snake."

"But I kissed my snake many times and he was always a snake."

"It's different with him. He likes being a snake. He's just a little man, normal, common, but he's a beautiful snake. He was Beesha's snake. She let him wrap around her neck just as you did."

"Beesha?"

"She was a moormit. She was my father's moormit in battle for many years, she was very powerful."

"I've never heard of a moormit before."

"They are different, especially their ears. Strange that you have never heard of them. They come from the Otherworld."

"The Otherworld?"

"Jennifer, my father was an amazing king. Our people loved him and followed him. He won many battles and united all our people but—"

"But what?"

"My father." Necalli looked down at the ground and he frowned. "My father." He took in a deep breath. Jennifer put her arm around him.

"It's okay, Necalli, you don't have to tell me."

"I just miss him. It's been so many years, trapped in this realm, unable to leave. I don't know what happened to my father or Moctezuma."

"Wait, Moctezuma was an Aztec king. How could you know him?"

"An Aztec king?"

"Yes."

"So he lived?"

"Necalli, he died fighting against the Spanish a few hundred years ago."

"So he made king. Amazing! But what of my father?"

"There's no mention of him after you … um … were sent here, I guess."

"So Moctezuma never mentioned anything about Malinche?"

"Not in any of my studies."

"I hope she died, but then… My father was standing right next to her when it happened."

"Necalli, how could you know Moctezuma and how can you be a thousand years old?"

"Many years ago, my father and Beesha had a plan to destroy Malinche and the many priests that followed her. They buried huge Ispus stones around a small spring to conceal them and called them to a meeting to try to quench their power. They were defeated, but their power caused something amazing to happen to the spring when the Ispus stones absorbed their energy. Unfortunately, Malinche escaped the priest's fate. Now anyone who drinks of the spring lives for a very long time."

"Wait! You mean like the fountain of youth—it's real?"

"It's here, Jennifer. In the realm."

"This is blowing my mind right now. I think I'm ready to wake up."

Necalli pinched her side.

"Hey!"

"See, you're not sleeping."

"Okay, so then now what?"

"Would you like to see the well, the forbidden spring?"

"Yes, I would actually."

CHAPTER 31

Necalli took her by the hand and they started to make their way to the spring. They climbed a set of stone steps carved into the cavern walls then walked down a long, narrow passageway. When they reached a large opening with a very high ceiling, they could hear screaming and shouting. A large, thorny, skinny leg stepped out into the clearing from a pathway around the corner.

"Wait here, Jennifer."

Necalli drew his sword and ran to help the men. Then it stepped into the large room. The spider was twice the height of the men. It trapped one man in a web and drove spikes from its leg into his back. He let out an excruciating scream. Necalli swung his sword and severed one of the legs in two. The men poked at the spider with long pikes as it lunged at them. It made a funny noise, almost like a high-pitched squeal with a chattering after. They managed to slice off pieces of the spider's legs leaving it flopping around on the stone floor. Necalli stabbed it repeatedly until it finally fell and rolled upside down. One of the men became lodged in between the dead spider and the cave wall. He cut at it with his knife like a handle trying to pull himself free, but he punctured an egg sack on the spider's back. About fifty dog-sized spiders scurried out in all directions. The men fought them, stabbing at them with swords, spears and pikes.

Two ran at Jennifer. She screamed and backed up with her heart pounding heavily. Akna ran in front of her but they both climbed right on him. Jennifer bit her lip hard and she reached out with her palm; a plasma bolt flashed outward killing one of the spiders, throwing it across the cave. Again she reached out and zapped the second spider dead. This time it went up in a puff of smoke. Akna got up and picked off pieces of dead spider stuck to his clothes.

One of the spiders lowered from the cavern ceiling by a web and landed on a man, it bit into the back of his neck. The man screamed and fell to the ground in pain. The spider chewed into his flesh and clean through his neck. His severed head rolled down the cavern floor passing under a log fence then fell deep into the abyss below.

Jennifer screamed and backed up further as she watched his head roll. She could see a spider hanging just above Necalli's head. She ran and threw her hands into the air releasing green eleamus, frying the spider to a crisp. It fell from the ceiling and bounced off Necalli's head. He turned and looked at Jennifer. She held up her arms and shrugged her shoulders as if to say, "I don't know." Necalli winked at her.

After all the spiders were destroyed the wounded men were carried off along with the dead. Necalli hugged Jennifer tightly. He could feel her shaking nervously.

"Are you okay?"

"I think so. That was so scary. Why is everything so big here?"

"They're not actually that big as much as we're very small."

A shiver ran across Jennifer's body.

"What do you mean?"

"When we're in the realm, we become very small."

"Umm, I think that's like 'need to know' information that would have been helpful."

"Sorry, it was hard enough to try to convince you we turn into frogs when we cross the barrier of the realm."

"And snakes, don't forget snakes. By the way, I really hate spiders!"

"You did really good though. You killed the one that fell on my head."

"I didn't want you to get bitten."

Necalli smiled and took her hand. "Shall we go see the forbidden spring now?"

Jennifer looked at him with a bubbly smile while trying to get the image of a severed head rolling past out of her mind. Necalli noticed her teeth were whiter than any he had ever seen. They stepped over pieces of spider legs with spiky, thorn-like hair. Akna was never far behind.

When they reached the opening to the spring and surrounding pool of water, Jennifer noticed chiseled pictographs and writing in the stone around the curved entrance. She ran the fingers of her free hand around the edges.

"Wow, it's so smooth and perfect. How do you do this?"

"Well, it's not too hard when you have thousand-year-old craftsmen with extensive knowledge."

"Oh yeah, right, I forgot you're an older man." Jennifer snickered a little bit under her breath. "But you look great, I would say about twenty-one or so."

"Wait until you try the spring water. You'll feel like you've never felt before."

She looked down at his hand in hers and said, "I feel fine already." She looked up and couldn't stop smiling, even if she wanted to, spiders or no spiders.

Necalli motioned Akna to stay at the mouth of the chamber. He frowned and went to sit down by the stone wall. After they walked in he kneeled down low and peeked around the opening to keep a protective eye on Jennifer. He missed being coiled around her soft, skinny neck. He was first turned into a snake by Beesha for disobeying the Ahau but liked it so much he asked to stay in the form to serve and protect her.

Now his desire was to serve Jennifer.

There was dim light in the chamber provided by four oil vessels burning in the corners that gave off a slight illumination. The flames flickered and danced with the draft from down below. They sat down on stones that mapped the circumference of the pool. Necalli dipped his hand in the water and swished it around while looking at Jennifer with a smile. She watched him playing with the water and smiled back.

"What's it feel like? It doesn't hurt, does it?"

"No, not at all. Quite the opposite actually."

"How often do you drink it?"

"Just once, that's all it takes."

Jennifer reached down to feel the cool, crystal clear water, but the moment her fingers touched it the water glowed brightly and little specs of light rose up from all over the pool and floated in the air. It glowed with an amber light that brightly lit the whole room and outside into the passageway.

"This is new. I've never seen it do this before," Necalli said.

Jennifer waved her hand around in the water and colorful rainbow looking streaks of light fanned out and followed her motions, dissipating off as she moved.

"That's amazing."

"Should I drink it?"

"Yes."

"But you know my father said to me, before leaving for this trip, not to drink the water in South America."

"Ha, ha, why not?"

Necalli dipped a wooden ladle in and took a drink.

"See, it's harmless."

Jennifer picked up the ladle and held it to her lips. She looked over the top of it at Necalli as she took a sip. The water tingled her mouth and tongue so strangely. She swallowed and could feel it running down her throat and into her body. Her back arched and her head tilted back and she let out a squeal. Her whole body tensed up then released all at once. Her head thrust forward and she rolled sideways off the stones. Necalli caught her and held her in his lap. Her eyes got really big and glowed bright blue. Her face lit up and shone with a brilliant amber glow. Necalli stared with his eyes and mouth wide open.

"What?"

It appeared almost as if light was flowing upward from her palms, illuminating dust from the realm as it floated. Light shone from her mouth and her fingernails glowed red. She held her head and whined, panting heavily and jerking her body. She wiggled around and squirmed in Necalli's arms until the sensation finally subsided. She put her hand to her head and pulled her long hair back, taking a very deep breath, and started laughing.

"Damn, that was amazing. Whew!"

"How do you feel?"

"Are you kidding? I feel wonderful. I feel like I could float."

"No one's ever reacted like that before."

"Wow, they're missing out. Give me some more."

"I think once is enough."

Jennifer pulled herself upright in Necalli's lap and looked into his eyes. He looked deeply at her for a few moments. They both slowly leaned in closer until their lips met. The spring glowed more brilliantly with little specs of light popping up, rising above the pool then bursting in glittery sparks all around them. Necalli's heart was in his throat. He almost couldn't breathe. They kissed passionately, forgetting about everything else. Jennifer felt like her body was on fire, but she couldn't stop. Necalli's whole body trembled from the electrical stimulation of Jennifer's body. Everything tingled and they didn't want to stop. The ground shook and they were startled and looked around.

"Did I do that?" Jennifer asked.

"I think you made the ground shake."

"No, I think that was you kissing me."

They started kissing again.

CHAPTER 32

Sean was in a deep sleep with Vicky lying on his chest. He jumped when the professor smacked on the side of the tent.

"Sean, Vicky, time to get up."

Everyone climbed out of their tents and started to pack up. The professor was frantic and hurrying everyone so they could search for Jennifer. He dreaded thinking about having to contact her parents to tell them she was lost to the jungle.

Sean stood up and leaned back to stretch in the cool morning breeze. He looked up at the lower canopy. It was very still and the jungle was surprisingly quiet.

"Professor, you hear that?" he whispered.

"Yes, the jungle is oddly quiet."

"It feels strange."

"I agree."

"Maybe it's because of the storm last night."

"That's what's so odd. Normally more animals are out and about after a storm. I haven't seen a single monkey. Yesterday there were howling from the treetops, today they're gone."

Vicky took out her cell phone. Only about 2% battery left and no way to charge it.

"Shesh."

"What's wrong now?" Sean asked.

"Guess it doesn't matter anyway. I haven't had signal since the last flight into this jungle."

"There's no one here, why would they even have cell towers?"

"For all the people like us, exploring the jungle and stuff."

"I don't think there's anyone else even here."

"At least my head isn't aching from all the noise now."

There was a strange noise in the distance. A kind of howling they had never heard before. It sounded like a monkey screaming as if it was being eaten alive. Then followed another strange noise of distress.

"Professor, are you hearing this?"

The professor picked up the radio that was charging on a solar battery hopping there was enough charge to get out a strong signal. He tried to signal the hotel but no one was answering, still. He tried to connect a longer detachable antenna and tried again but still no response. All the students stood around, ready to depart, waiting on him. He went to put the radio into his belt radio holster when there was some crackling on the radio. Someone pushed the transmit button but didn't speak. It was only for a moment. The professor fiddled with the radio and tried to contact them again, but there was nothing, not even static.

One of the students asked, "Why can't we reach them?"

"I don't know, it sounded like someone was trying to transmit for a moment there, but then it stopped."

"Can we try anybody else, Professor?"

"No, there's no one else in range this far into the jungle. I'm afraid we're on our own."

"That's great. I hope nobody gets hurt or bitten," a student said.

"We will divide up into three groups to start searching, but I don't want anyone to wander out of shouting distance."

"What! Are you kidding me? Either we all stay together or I'm not going anywhere," Vicky said with zero empathy.

"Agreed," several other students added.

The professor thought about it for a second.

"You're right. I wasn't thinking. I want everyone safe."

He took a deep breath and let it out. There was another loud deadly howling coming from deep in the distant jungle. It was a suffering cry. The professor turned away from the students and held out his hands, they were shaking. Vicky tried to put her arm around Sean, but he pulled away from her.

"Sean, baby, please stop."

"You just don't get it, do you? You don't take any responsibility."

"For what? I didn't do anything," she said sternly.

"You just couldn't leave her alone."

"It's not my fault she's a freak and ran off into the jungle in the middle of the night."

The team started off to search for Jennifer in her last known direction. There were a lot of downed trees from the storm and some snakes, displaced from their dwelling, within view as they walked. They tried to find any signs of disturbed underbrush or tracks, but the storm ruined any chance of that. They fanned out in small groups of three within close sight of each other. They searched for hours calling Jennifer's name as they walked. The jungle was deathly silent. Then they heard another deadly howl, not too far away.

"I don't think we should be out here," one of the students said.

One of the girls screamed and her group ran quickly to the professor.

"What is it?" he asked.

"There was something running fast in the jungle—scared the crap out of us."

"Could you see what it was?"

"No, it was a dark object moving fast. I think it was upright like a person running, but it was so fast."

"Do you think it could have been Jennifer?"

"I really don't think so but maybe. We couldn't see who or what it was."

They all walked in that general direction together, calling for Jennifer. They searched around but couldn't find anything. They continued walking deeper into the jungle in a zigzag pattern. About an hour later, they came upon a clearing by a lake. The grass was very tall and cut at their hands and ankles.

"Over there! Look!" one of the male students called out. "There's something floating in the water."

They all ran to the bank and looked intently.

"Can anyone tell what that is?"

"We need to get a closer look."

"Who's stupid enough to go into the water with crocodiles, piranhas, and snakes?"

"Nobody's going into the water. Give me some rope," the professor said.

He used a machete to chop a fallen branch to use as a dual hook. He gave Sean the hook and rope.

"Try to throw this over it so we can pull it in."

Sean made several attempts to hook the object, but he kept missing to the left or the right or throwing too short. Finally, he was able to get the line over it.

"Pull it in gently," the professor said.

It was something heavy and took a bit of tension to get it moving. As the object floated closer they could tell it wasn't a human, it looked like a mangled crocodile. The professor dropped down his head in relief.

Several of the girls teared up, relieved it wasn't Jennifer but concerned she was dead alone in the jungle somewhere.

One of the students heard soft footsteps behind her. She turned around and arched her body, moving slowly back holding her hand out in front of her. She bumped into some of the other students.

"Shoo. Get," she said with her heart pounding, flicking her hand at it.

The students turned to look. A jaguar was standing right in front of them, panting heavily. There was another deadly howling screech in the distance. The jaguar perked up its ears turning its head toward the sound then took off, running in the opposite direction. They stood there in disbelief for a second then could hear something running toward them. It got louder and louder. The sound of stomping and scuffling. The pounding of many feet. A large number of white-tail deer, jumping high in the air as they entered the clearing around the lake, dashed past them. Many more were seen in the woods beyond the clearing. Dense patches of leaves fell from the trees all around them as large troops of howler monkeys fled along the treetops.

"What the hell is going on?" the professor exclaimed.

The radio squawked and a voice spoke in an unknown language for a few moments then he screamed... The radio went silent.

"Professor, I think we should get back to the hotel," Sean said, disheartened, in a desperate voice.

"Agreed."

A sound of distant thundering like stomping could be heard beyond the woodline. They all stopped and listened, waiting.

"Now what?"

The sound grew louder like a stampede thundering their way. Then, through the jungle, they could see something running fast. Very fast. Then many more but they were moving so fast in the distance it was hard to see them through the trees and scrub but they looked dark and appeared to be standing upright. There were so many of them the sounds of their rumbling carried through the jungle.

The group found themselves huddled together, sweating and breathing heavily. The smell of death and decay was in the air. They wrinkled up their noses and looked at each other, waiting for what would come next. One of the young ladies asked, "What could they be?"

"The only thing that comes to mind is the myth of the Mayan Balam," the Professor said.

"What's that?"

"Never mind that, let's get to the hotel. Drop anything we don't absolutely need and hurry it up."

CHAPTER 33

When they reached the hotel, it was in a shambles. Windows were broken and drapes were flapping in the breeze. The glass of the front door was shattered and scattered all over the floor. Several cars were parked near the front with their doors and trunks opened. One of the girls whimpered when they saw a well-dressed, nicely tanned woman with fancy jewelry lying on her back halfway out of a front seat lying back, motionless. She had teeth marks in her neck and her chest was covered with blood.

They all moved closely together toward the front door of the hotel.

"We shouldn't go in there," a young student whispered.

"We need a phone with a hard line to call for help," the professor said.

When they walked into the lobby, they could see bodies lying on the floor. Two of the girls became hysterical and completely freaked out.

"Shhh! You don't what to draw attention," several of the students said and tried to calm them. The professor found the valet keybox and took out several keys for the hotel's Land Rovers. Sean picked up the phone at the front desk and pressed the off-hook button several times, but there was no dial tone.

"Darnit! The phones are dead."

Everyone turned silent when a scraping sound came from the seating area around the corner. It was loud like someone scraping an iron bar across the marble floor. Sean pulled out the machete. The professor waved his arm for them to head for the front door. They hurriedly, but softly, moved together. They turned when hearing the scraping again. A jaguar was eating a man, dead on the main staircase. It ripped off some flesh and swallowed it down. Moments later, the flesh fell from its belly to the floor. It lifted its head and looked at them. Its bones were showing through on one side exposing its innards. Flesh hung off its body. It opened its mouth as if to roar but no sound came. It seemed to move in slow motion. It ignored them and went back to chewing on the dead man. They all ran out the door and squeezed into two vehicles. Their only concern at that moment was whether there was enough gas in the tanks to make it to the small airport.

Sean held Vicky close. She was shaking and very quiet with a blank face. They were all jumpy every time overhanging branches smacked against the windshield.

Not wanting anything to delay their departure they devised a plan to clean themselves up and present themselves as if everything was normal, but when they reached the small airport everyone was gone and the offices were torn up. There was a dead body hanging halfway out of an airplane.

"What are we going to do now?" the students asked quietly.

"I guess we find more gas and continue driving," the Professor said.

"That would take forever."

"I'm open for suggestions."

"I can fly," Geramie, one of the students, said. "I've been taking lessons."

"Do you have a pilot's license?"

"Almost."

"Are you absolutely sure you can fly one of these?"

"I think so. These planes are bigger than I am training on."

"What have you flown?"

"Single engine fixed wing. These are large two engine turboprops, but the principles of flight are all the same."

A distant roar and commotion echoed from within the jungle.

"I vote we risk it," Sean said rapidly.

There was no opposition. They snuck around the small airport until they could find a plane already fueled. They loosened its ground restraints and climbed aboard. Geramie positioned the large turboprop in the center at the edge of the runway. Once in position he moved the two throttle levers forward to full thrust. The plane picked up speed very fast, pushing them back into their seats, but it veered to the right edging close to the dirt on the side of the runway. They started hitting clumps of grass, bouncing them in their seats, just as Geramie pulled back hard on the yoke taking them to the sky.

The citizens and tourists of Merida, Mexico were enjoying shopping at an outdoor market. Two girls were looking though oranges when they noticed some wiggling around. Then a small mound of oranges seemed to form in the center. They were curiously looking on when a skeletal head popped up in front of them. They screamed and the skeletal creature screamed back. Out of instinct, one of the girls stuck an orange into its mouth and they took off running down the street. Everyone standing around was curious as to what all the commotion was about when they felt a small earthquake under their feet. Shortly after came a larger quake. The road started to lift up in a large mound, cracking and breaking with thumping sounds. The smell of death burst up in a dark mist from the cracks and skeletal creatures squeezed up from the crevices and ran down the street.

Stunned citizens watched as they ran past. One was running with a black cat under its bony arm and another running next to it with an encyclopedia under one arm and the encyclopedia salesman's head under the other. The creatures were turning over cars with people still in them, screaming in disbelief. They went after anything that moved with daggers, sharp sticks, and rocks. The skeletal creatures infested the city, uncontrolled, tearing up everything and terrorizing the citizens.

Local news crews took to the streets to capture the incredibly terrifying phenomena, but they only captured limited footage as they were all killed moments later. One camera was picked up by a skeletal creature. The feed was live casting unbelievable images back to the newsroom. It didn't take long for the footage to make the national news. The world watched in horror as Merida was inundated by the living dead, killing anyone caught out on the streets, trapping people in their cars, busses, trains, and in their homes.

CHAPTER 34

The morning sun shone through several round holes high up in the cave ceiling. Jennifer was snuggled up in Necalli's arms, warm and content. Her head nestled against his neck with sleepy eyes and his arms enclosed her skinny waist. They stayed up most of the night next to the spring, talking and kissing, only catching a few hours of sleep in each other's arms. Jennifer leaned back and yawned with her hand over her mouth.

"It's morning already?"

"It is."

"Shesh, it felt like a couple hours to me."

"Jennifer, will you help to free my people from the realm?"

"Humm. Just a little while longer. I wish we could just stay here forever."

Necalli was okay with that. He loved her smell, so sweet. She took his breath away. He took a deep breath, inhaling her into his lungs, and rubbed her back. She arched her back and kissed his lower cheek. She held her stomach for a moment and looked up at him with grim lips and wrinkled eyebrows.

"Jennifer, what is it?"

"I don't know, something doesn't feel right."

"Are you okay? Are you hungry?"

"No, it's something else, uneasy. I feel like something's wrong—it's just an eerie feeling like when you forget something and can't remember what it was."

"Maybe you'll feel better after you've eaten something."

"I am hungry."

"Then we can free my people."

"Necalli, I don't know how and I'm not kissing everybody."

Necalli laughed. "You won't have to, you just need to concentrate. I know you have the power."

"Okay, I'll try."

When they finished eating, Necalli took her up to the main entrance to the realm. It was bright white with a semi-solid energy field over it, not dissimilar to the cover over the well in the temple where Jennifer battled the black panther. The exterior was glistening and shimmering with shades of white fluctuating across the surface. Jennifer reached out to touch it.

"Ahem."

Jennifer and Necalli looked behind them.

"What is it, Akna?"

Akna spoke in their ancient language. "Ah-ka namen la hissa."

"No, Akna, she'll be fine." He turned back to Jennifer.

"What'd he say?"

"He's a bit protective of you. He's afraid you might pass out again if you touch the doorway."

"Maybe I'll wake up in Kansas," Jennifer said, snickering.

Necalli looked at her strangely.

"Nevermind, twentieth century joke."

"Oh, I was going ask who Kansas was."

"Kansas is a place not a person, silly."

Necalli smiled at her silly demeanor. She reached out and touched the luminescent barrier athwart the doorway. As soon as her fingers were near, lightning feathered across it, fluctuating over the surface building up a charge that made it shine brighter.

BANG!

Jennifer screamed. A bolt of lightning arced through the air from the doorway to the ground in front of her. She reacted with nervous laughter.

"Well, I guess it won't disappear like the one in the temple."

"What temple?"

"The Temple of the Jaguar. There was a covering over a pool that looked almost like this one only it was very faint and not full of all this energy. It was over a pool not a doorway."

"Temple of the Jaguar?"

"You don't know of the Temple of the Jaguar?"

"Not by that name, no."

"Maybe a different name. It said only a guardian could open it."

"Ugh! The Well to the Otherworld, you're talking about the Well to the Otherworld."

"What's that?"

"It's where the moormits come from—Allusshia, Beesha, and the others."

"Wait a minute. I know that name, Allusshia. I've heard it before."

"How could you?"

"It was in a dream, walking in the woods and this bright, glowing bug flew in front of my face and just hovered there. It was daytime yet it was so bright, like the sun. I held out my hand and it landed on my palm, only…"

"Only what, Jennifer?" Necalli asked, fascinated, as he ciphered his thoughts. His cognition was of Tepin, so many years ago.

"Only when it stood still, it wasn't a firefly at all. It was a tiny little girl. She had long, blonde hair, longer than her body, and it glowed intently. It wasn't until she landed and took a few steps that I could see her tiny, cute little body uncovered from her hair. Then I heard her speak in this faint, cute, little voice."

"What did she say?" Necalli asked with wide eyes, raised eyebrows and a grin that wouldn't quit.

"She said her name was Brittany and it was important that I followed her. She took off flying fast; I ran after her. Before long we ran up on a wall of glistening reflections in the jungle. It was like a wall of wavy water. She motioned for me to walk through it, but I was afraid I would drown. Then she flew into it and disappeared. I was so sad in my dream. I almost cried. I said, 'Okay,' and took a deep breath, held it in and I walked into the wall. It was like trying to push through a wall of thick gelatin. It was hard to move.

"When I got to the other side, it was so bright it took a moment for my eyes to adjust. Everything was so brilliant and beautiful. I saw strange and fascinating creatures that I had never before seen in my whole life. It was like another world. The sounds were like distant high-pitched singing, like birds only not. It was like a song or notes played by birds. I had to watch where I walked because there were little plants that looked like aloe but their limbs were moving around like little upside down octopuses all waving around. The air smelled fruity kind of like a fresh peeled peach right off the tree. There were fluffy little flying puff balls of different colors that played in the air, dancing about and a purple, two-headed lizard looking thing. I swear, it smiled at me! There were many more of the glowing little fireflies. I'm guessing they were all like Brittany, but they flew so fast all I could see were streaks of light.

"Then I heard this strange noise in my ear. I turned and there was this sparkly silver butterfly thing with a beautiful lion's head. It had such a cute little roar. I remember being so warm and tingly all over. Brittany led me to a little hut where a funny looking girl lay in a high bed. I heard her speak and say her name was Allusshia. Then I woke up."

"Jennifer, this is so important—when did you have this dream?"

"I can't remember exactly, I know I just had it but ... but ... wait! Necalli, it was when I passed out after—"

"After?"

"Umm, when I woke up from the dream, you were standing above me, looking down, asking if I was okay."

Necalli wiped his face. He ran his hand slowly though his hair in deep concentration.

"Necalli, what is it?"

"Hatsuts," which is to say sweetie in Mayan, "it wasn't a dream. Allusshia, she's alive, I've been there—to that place. I met Beesha there to get this Ispus."

Necalli pulled the Ispus out from under his shirt. Jennifer reached out to touch it, but she pulled her hand back when it lit up bright green. Her hand felt like it was in a static field whenever her fingers were near it. It was the oddest feeling and almost made her arm go numb.

"Jennifer, will you come with me to see Allusshia? She will know how to free my people."

She looked up at him and smiled. "Necalli, I would follow you anywhere."

Necalli smiled back at her and turned a little red. He felt warm all over. He put his arms around her and hugged her tight. His heart beat heavily and his palms felt clammy.

"Thank you, Jennifer. My people need you—and I need you."

"I need you too, Necalli. More than you know. I think I was meant to find you."

Necalli took her by the hand and motioned at her to walk through the barrier. "Are you ready?"

She stopped. "Wait. Is it gonna hurt?"

"Here, watch Akna."

He motioned Akna to go through first. As he walked through the white light surrounded him and it sparked and sizzled a little, bit then Akna was gone, on the other side out of view.

"That didn't seem too pleasant."

"It's nothing, we do it all the time."

CHAPTER 35

Jennifer took a deep breath and held it in while they walked through the opening. Everything went black. She felt as if she was floating again in utter darkness. Moments later, she opened her eyes and looked up at Necalli holding her in his lap. She reached up and rubbed her head.

"Let me guess, I passed out again?"

"Sorry, hatsuts. It doesn't bother us that way. Are you okay?"

"Yes, I think. My head's pounding."

"I thought you were going to be a frog and I had to kiss you."

"I guess you already set me free, but you can still kiss me if you wish, I really don't mind."

Jennifer twitched when she felt an electrical tickle on her leg. It was Akna slithering up her body. He gently coiled himself around her neck.

"Long as Akna doesn't mind."

"I'm sure he's fine with it."

They kissed with tingly lips from the electrical charge about Jennifer's body. Necalli smiled looking into her eyes. "Hi."

"Hi."

He helped her to her feet and took a look around. He listened to the silence and the aura of the air.

"Something's wrong with the jungle," he said.

"I know, something's not right. I can feel it in my tummy again."

"And where are all the animals?"

They searched the canopy with their eyes, but they couldn't see a single animal.

"Let's find Allusshia, we need a horse. Can you summon one?"

"Necalli, I don't know how to do these things."

"Here." He held her. "Close your eyes and concentrate. Think about a horse."

Jennifer closed her eyes and leaned her head back. She thought about a big horse. She imagined it walking out of the woods. She imagined petting it and feeling his mane. She opened her eyes. Nothing...

"I tried. I really did."

"It's okay, we can walk. It's just going to take a while. It's at least a day's ride from here."

Just then they heard something walking in the jungle. Heavy footsteps. Necalli put his hand on the hilt of his sword and positioned himself in front of Jennifer. A horse's snicker carried on the air. It stomped over the underbrush and into the clearing by the lake. His eyes were funny, they glowed with a lustrous purple. He was dark black but his coat shone in the sun and he was tall with strong legs and a full tail arched in the air. He marched with his legs.

"What a magnificent creature," Necalli said. "He's obviously had training to march in such a way."

"He's so pretty," Jennifer said as she walked over to touch him.

Necalli grabbed her arm. "Wait, hatsuts, we don't know his temperament."

"Aww, he wouldn't hurt me, would you, baby?"

She reached up and touched his face. The moment she touched him his eyes returned to normal. Necalli petted his neck and whispered into his ear.

"You're a good boy, aren't you?" He shook his head and snickered. "He's a big sweetie."

Necalli picked up skinny little Jennifer and lifted her onto the horse. With no saddle it was hard to climb on. Necalli tried several times to jump up and finally made it when Jennifer grabbed him by the waist and helped him get his leg over.

"It's been a while."

They rode at a brisk pace and covered much distance with the horse's long stride. Jennifer held Necalli around the waist and put her cheek against his back to rest. She was so tired. As they rode a large troop of monkeys moved quickly past them overhead. Leaves and vines fell and floated down all around them. They were irregularly quiet.

"What's going on?"

"What is it, Necalli?"

"The monkeys are acting very strangely."

"What's wrong with them?"

"Normally they're annoying and loud."

They rode as far as they could until dusk then stopped to make camp. Necalli helped Jennifer down and kissed her forehead. Akna hissed at him.

"What was that, Akna? You want to be dinner?"

Jennifer laughed. "You're not eating my Akna."

"I always figured he would be quite tasty."

"Aww, don't listen to him, Akna. We're not going to eat you."

She smacked Necalli. "Stop teasing."

Jennifer yawned, covering her mouth, when something caught her attention. There was something dark in the shadows, moving slowly behind a bush. The horse snorted and became alert, turning his ears toward the sound. Just as Necalli turned to look the thing ran at him, out of the brush, moving quickly. Jennifer reached out with her palm and a bright flash arced outward and struck it with a POOF! It disintegrated into dust. A thick, brown cloud of particles floated with the air and dusted them. Necalli took a snort full and it embedded deep into his nasal cavities and lodged there like an irritant. His nose wrinkled and he held his breath. He quickly placed his finger under his nose, but it wasn't enough. He gasped for air and violently sneezed.

"What was that?" Jennifer asked.

"I don't know. What'd you do?"

"I don't know. It scared me so…"

"Guess we'll never know now."

"Ewh, it smells like burnt hair, yuck."

Jennifer helped Necalli gather some wood and start a fire.

"I'm going to have to stay awake on guard duty tonight. The jungle is weird and there could be more of whatever that was out there."

"No, no, you're too tired. I can take first watch and wake you up in a little while."

"Are you sure?"

"Yes, I have Akna to keep me company. You really need to sleep. Here, come here and lie down."

Necalli laid his head in Jennifer's lap. She played with his rough-cut hair in her hand. Necalli looked up at her with the light of the fire flickering about her face.

"That feels nice. Relaxing. You're going to put me to sleep."

She leaned down and kissed him.

"That's the idea."

"You're so beautiful."

Jennifer smiled and kissed him again. Necalli fell asleep pretty fast and breathed heavily, filling his lungs with the cool evening air. Jennifer whispered softly to Akna. She just talked about everything that happened. He already knew about Vicky and that she was nasty, but he didn't understand much English. He watched the woods closely for any signs of danger as Jennifer rested her head for a second and fell asleep.

CHAPTER 36

Geramie was able to raise the control tower at Merida Airport over the radio. He explained the situation and that he needed instructions for landing the plane. Earlier in the day they would have laughed and thought he was joking, but now there were skeletal creatures running around the city. The Mexican Army had been called in to handle the situation. They stood guard around the airport for what little good it did. It was getting dark and there was a language barrier, but they successfully worked through the landing procedure for that aircraft.

Geramie had a hard time keeping the plane above stall speed and had to keep forcing the throttle. He aligned perfectly with the runway but touched down hard, causing the aircraft to veer off the runway into the grass. The girls screamed when they hit a gully and bounced up into the air and back down again. The plane was still moving fast and he tried reversing the blade pitch and gunning the throttle. They passed the end of the airport and started down a steep hill. He pushed both pedals as hard as he could with his legs extended for full breaks and they almost stopped, but then the front wheels caught and the tail lifted into the air such that the nose was almost looking into the ground. Everyone screamed and held hard on to their seats thinking the plane was going to tip on its end, but then it fell back to a stop. It took a few minutes for everyone to remember to breathe and gather their thoughts.

⨂

The student team tried to purchase tickets home, but there were no flights going out and incoming traffic was diverted. The students were able to call their families to let them know they were okay. Jennifer's parents, along with Allie, waited for any news, but the professor procrastinated in making that call; although he held out little hope of Jennifer being alive, he didn't want to make an assumption he would later regret. The whole team sat in the airport embarkation area watching the news in Spanish.

The army sustained heavy losses trying to fight the creatures. Bullets had no effect on them, but explosives and bombs worked fairly well, blowing them apart. They systematically managed to kill many of the creatures, and then they used bulldozers to shovel them all into a shallow grave. Moments later, they could see arms digging up through the fresh-turned soil. They climbed up out of the grave killing the heavy machinery operators. Most of the soldiers hid within tanks and armored vehicles, but the creatures were getting smarter somehow and were taking hand grenades from dead soldiers and throwing them down tank turrets, causing the internal ordnance to explode.

The media picked up on huge explosions as it grew dark from the buildings above. The world watched in disbelief.

The professor and the students tried to get some rest while hoping for a flight out. Vicky and some of the other girls were crying and nervously shaking, unable to sleep. Sean tried to comfort her, but she was too frantic to be calmed.

⨂

Necalli woke, jumping up. Jennifer never waked him to take watch. She was sleeping peacefully so he let her sleep a while. He looked around; the jungle had not changed from yesterday and was still deathly quiet.

"Akna, we need to catch something to eat."

Akna slithered off for a while and Necalli watched over Jennifer. He sat next to her and pulled her long hair from her face. Soon Akna returned with some food in his coils. Necalli stoked the fire and skinned a rabbit for breakfast. He woke Jennifer, gently shaking her. She covered her eyes from the sun with her hand and stretched.

"Ooh, I fell asleep, it's morning already?"

"It's been morning for a while. You hungry?"

"Starving."

Necalli gave her a stick with some grilled meat.

"Umm, this is good. What is it?"

"Rabbit."

"Aww, it's a bunny. I don't want to eat a cute, fluffy bunny."

"Don't think of it as a bunny. Think of it as a jack rabbit that wants to bite you."

"Well, long as it's a mean bunny, I guess I can eat it."

Necalli finished eating and put out the fire.

"Necalli, how do you know English so well?"

Necalli laughed. "After many years of listening and watching visitors to our land we have learned several languages—and endured many life-threatening situations we could do nothing about."

"Like what?"

"It's hard to watch when someone is being kidnapped and dragged off when you can't do anything about it. We have been imprisoned in the realm for so long. It feels good to breathe the air as a man again and feel the sun on my face."

"I couldn't imagine what it was like for you all these years. I wish I knew how to set your people free."

"You will. Allusshia will teach you."

"But how do you know she's still alive?"

"Because you've seen her."

"But that was just a—"

A glowie flew by them and circled around Jennifer.

"Hey!" She smiled. "Just like my dream."

She held out her palm and Necalli watched it land. He squinted hard to see tiny little Brittany walking up Jennifer's hand. She motioned with her tiny arm for them to follow and took off into the air. Necalli lifted Jennifer onto their horse and they followed Brittany up a path. They walked for a couple miles then Necalli stopped and helped Jennifer down. He had a blank expression and kept a watchful eye. He felt the Ispus under his shirt with his fingers to make sure it was still there.

"Necalli, what's wrong?"

"Last time I was here there was a great beast, just up ahead."

"It wouldn't be there still, would it?"

"It was very old from the past. It had an armored head and two large horns on its armor and one on its nose. Its roar was tremendous and it shook the ground when it ran."

"Hmm, that sounds like a triceratops, a dinosaur, but they've been extinct for thousands of years."

Brittany buzzed around them motioning them to come.

"I think she's being impatient, Necalli."

Jennifer stood up and walked up the path.

"Jennifer, wait!" Necalli ran after her.

"There's nothing here. Doesn't seem like there's been anything here for a very long time."

"It would lie right here in this streambed."

"Whoa, it must have been huge."

They both climbed back on the horse and rode for the sound of the waterfalls. Brittany continued to lead until they reached the shimmering wall of reflections. They pushed through on the horse. Jennifer was wide-eyed. It was just like her dream. Necalli helped her down and she kept peeking around.

"What you are looking for, Jennifer?"

"My little lion butterfly. Where is he?"

There was a voice coming from a small cottage. Necalli took her by the hand and they walked inside. They were standing next to a little girl in a high bed.

"Are you Allusshia?"

"Necalli, you look exactly as I remember you. You haven't aged at all."

Necalli walked up next to her and gave her a hug. It felt like he was hugging Jennifer. His whole body tingled.

"I thought I would never see you again, Necalli. I searched for centuries. I knew you were alive somehow, but I couldn't find you."

"Allusshia, what happened?"

"The guards gave me some kind of drink and it made me lose my head. Malinche got free and started killing everyone. By the time I was conscious you were in battle with her and then everyone was gone. I searched and found your father, but I couldn't save him. His mind was lost to Malinche. Moctezuma survived and together we fought her. She was so mad it made her more powerful. I don't know, we couldn't defeat her so Moctezuma devised a plan to capture her. She chased me into the Otherworld, so she thought, only it was a trick. When she entered the well, I sealed her inside. She was trapped there for almost a thousand years."

"At least we're safe from her now."

"No, Necalli. She set her free." Allusshia pointed to Jennifer.

"Me?"

"Yes, you fought with her."

"You mean the black panther?"

"Yes, that was the form she was trapped in for all these years. If she actually knew who you were and what you are she would have killed you. "

"Allusshia, what do you mean?" Necalli questioned with his eyebrows lowered and a wrinkled forehead.

"Necalli, she's Tepin's grandchild."

"What?" he asked with big eyes.

"She's a moormit, Necalli. Well, half moormit and half human."

"I'm confused."

"After you disappeared Tepin met a moormit and they fell in love. They secretly had a child many years later, which was strictly forbidden after what happened with…"

"With what?"

"Wait! My grandmother was married to a moormit?"

"Yes, child. Your grandmother was an astonishing woman."

"I can't believe you knew my grandmother."

"Where is she now?" Necalli asked.

"She died in a car crash when I was very young. She used to tell me the most amazing stories."

Necalli lowered his head and his eyes teared up.

"I'm sorry, but this doesn't make sense. I can't be a moormit. I mean what about my mother or sisters?"

"Child, there's a reason why moormits are forbidden to have offspring with humans. The results are unpredictable. Quite often the power is selective and can skip several generations. Not to mention…"

"Not to mention what?"

"I've said to much already, Necalli."

"I can't believe Tepin was alive all these years and never drank from the forbidden spring."

"She lived in this realm most of her life. Humans don't age much here. And I can never leave or I will die. I am near the end of my days, Necalli."

Necalli knelt down and put his head in his hands. He didn't want Jennifer to see him cry, but he couldn't hold it all back. His face turned bright red and his lips turned down. Jennifer kneeled in front of him and hugged him.

"It's too much. So much is lost. Everyone is gone."

"Not everyone, Necalli," Allusshia said. "Your people, they wait for you even now. But you need to free them soon because Malinche has risen her army and soon will have full control over them. You must stop her and kill her."

Necalli wiped his eyes.

"I've tried and failed. Can she even be killed?"

"With the help of this young moormit she can be defeated."

"No, I'm not losing anyone else I care about."

"You can't do it without her. She is strong, very strong. I can feel the power within her and she may be the only one who can defeat Malinche because they are…"

"They are what?"

"No, I've said too much."

"Necalli, Let me help. I would give all for you," Jennifer said.

Necalli hugged her tight.

"That's what I'm afraid of. I can't lose you. I have grown so fond of you in such a short time. I feel like you're the one I have been waiting for all my life."

"Necalli, come closer," Allusshia said.

He leaned down next to her.

"Do you still have the Ispus?"

Necalli pulled it out from under his shirt. Allusshia touched it with her tiny fingers and it glowed bright green.

"You know what to do. Get it around Malinche's neck then end her for good. She will destroy the world if you don't."

"No pressure," Jennifer said.

"Child, take my sister's staff from the corner."

Jennifer looked around but didn't see anything. She walked to the corner and noticed a stick covered in years of dust and cobwebs.

"Ewh. Do I have to touch it?"

She curled up her lips and looked at Necalli. He got up and picked the staff up, wiping off the years of sediment, and cleaned off the stela-stone, blowing dust from the crevices. He handed it to Jennifer. When she touched it, she felt her whole body surge and she dropped it on the floor. Allusshia cringed and leaned her head forward fearing the stone would crack.

"Sorry."

"Easy, child. You're so jumpy. You need to relax."

"Sorry."

"Take a second, close your eyes."

Jennifer relaxed and tilted her head back with her eyes closed. The stone in the hilt lit up bright blue and the staff floated up into the air. Jennifer could feel that burning ember inside her, but the heat left her body and was absorbed by the stone. It felt like warm flowing water across her body. She floated into the air until she opened her eyes and realized she wasn't touching the floor then fell. Necalli caught her. His eyes were open wide and he was breathing heavily. Jennifer reached out and took the staff from the air. Her whole body tingled with energy. Necalli could feel it while holding her. He tingled all over too.

"Very good, child. Now you go set the people free, unhide them and protect the world from Malinche."

"But how do I free the people?"

"Jennifer, you have the power. You always have. You just need to focus your thoughts and energy. The staff will do that for you. Just concentrate on the energy surrounding the realm and you will bring it down. Just don't do it here, I kind of like my realm," she said with a smile.

"Allusshia, isn't there anything Jennifer can do for you?"

"No, I'm afraid it's my time, Necalli. I wish it weren't. I've missed you these many years."

Necalli hugged her and gave her a kiss on the cheek. It brought back memories of when Allusshia was young and tall with her flowing gown and magnificent power.

"I will miss you too much."

"You must go now. I can feel Malinche's power growing by the minute. And Necalli…"

"Yes."

Allusshia whispered into his ear, "Trust her. She is more powerful then she can ever imagine. She just doesn't know it yet. Be patient with her, she needs to have confidence in her ability. I dare say she could equal that of Beesha. And Necalli, make sure she feels loved. Trust me when I tell you from experience, you don't want to break her heart."

"Wait, another thing." She called out, "Malinche, she is building her army to the northeast, not far from the ocean." Allusshia looked funny and became almost transparent then vanished into a swirl of light.

"Where'd she go?"

"She's gone."

"You mean dead?"

"Moormits don't really die, they just grow little and then change to energy or something. Eventually they can no longer appear when their energy grows too weak."

They both frowned. Necalli felt a lump in his throat. He wiped a lone tear from his eye and they climbed onto the horse and rode back through the barrier with Akna and Brittany. They moved quickly. Jennifer held the staff tightly in front of her. The stone in the hilt never stopped glowing bright blue. From time to time it would spark with little lightning bolts jumping into the humid air with a little flash.

Before long the sun began to set beyond the canopy. Jennifer held the staff high over her head to light the way. Brittany led them in the right direction in the dark of night. The more Jennifer focused the brighter the stone shone.

They stopped to water the horse. Jennifer walked into the woods to relieve herself, setting the staff against a tree. When she stood up, something jumped on top of her, knocking her to the ground. She screamed and cried looking up at a half eaten brain and a rotted tongue hanging out of a skull. It stunk like rotted flesh and was full of maggots. Necalli drew his sword and chopped off its head, sending it bouncing some distance. The carcass lay still on top of Jennifer. She screamed, frantically trying to push it off, but it was heavy dead weight. Necalli pulled it away by the arm and helped her to her feet. Tears rolled down her face and she couldn't stand, still shaking her goose bumped arms.

"Jennifer, Jennifer, it's okay, hatsuts. It's dead."

She said loudly, "Why was it alive?" She cleaved on to Necalli.

"That's one of Malinche's creatures."

"Zombies! Are you freaking kidding me right now? We have to fight zombies?"

Jennifer was freakishly crazy for about an hour after that. Necalli held her close and stroked her hair to calm her. She wiped her nose and cheeks and held her face against his chest. After giving her sufficient time to come to terms with the reality of the situation, he said, "Now you see why it's so important we set my people free. We fought these things before and won. They are easy to kill, once you know how."

"I'm scared."

Jennifer was shaking and all welled up inside. The stone in the staff no longer glowed.

"It's okay, Jennifer. Just free my people and we can do the rest."

"No, wherever you go, I go. No matter what. I'm never leaving you."

She wiped her eyes again and stood to her feet. She took a deep breath and reached out for the staff. It flew off the ground and into her hand, surprising her. The stone in the hilt lit up brighter than ever. She felt her power through the staff and felt powerful. She stood up tall and looked at Necalli.

"Okay, let's do this."

Necalli smiled and kissed her then lifted her up onto the horse. They rode deep into the night. Jennifer held the staff high the whole way to keep the path lit. She was alert, watching and listening to every sound of the jungle. Almost to the realm, Jennifer heard grunting sounds behind them. The sound grew nigh. In an instant two skeletal beings ran out of the jungle moving fast. Jennifer's whole body shuddered and two brilliant sparks flashed out of the stela-stone.

POOF!

POOF!

Two large, brown puffs of smoke floated toward them. Jennifer's heart was pounding. She breathed heavily.

"Did you see that? I got both of them."

"That was impressive. I think we really have a chance."

"Whew, they really stink."

Necalli wrinkled up his nose. "Yes, they really do."

Jennifer giggled. "I feel much better now."

She wrapped her free arm around Necalli and hugged tight. Akna laid his head down on her shoulder to sleep. It wasn't much longer before they reached the realm. They stood before the small cave entrance.

"It's so funny how it's so small out here and so massive inside. The energy doesn't seem so intimidating from out here."

"You ready to give it a go?"

"Yep! Stay back."

Jennifer moved the staff to her right hand, but as she was moving it she noticed the white barrier over the entrance deformed with her motions. She walked closer and moved the staff back and forth to find a point where part of the barrier was pulled aside and they could see the dark of the cave.

Necalli squatted down by the opening and called out, "Le-ma op calleggraa," meaning, "My people, come forth!"

Jennifer held very still trying to keep the opening stable. A group of tiny Tenochcan people gathered at the threshold inside the realm. The first brave walked through.

Spark! Pop! Flash!

He exteriorized to normal size and jumped up and down. He walked over to Jennifer and hugged her smiling widely. He stepped back to make room for the next to cross. One by one they came, big and small, men, women, and children. Jennifer tried her best to hold the staff still, but after half an hour her arm was getting way too heavy.

"Necalli, how many more? I can't hold this open much longer."

"About two hundred thousand."

"What? That many!" she said with surprise. "Necalli, I can't hold it that long."

"Let me help you."

Necalli grabbed the staff. There was a bright flash and he was thrown about ten feet away to the ground.

"Necalli!" Jennifer ran to him, kneeled down and put his head on her legs.

"Baby, are you okay?"

"I feel like I was kicked in the horse by a chest. Wait, what did I say?"

"I think you meant to say you felt like you were kicked in the chest by a horse."

"Yeah, what you said."

Jennifer rubbed his chest.

"Poor baby."

She put her head against his.

"Remind me never to do that again. Touching a staff when a moormit is using it, very bad."

"I'm sorry, baby. You feeling any better?"

"I just need a minute."

"I think I have an idea."

Jennifer walked to the covered cave entrance and closed her eyes. Her head tilted back and she concentrated. She could feel that hot ember inside her and the stela-stone glowed bright. She opened her eyes and a blast of energy struck the barrier like a stream of lightning continually flowing. The barrier became brighter as if it was strengthened even more.

"Okay, that didn't work the way I expected. Let me try this."

She squinted her eyes and bent her head forward concentrating on the doorway. She felt the pull of energy on the staff. Light streaks of white floated in the air from the doorway and were absorbed by the staff. She kept focusing and pulled more and more power away. She could feel the energy entering her body. There was a deep rushing sound that got louder and louder. The barrier become thinner and thinner. Jennifer felt like her insides were on fire. The doorway went dark. She turned and looked at Necalli with big, red, catlike eyes and her face shone amber. She stumbled but waved Necalli off. She spoke in a strange deep voice. "Don't touch me."

She walked past everyone into the jungle and raised the brilliant shining staff high into the air. She released the energy with a crashing lightning bolt that struck high up in the canopy, bringing down several trees that fell to the ground. The bolt continued up into the clouds and made them glow bright as the energy fanned out and was absorbed by the atmosphere. Everyone took a few steps back. When all the energy was released, she fell to her knees. Necalli rushed over.

"Hatsuts?"

"I'm fine." She held her head. "Shesh, what a headache."

With the barrier open, all the Tenochcan people were able to walk out and transposed to their old selves. Freed at last.

"Now what?" Jennifer asked.

CHAPTER 37

Necalli greeted his people as they exited the realm.

"Now we fetch our weapons from the temple armory and take our revenge on Malinche. I have the Ispus, her time will come to an end."

The people cheered and bowed before him. They made their way to the great Temple of Naranjo. The women and children set up camp. The warriors followed Necalli to a hidden entrance to the temple. They had to dig down into the soil and sand that had shifted over the last millennium. Many were surprised that their structures were still standing. Not in the best of shape but still standing after a thousand years. Once uncovered, Necalli and Jennifer along with Akna walked down before a large engraved set of stone doors. Necalli pressed and pulled on several pieces of pictographs and the doors cracked open but not enough for a man to fit through.

"Let me try," Jennifer said.

They all stepped back and she focused her mind. The stela-stone glowed bright white and a burst of energy blasted the doors, forcing them open. Once inside Necalli and the men lit torches and oil pots along the walls as they walked. The corridor led deep underground to a large, empty room.

"Now we need you, Jennifer."

"Me?"

"Yes, only a guardian can open the armory."

"What do I do?"

"Can you read the inscriptions?"

"Can't you?"

"No, it's the language of the moormits, only you can see the words in your mind. The writings look different to every person who looks upon them except for the moormits."

"Oh, okay. I feel special."

Necalli laughed and hugged her. "You're very special."

Jennifer read with her lips mouthing the words silently as she ran her fingers along the engravings. She thought for a few minutes and rubbed her head. She then lifted up the staff and tried to turn the glow red, but she didn't know how. She was able to make it white, green, blue, and violet but not red. She huffed and smacked the wall with her hand then held it because she hurt herself.

"Hatsuts, what's wrong?"

"I don't know how to make the staff red."

A black shadow swirled overhead and down into the wall. Jennifer screamed and stood with Necalli.

"Did you see that?"

"What?"

"That black shadow."

"I didn't see anything."

"This place is creeping me out."

She stomped the staff on the floor and tilted her head with her hair hanging down. She shook her head. She took a deep breath and closed her eyes for a moment. The staff glowed red and the doorway opened. The men cheered.

"Did I just do that?"

Necalli smiled and kissed her.

"Uh-ha."

They walked into a huge multi-room armory with stone carvings on the walls. There were treasures and weapons, a great many weapons, and cash set aside after many hard-fought battles followed by a great time of peace. The men gathered the swords, pikes, bows, shields, oil, and war instruments.

The troops assembled around the temple. They found several horses for Necalli, his moormit, and his personal guard outfitted with saddles and war armor. Necalli took Jennifer by the hand and led her to the top of the temple. The one hundred thousand warriors below bowed down before them. Necalli spoke to them in their language, inspiring them for their quest. He told them to rise. Necalli took Jennifer's hand and held their hands up in the air. The men cheered and were anxious for battle. Jennifer smiled and for the first time in her life felt important. She was determined to make a difference.

The army assembled. Jennifer watched with fascination while the musicians prepared their instruments. Each drum crew consisted of five men, four to hold up the drum platform on their shoulders by two long posts on either side and one drummer that sat up on the platform behind a huge drum. He held two thick, heavy, oak drumsticks and pummeled the leather with a powerful war beat as they walked. There were bamboo flutes and pipes of varying sizes. Some were thick and long and produced a deep, deep tone and others were medium in size and played a light melody. The war drums marked the march and the Tenochcan Army began their long trek toward the Northeastern Coast. Strong men walked ahead clearing any vegetation blocking their way.

Jennifer rode at the head of the army next to Necalli with Akna coiled around her neck. Necalli had found one of Beesha's pretty, blue, light flowing gowns in the war chamber of the temple and given it to Jennifer. It was partially transparent but had several layers with flowing material that danced in the wind. He thought she would appreciate it because it matched her beautiful blue eyes. He turned to stare at her often. Jennifer smiled and was actually looking forward to the adventure, but she had a distant eerie feeling that she couldn't shake in the back of her mind. Still, she felt empowered by the war drums and could feel them deep in her chest.

BOOM – Botta Botta – BOOM – Botta Botta – BOOM – Botta Botta – BOOM

CHAPTER 38

The professor and the team were still waiting for a flight out of Merida. Several days had passed and the skeletal invasion upon the city and the surrounding areas had escalated to the point of bringing the city to a standstill. Citizens hid in their homes. Anyone daring to venture out onto the streets was killed. Malinche was still gaining power and did not have full control over the creatures. It was total chaos, people trapped in cars and busses, starving while being still and quiet so as not to draw attention being in horrifying fear. Many homes were surrounded by the creatures trying to get in. Families cuddled in closets, out of sight, being as quiet as they could. The army hid inside their armored vehicles or flew far above the city in helicopters, not daring to land within the infested areas. Some of the commanders and soldiers were enticed by Malinche to join her army, but she had not yet made an appearance before the world.

The soldiers still guarded the airport runway as best they could, but they were overrun at times and fought hard to keep their position, but then the creatures would lose interest and run somewhere else. A military jet from the States landed with several pilots aboard to evacuate as many as they could.

The professor and the team were able to get on one of the first flights out on one of the commercial aircraft. They sat in their seats praying they could get off the ground quickly. Sean held Vicky tight. She leaned on him, almost lifeless, with a distant stare in her eyes. Their spent nerves wore on them heavily with depression and exhaustion. The young lady who was attacked in the jungle was in bad shape and had incurred infections from the tears in her skin from the fleshless fingers of the skeletal being that attacked her.

The plane's engines spun up and fired. They began to taxi down the runway and made a turn for departure.

"Vicky, it's okay now. We're taking off," Sean said.

Vicky looked around and sat up in her seat. She smiled for the first time in days. Some of the passengers cheered as the jet quickly sped up, pressing them back into their seats. About halfway down the runway the plane jerked hard to the right and everyone screamed. The right engine exploded venting fire down the side of the aircraft. A skeletal being had been sucked up into the engine. The plane yawed hard right and bounced off the runway at ninety miles per hour. The landing gear buckled and the fuselage slid over hills and ruts. The plane struck a pole that ripped off the right wing. Hot trails of fire followed after the wreckage. The plane spun around hard tearing off the aft fuselage with passengers still strapped into their seats. Some of them flew out the opening and into the blazing fire. The plane rolled a few times then slid to a stop.

Sean white-knuckled his fingers hard to his seat and was frozen in place, breathing heavily. Vicky started screaming hysterically as dense smoke filled the plane. The passengers that survived the crash scampered to get their seatbelts unfastened and get off the aircraft. It was difficult because the plane came to rest partially sideways.

Sean and Vicky got out before the plane ended up totally engulfed in flames. Vicky fainted into Sean's arms. When she woke moments later, she felt moisture on her upper lip. When she wiped it, she saw that she had blood all over her hand.

"Sean, I'm bleeding," she cried.

Sean pulled her hair back and there was a gash on her head. He held his hand over it as they walked. The survivors walked back toward the airport but were very exposed. Vicky whimpered and felt his hand over her wound.

"Shhh. Tell her to be quiet. Those things are everywhere."

No sooner did the passenger comment than several skeletal beings ran at them from multiple directions. They surrounded them and started closing in. Vicky fell to her knees and didn't have the strength to get up. Sean kneeled down next to her. The skeletal figures moved ever closer with knives, sticks, and stones in their bony hands. Vicky cringed with wide eyes at their sight. They charged in fast grunting and wailing, those that still had lungs, but then they stopped dead in their tracks. There was a strange sound coming from the jungle around the city. It grew louder. It was a distant rhythm. Many of the skeletal creatures ran and gathered in a large open field north of the city.

The citizens trapped in their cars and homes at the south end of the city could hear the sound of drumming then the deep sound of bamboo flutes. The Tenochcan Army, one hundred thousand strong, emerged in a long parade, marching to the beat of the powerful war drums. The citizens could hardly believe their eyes. They noticed the beautiful blue woman with the emerald boa coiled around her neck leading the army with her glowing staff at her right side. Two skeletal creatures terrorizing a bus full of people ran at them. Before they could get close, Jennifer tilted her head and flexed her muscles. Two brilliant streaks of light sparked from the staff. POOF! POOF! Both skeletal beings were evaporated into dry dust that floated in the air.

Some of the soldiers ran ahead to kill the scattered scourge while they marched forward. Most of the skeletal creatures ran away, north of the city. Citizens watched in awe from their rooftops and balconies as the powerful, ancient Tenochcan Army marched past. The war drums could be heard all the way to the coast.

News media picked up the event. They zoomed in on Jennifer then panned down the assembly that stretched for a mile in length. So many ancient warriors in full battle dress.

"This is ACCZ reporting live with new information about the situation in Merida, Mexico. Just moments ago, an amazing turn of events. An unknown army of incogitable size just appeared out of the jungle. They are driving off the living dead that have laid siege to this city for the last several days. The sound is incredible. They approached from the south, marching in formation to a powerful set of drums and are playing what sounds like some sort of jungle music, as best as it can be described. Most of the living dead have either fled or have been slain in the streets. Where did they come from? Your guess is as good as mine, but the scene looks like something out of the past; one could surmise that they are some sort of ancient power, right out of history, with swords and shields."

The news media zoomed in on Jennifer as she was annihilating several creatures, turning them into dust. Many of the citizens left their homes and followed the army through the streets in amazement. The army reached the point north of the city just above the gathering of the skeletals. The creatures were still randomly acting out of control as if Malinche was still unable to keep them under control. They were grabbing at each other and spasmodically moving about. The Tenochcans marched up a hill to where they could fully see the horde of the dead below. When they crossed the summit, Necalli sat with his mouth open staring intently. Jennifer shared a similar expression and slowly turned her head towards him while watching in her peripheral vision.

"Oh, crap! Necalli! Are you seeing this?"

"I wasn't—"

"How many do you think there are?"

"I would guess about five hundred thousand."

"Why is the Mexican Army down there with them?"

"Malinche can entice men into doing her will."

"Where is she?"

"She never shows herself on the battlefield. She's either hiding or sheltered somewhere. That's just her way."

Necalli motioned to his general to deploy the Tenochcan Army. Some of the Mexican Army, not under Malinche's control, climbed out of their tanks and armored vehicles and watched, desiring to join the battle with their ancient brethren. They were very reverent toward them.

The war drums stopped. The men stood quiet, waiting and watching, confident from past victories but bewildered by the increasing size of the amassed enemy forces.

"Necalli, what's that?" Jennifer asked, pointing to the far side of the battlefield.

"What is that?" Necalli asked in wonderment.

They both tried to focus far across the large field, something was moving. Three large, armored war elephants with riders walked out of the woods. All of the skeletals stopped moving about and stood still looking their way. The elephants marched up to the rear of the enemy and stopped. Necalli hardened his stance and stiffened his lower lip.

"It's Malinche!"

"I thought you said she hides in battle?"

"Normally she does, but that's her."

"Oh, SNAP! Look at that amazing dress. I want one like hers."

Necalli gave Jennifer a funny look. She shrugged her shoulders and giggled. "What? It looks hot."

Malinche wore a long, white dress with pleated layers and black edges. There were long, white fabric strips blowing in the wind like streamers. She had a white and black shawl wrapped around her shoulders held on by a leather strap. The front of the dress had a magnificent black tree like pattern that stood out, even from a distance.

Necalli smiled and shook his head at Jennifer, thinking, *Well, she is young.*

"This isn't like Malinche, she's up to something."

"Maybe she's learned something new."

"It must be a new tactic."

Jennifer could see the worry on Necalli's face.

"Babe, don't worry. We got this."

CHAPTER 39

Necalli didn't want to give Malinche too much time for tactics so he gave the command to advance. He and Jennifer stayed back on their horses watching along with his prince's personal guard and reserve troops.

The advancing soldiers seemed to have a hard time walking, like the ground was squashy or something. The first few rows of men started sinking into the ground up to their knees. The advance halted and they tried to free themselves, but the men behind them started sinking as well. Malinche was flaunting her staff in the air doing something. The ground started to act like quicksand; thousands of soldiers were stuck and sinking fast, yelling out for help.

"Er, Necalli? What can we do?"

"Humph!"

Necalli put his hand on his sword thinking of a way to get to Malinche to stop her. Jennifer closed her eyes and leaned her head back. She focused her mind on Malinche. The skeletal forces were loose and ran up the hillside toward the trapped soldiers. Jennifer opened her eyes and pushed her staff slightly forward. Several energy pulses flashed outward like miniature white comets with streaming tails, not really noticeable in the scheme of things. Malinche was completely caught off guard when they struck her, knocking the staff from her hand and knocking her backward with an unpleasant shock.

"Jennifer!" Necalli said with amazement. She winked at him. Up to this point Malinche didn't know of Jennifer's existence and was too weary to remember her when she was freed from the Well to the Otherworld. She lost her concentration and the soldiers were able to work themselves free of the ground but not before the dead were upon them. Jennifer was having a bit of fun with this and lifted her staff into the air. She tensed her body tightly and the stela-stone glowed bright blue. A distant crack of thunder was espied in their ears. A lightning bolt struck the ground behind them and seemed to roll with sparks across the ground.

Jennifer swung her staff down and caught the lightning. She could feel the immense power flow over her body. Necalli leaned away, watching out for any flashes of energy from the staff. Jennifer released the built-up power all at once as thin strands of light splintered out in all directions over the heads of the soldiers. The advancing skeletal beings were running full force. The soldiers braced themselves for impact, but the lightning strands struck the dead first and they dissipated into dust that just blew into the soldiers' faces like a cloud of sand.

Malinche grew angry and spun her staff in the air until she amassed large swirls of green eleamus.

"Jennifer, that's what she did when she banished us into the realm! You have to stop her," Necalli said with great concern.

Just then Malinche released the eleamus that whisked across the sky and hit Necalli and Jennifer, knocking them from their horses. The eleamus continued flowing then sliced one of the generals behind them in half. Jennifer screamed when the upper part of his body fell in front of her as she sat up on the ground. Necalli's leather armor was on fire and blackened; he pulled the burning Ispus from his neck and patted out the flames on his leather. The Ispus was smoking hot, having absorbed most of the eleamus that hit the two of them.

Jennifer's nostrils flared and her pulse elevated. The ember was burning inside her. She picked up her staff and looked at Necalli with flaming red catlike eyes with a vertical iris. Dark clouds started to form in the sky and the wind blew. She walked down the hillside. Necalli drew his sword and ran after her. She held up her staff and her body twitched as red flames shot out of it. She twirled the fire around in the air until it built up so dense it scared her. She motioned forward and it scorched through the sky with a loud whistling sound. Malinche saw the ball of fire and materialized what looked like an energy barrier, but even she didn't realize Jennifer's power and then some of the flames burned her dress and singed a good portion of her long, dark-and-silver hair leaving a pungent odor.

Malinche marched forward on her war elephant circling the tip of her staff around in the air. She was smiling, sitting tall with confidence, high up on her mount. Black clouds of darkness swirled out from the stone hilt and floated in the air above her skeletal army.

"What now?" Jennifer asked harshly.

Something swarmed out of the cloud en masse and flew at the soldiers. They tried to swat them away, but there were so many. The orange-and-black scorpions with dragonfly wings landed on some of the soldiers, stinging them. They collapsed to the ground dead but rose again moments later with gray eyes and vacant expressions. The first one that rose rammed his sword through the gut of the soldier standing next to him. They began to fight against each other. A small swarm flew after Jennifer. She screamed and ran then ducked down with wide eyes and raised eyebrows. Her body shivered with goose bumps and her insides heated up until the stela-stone in her staff glowed bright white. A scorpion landed on her back and stung her. She screamed out in pain and Necalli cut it in two with the tip of his blade. Jennifer reached behind and tried to rub the swollen area of her back but couldn't reach it. She could feel the venom in her body. The ember inside her burned and the stela-stone turned blood-red. She released the energy that blasted out with a loud, low-pitched vibrating sound. All of the scorpions fell from the sky and struggled for life on the ground. They were stamped out by the soldiers. The living dead soldiers were slain and beheaded so that they would not rise again.

Malinche opened her mouth with her hands in the air and let out a guttural roar. She looked up at Jennifer standing on top of the hillside with a death stare and glowing green eyes. She smiled with an evil grin and swiped her staff forward. A clear reflective substance flew through the air rapidly striking Jennifer hard. It knocked her to the ground and surrounded her with a translucent barrier, pinning her to the ground. She could still hear the sounds of war around her, but everything was muffled. She pushed up against it with her hands and kicked at it with her feet, but it didn't budge. It was only inches from her face. Necalli tried to chop at it with his sword, but it just bounced off with a muffled thud in Jennifer's ears. She could see his lips moving but couldn't understand what he was saying.

It became hard to breathe as she was running out of air. The ember inside her grew hotter and felt like it was burning through. Poisonous snakes came up out of the ground biting her on the legs. She screamed and cried with each bite so that tears ran down her face. Akna uncoiled from her neck and swallowed up the other snakes. Jennifer's legs started to burn from the venom. Everything started spinning around in her head and she could feel herself slipping away. She saw her staff lying on the ground outside the barrier and the stone was still glowing white. She leaned her head back and closed her eyes. The staff started absorbing streaks of light out of the air around it. Necalli stepped back when sparking electrons were ripped out of the atmosphere with loud pops. The stone glowed brighter and brighter until it was so intense that even Malinche, hundreds of yards away, could see streaks of light shooting upward toward the darkened sky. It was so bright that it lit up the clouds over the battlefield.

Jennifer ran out of air and passed out. The energy in the staff erupted with a massive pulse. Necalli was thrown through the air and landed halfway down the hill. The blast wave burst out in all directions ripping away the barrier surrounding her. It continued down the hillside knocking down all the soldiers and disintegrated every one of the skeletals into clouds of floating dust. The Mexican soldiers enticed by Malinche were knocked down and freed from her mind control. When the blast reached Malinche, it knocked her off her war elephant such that her foot caught in a stirrup leaving her hanging upside down.

The men on the other two elephants were knocked to the ground and their minds were freed. They went after Malinche to kill her, but she waved her hand in the air forcing them upward. The two men flew high in the sky and splashed down several hundred yards out into the sea. Necalli saw his chance while Malinche was distracted and jumped on a horse, but he couldn't leave Jennifer lying on the ground on top of the hill. He turned and galloped up the hillside but then saw her float over the crest of the slope with her gown flowing in the wind behind her. Her head was tilted back and the stela-stone was dark black. Lightning started striking the ground and the clouds overhead swirled around like a hurricane. All the color in Jennifer's dress faded into a pure, silky white. The ground shook under their feet and cracks appeared in the soil. Necalli's horse bucked, throwing him to the ground.

Malinche had gotten herself freed from the stirrups and levitated toward them. Necalli drew his sword and ran down the hill. Malinche lifted her staff in the air and tilted it forward toward him. Jennifer had built up so much power that she felt herself out of control and opened her eyes. She squinted and wrinkled up her nose at Malinche and a lightning bolt lashed out from the clouds striking Malinche's staff. It knocked it violently from her hand burning her skin. She leaned forward holding her wrist in pain.

Necalli caught up to her with his sword steady. He slowed in caution and walked up to her. She smiled at him and held up her left palm as if to say, "Stop," while reaching in the air with her right. A sharp, ancient looking sword materialized out of nowhere in her hand as she turned and thrust it through Necalli's chest and out of his back. He moaned, arched his back, and fell to his knees. Jennifer gasped deeply putting her hands to her quivering lips.

"Noooo! Necalli, nooooo!"

She fell to her knees holding herself up by her staff. Tears welled up in her eyes and her insides turned. Her chest tightened up and her back stiffened. She couldn't breathe and she felt the ember inside her consume her whole body. Her skin turned bright red and flames flashed about her. Only a moment passed, but time seemed to stand still. Everything moved in slow motion. She stood to her feet and her lips drew together tightly. Her grasp on the staff tightened. Her body began to glow. She looked right at Malinche with an unbreaking stare and lifted the staff toward the sky then pounded it on the ground with her teeth gritted together.

The stone in the hilt glowed blue and became so intense that it was as bright as a supernova. Everyone shielded their eyes and ducked to the ground. The stone pulsed with energy and a low-pitched thrusting sound. Rings of light resonated outwards like circles of translucent mist. The stone turned red with stela-matter spinning around.

Malinche stepped back several steps with her eyes opened wide. Her hair stood up on the back of her neck. Even the soldiers moved away in fear. The pulsations and sound grew louder and louder until the stone shattered into a thousand razor-sharp red shards pulsing with energy. Jennifer dropped the empty staff and held her hands forward. The shards darted through the air like a supersonic jet pulsing with energy. Malinche ran, but within a millisecond the shards tore into her body. She screamed and screamed as the shards tore her insides apart and tormented the spirit within. Her whole body had a red hue about it just before it blew apart and evaporated into red mist.

Malinche's dark spirit shadowed upward, floating above the ground. Jennifer twirled her hand around above her head creating a thick, swirling, red mist. Everyone watching stepped back in fear. The storm clouds overhead intensified and huge lightning bolts cracked through the sky in all directions. All at once the lighting and the red mist struck the dark shadow, first shrinking it to the size of a grain of sand, and then it exploded like a bomb. The explosion turned the very soil, knocking over tanks and splitting trees in half as it raged outward. It reached the sea and splashed water columns hundreds of feet into the air that then came crashing down, pulsing a large wave up the coastline.

The dark clouds cleared and sunlight started to shine through. Jennifer fell from her levitation and landed on her feet. She ran down the hill crying. Her face was soaking wet being so choked up inside she couldn't speak. She lifted Necalli and laid his head in her lap. The sword had vanished leaving a hole through his chest. Her tears dripped down onto his face. His lifeless eyes were open, looking up at her.

"Why'd you have to die, Necalli, Why? You can't be dead because I love you too much."

Jennifer tilted her head back and closed her teary eyes. She rocked forward and back in place with him dead in her lap. Her insides turned and burned like never before. Many of the soldiers gathered around them, most of them in tears over their prince.

"NOOOOOO!" she screamed with all her lungs.

She put her hands on Necalli's chest and screamed, "NO! This isn't happening."

Necalli's body jerked, his fingernails lit up, his eyes glowed; then there was a brilliant flash of light. Then darkness. Jennifer felt that familiar feeling of floating in darkness. She tried to open her eyes and she was floating, kind of bobbing up and down a little. She could see the waves of the beach crashing on the sand and the white foamy stuff washing up on someone's feet. Her arms were hanging out to her sides and her head lying back, bobbing around. Someone was carrying her. She finally came to and lifted her head up to look.

"Is that really you?"

"Hey, hatsuts. How are you feeling?"

"Please tell me you're real and this isn't a dream. And if not then never wake me."

Necalli placed her hand on his chest so she could feel his heartbeat. "I love you."

He helped her to her feet and they kissed, standing in the warm surf with bright streaks of amber light swirling out from Jennifer's feet across the wet sandy beach like little sparks of glimmering lightning.

The Tenochcan people reclaimed their jungle home. Over time, they united with surrounding countries to form a large kingdom. They were quick learners of modern technologies and, combined with their own, advanced into one of the most technological nations of the modern world.

Necalli and Jennifer decided to do a little joining of their own. The wedding was spectacular, especially when Allie and Jennifer reunited with hugs and tears. Allie had watched as the events unfolded on national news and felt really bad that she had abandoned Jennifer. She was so relieved and excited when she received the invitation to the wedding. She had traveled with Lee, Lilly, and Jennifer's sisters who had no idea who Jennifer really was or the reality behind her strange behavior and struggles growing up.

Sean and Vicky were invited to attend but only Sean showed, with a beholden heart, grateful to be alive and happy that Jennifer was willing to forgive him for being so stupid. He very much sought her forgiveness and thanked her for saving his life by drawing away the skeletal creatures after the plane crash. He and Vicky never got along after their terrifying experience and separated for good, after which Vicky had to be admitted for psychiatric evaluation due to recurring nightmares. All in all the wedding was fantastic and the whole world watched in amazement as the seemingly young couple spoke their wedding vows in ancient Mayan.

Great King Necalli, son of King Ah-Cacaw, sat upon the high throne protecting his people with his jungle queen, a moormit from Virginia Beach, sitting at his right side with an emerald boa coiled around her neck and a new handmade staff in her hand. Necalli's only regret was not knowing the fate of his sister Dacey or her tribe as they were not expelled into the Frog Realm with the rest of the Mayans when Malinche's powerful conjuring backfired. All it took was a simple tingling touch of Jennifer's hand to draw away any grief in Necalli's heart and put a beaming smile on his face.

"Necalli, I think this is the end."

"Yep, I think so."

"That's so sad."

"That's okay because we will live happily for a very, very, very long time."

"I can live with that."

"Just don't tell anyone where the tiny little forbidden spring is hidden."

"I won't if you'll pose for a selfie with me."

THE END

MEET THE AUTHOR

George Babec is the author of Voncara Cove, an adventurous steampunk novel with pirates, tall ships and blazing cannons. He has always been adventurous at heart and his mind is always in overdrive as he continuously pursues every opportunity to fulfill his passions to invent something new. George is a professional electronic engineer, having designed control systems for space based laser systems, media routers, industrial controls, and fiber-optic transmission systems. Learning is his greatest passion.

He loves thunderstorms, ocean waves crashing on the beach, and exploring new and exotic places. George currently lives just outside of Gatlinburg, Tennessee with his family and enjoys the early morning mountain views and fresh air.

FROM THE AUTHOR

I hope you enjoyed reading Frog Realm as much as I enjoyed writing it. The story came to me while thinking about one of my daughters who loves frogs. And yes, she calls them her "little babies." There's a scene in the book where the back yard was destroyed by the father when Jennifer's frogs wouldn't shut up. That was based on a true event. Yes, I destroyed the yard because the stinking frogs wouldn't stop. Where's Jennifer with a wave of her hand when you need her?

Authors survive by reviews. If you enjoyed reading Frog Realm then please leave a review. I would much appreciate it!

Feel free to stop by my website and say hi or view my other works.

Visit George Online:

Amazon: Author George L. Babec
Web: http://www.GeorgeBabec.com
Twitter: https://twitter.com/AuthorGBabec
Facebook: https://www.facebook.com/GeorgeLBabec/

WRITING OF FROG REALM

Some interesting things happened while doing research for the development of Frog Realm: Artifact of Protection. In fact, the entire storyline changed drastically from the original concept because of one old history book. The opening scenes had initially been conceived based on the events of the discoveries of the Ancient Maya and how the jungle consumed their amazing structures and temples. Several books were purchased for the research that quickly put this author to sleep, but there was another book. It was quite expensive so a search was commenced to try to find it elsewhere for a lesser investment. After spending much time it was determined that there was only one copy available anywhere as the book was much older and not really used anywhere.

The decision was made to purchase the book despite its higher cost. After opening the book and learning some of the true secrets about the Mayan people this author stood amazed that there weren't more books and movies created pertaining to these amazing people. Let's face it; the Egyptians and their history have been done to death, but the Ancient Mayans are just as amazing except for the added mystery surrounding their sudden disappearance. No one can explain what cataclysmic event happened to cause them all to disappear at the same time in history. What was learned was so amazing and inspired the actual storyline. What makes the things described in the story so astonishing is that some of them are real. The ancient names, Stela-stones, Tree-stones, the Otherworld, stunning structures and lingual references plus the chiseled stone imprints of skeletal creatures are all part of their ancient past. We know that skeletal creatures don't really exist, but how fascinating is the fact that they are imaged upon their structures and other symbolic monuments, some of which I won't mention because they tend to be too dark. The Mayans are amazing and the expensive history book provided a look into the Mayans that truly sparked the imagination and the desire to use as much of their true history and culture as possible.

VONCARA COVE

With the Pirate Fest competition only days away; Nattie and Jase search through a rustic bookstore hopping to find inspiration. Their search wasn't going well until they found an old leather bound book with secrets to the ancient past. They set off on the greatest adventure of their lives, hoping to find buried treasure but end up surviving on the edge. Hunted and chased by their new found nemesis. They make a startling discovery that threatens their entire planet. With only their love to hold them together; they try to survive and save their world.

ISBN 978-0-9970222-2-3

Available from Amazon.com and other retail outlets

Voncara Cove on Amazon

www.ingramcontent.com/pod-product-compliance
Lightning Source LLC
Chambersburg PA
CBHW021003120726
47905CB00009B/2837